"T... your stipulations, Grace."

"That you become *very* involved in her life. Take her places, join us for dinner, call her, look over her schoolwork… Be her father."

David scrutinized her for the longest time. "I'd be over here constantly."

"That's okay." *Was it*? she asked herself, with a faint sense of panic. Too late.

"Claire won't want me here."

"But that's the deal," Grace said firmly. "She has to promise to work at being your daughter. One of my rules is that we're all polite to guests."

"Guests." He tasted the word as though it was questionable wine.

And who could blame him? His position would be awkward, to say the least. His daughter was choosing to live with someone else. He gave one of those offputting nods. "I'll talk to Claire."

Grace hardly had time to say goodbye before he was gone, leaving her with the horrifying realization that she'd gotten herself into something she wasn't at all sure she wanted to do.

It should have been Claire she was thinking about. Unsettled, Grace had to admit, if only to herself, that she was far more worried about dealing with the grim father than with the sulky teenage girl.

Dear Reader,

The Daughter Merger came naturally to me, and let me tell you why: I have two teenage daughters. The bickering, the repartee, the gossip about school, all are the stuff of daily life for me. The rehearsals are familiar, too, since both my daughters act and I am, of course, their chauffeur.

Let me hasten to say here that my girls have more in common with Linnet than with Claire. They're top-notch students and my best friends. So here's my real secret: I was Claire, not Linnet. At twelve, my mother tells me, I was a nice kid. At thirteen, I woke up one morning a monster. I wept at sad songs, I stormed at my parents' refusal to let me date, I screamed at them, I spent the night at friends' houses and... Well, never mind. My mother might read this, and I wouldn't want to horrify her too much! Fortunately, at about fifteen, I awakened one morning to discover I'd grown up.

The point is, Claire came from my memories of that sad, tumultuous age. She has some reasons to be sad, as her father has reasons for his emotional detachment. Those of you who have read my previous books know that I love heroes who have difficulty expressing emotion— the strong silent type. What makes David Whitcomb a hero is his willingness to learn, to risk and, ultimately, to love passionately. This guy is one of my all-time favorite heroes. Claire is a lucky kid.

Now that you're in on my secrets...

Janice Kay Johnson

P.S. You can reach me at www.superauthors.com

The Daughter Merger
Janice Kay Johnson

HARLEQUIN®

TORONTO • NEW YORK • LONDON
AMSTERDAM • PARIS • SYDNEY • HAMBURG
STOCKHOLM • ATHENS • TOKYO • MILAN • MADRID
PRAGUE • WARSAW • BUDAPEST • AUCKLAND

ISBN 0-373-70944-7

THE DAUGHTER MERGER

For Nan Hawthorne, Jim Tedford
and the real gang: Lemieux, Stanzi and Kitkat

CHAPTER ONE

NOTHING LIKE FINDING OUT your teenage daughter had cut school to foul up your day. David Whitcomb's mounting tension was laced with anger. He didn't have time for this.

But fear was his strongest emotion. Had Claire hit the road again? How far would she get this time?

His gaze found the dashboard clock. Eleven forty-three. School had started at 7:10. That gave her a four-hour head start. If the Attendance Office had notified him sooner...

The garage door was already rising in response to his signal before he turned into his driveway. David killed the engine, set the emergency brake and leaped out, his long stride carrying him into the house.

"Claire?" he bellowed. "Are you home? Claire?"

The kitchen was quiet and dark; a cereal bowl sat in the sink. Loading it into the dishwasher was beyond her. At least she'd had breakfast.

"Claire?" He took the stairs two at a time. No pounding beat of music welcomed him. He slammed open her bedroom door, already knowing what he would find: an empty room.

Covers were tidy, but he knew better than to think Claire had made the bed. She was a quiet, still sleeper, had been since she was a baby. He remembered, with a pang he ignored, how she had sometimes scared him when he checked on her and at first glance thought she'd quit breathing.

Closet doors stood open, and clothes spilled out of drawers. *Damn.* Her binder and a social studies text lay on the desk. So she never had set out for school. The day pack was gone, as was the framed photo of her mother that usually sat beside her bed.

Fear finally swamped his anger. A thirteen-year-old girl, out on her own, trying to—what? hitchhike?—to California. Last time she'd made it to Portland before an alert cop had picked her up. What if some psycho found her first?

He'd have to call the police. But for an instant David stood looking around his daughter's bedroom, bafflement and helplessness holding him captive. What was he doing so terribly wrong that she wouldn't even give him a chance?

The police came and went, as they had the previous two times Claire had run away. They promised to put out a bulletin, but this time they kept asking questions and David felt the rising tide of suspicion and judgment.

Did he know why his daughter was so determined to leave his home? Here they scrutinized him carefully. Had he considered counseling? Did she have friends in whom she confided? Had he contacted her mother in California? Did he discipline Claire physically?

Hell, no, he didn't know why she hated his guts. David did understand, sort of, that Claire felt her mother needed her, that he was the bad guy who was keeping mother and daughter apart. Yes, he'd tried counseling, but Claire wasn't cooperative. Friends? Reluctantly, he decided he would have to call the mother of the one close friend Claire had made in the four months she'd lived with him here in Lakemont. No, he hadn't yet contacted his ex-wife. No, he never laid hands on his daughter. Literally, as she wouldn't accept even a hug from him.

Assuming he'd felt comfortable offering one.

The pair of police officers left, and David picked up the phone. He had only a home phone number for Claire's friend Linnet, but the answering machine suggested that if he urgently needed Grace Blanchet, he should try her work phone number. He did, and she answered.

He had met the woman a couple of times when he was at her town house picking up Claire. What little he knew about Grace Blanchet had been extracted from his sullen daughter. She was a legal secretary for some high-powered firm in neighboring Bellevue. She was a widow, Linnet was her only child.

His lightning impression had been of a tall, slender woman with shiny, thick, light brown hair cut at shoulder length and worn tucked behind her ears. The hair danced when she moved, distracting the eye from a face a man might call plain. Pretty eyes, though, he recalled: a deep blue. And her smile was warm enough to make him feel like a jerk for his cool, answering nod.

"Grace Blanchet," she said now in a rich, distinctively husky voice. One that, upon first hearing it, had instantly made him imagine darkness and a throaty laugh, tangled sheets and satin skin.

It had the same effect this time, despite everything.

Disbelieving and annoyed at himself, he said, "Ms. Blanchet, this is David Whitcomb. Claire's father."

"Yes?" She waited, not making it easy. Apparently she had noticed how cool his previous greeting had been.

"Claire didn't go to school today," he said bluntly. "I think she's run away. I'm wondering if you can find out whether she told your daughter anything."

"Oh, dear." That voice resonated with compassion. "Linnet told me that Claire has done this before. She's so young!"

"Yes." Images flashed before him. His small, dark-haired daughter beside a busy highway, her thumb out. A truck slowing, stopping. Fear and resolution on her face before she gave a nod and climbed in with two men.

He squeezed the bridge of his nose.

"I'm sorry," she said. "You must be terribly worried. I'll call the school and have them get Linnet. Are you at home?"

He didn't want to be. He ached to do something. Anything. Check out the Greyhound bus station. Cruise the freeway entrances. But he knew Claire was probably half a state away by now. The cops were looking. They'd found her before.

"I'm home," he said. "In case she tries to…" Get in touch with own father? Never.

Grace Blanchet promised to call the moment she'd spoken with her daughter.

David dialed again, this time his ex-wife's number. The very sound of her on the answering machine message was enough to make his teeth grit. In contrast to Grace Blanchet, Miranda managed to imbue even her voice with a feminine plea that pushed every man's buttons. *What can you do for me?* her voice seemed to ask. Her big, velvet-brown eyes had asked the same question. Men fell in line to answer. David had trouble believing he'd been dumb enough to fall for it himself.

Sometimes he wanted to shake Claire and say, *Can't you see how she uses people? She has no damn right to use you!*

He clamped down on the words every time. Miranda was Claire's mother. A child should grow up with some shred of respect for her own mother. He wouldn't be the one to take that from her.

A call to the police gave him what he'd expected. Yes, sir, they had checked the bus station. No, sir, no sign of a girl answering the description of his daughter.

David called his office to find out what chaos was brewing there, but though he got so far as sitting down in front of his computer, he couldn't work. Pictures of Claire trudging down the shoulder of the freeway kept intruding.

Damn it! She was so small, so childish, even for thirteen. Too childish to interest a rapist, he tried to convince himself but knew better. David tried to focus on the future, when—*when*—she was home again. A different counselor? She hadn't given the first or second one a chance, and the latest wasn't showing any more promise. A nanny who escorted her to school and picked her up afterward? He knew how that would go over.

"I'm not some stupid little kid!" she liked to yell at him, just before she stormed off to her bedroom. "Quit treating me like I'm in kindergarten!"

David was restlessly pacing when the phone rang. He pounced. "Yeah?"

"Mr. Whitcomb?"

Grace Blanchet. No mistaking that voice.

"Yes," he said tersely. "Were you able to talk to your daughter?"

"I was, but she doesn't know anything about Claire's plans." She sounded apologetic. "Linnet assumed she was home sick."

"And you believed her?"

A momentary pause told him he'd offended even before she said crisply, "My daughter does not lie to me."

David bowed his head and rubbed his neck. "I'm sorry. She was my best hope."

Her voice softened. "I understand."

Strangely, he suspected that she did. Damn right he preferred to think her kid was lying. He didn't want her to be everything his daughter wasn't. He didn't want to give up hope that she knew how he could find Claire.

"If there's anything I can do..." Her sympathy and kindness were as tangible as a touch. Most people didn't mean it when they said that. She seemed to be an exception.

"There's nothing." David hated his own brusqueness but couldn't seem to help himself. "The police will find her."

"Yes. Of course they will. Please do let me know. We'll...worry."

We. Her good little girl and her.

David swore as he hung up the phone.

The deep wheeze of a truck climbing the hill outside turned his head. He didn't give a damn whether some neighbor was moving or had just bought a living room full of new furniture. Still, big trucks with air brakes didn't make it into this exclusive Lakemont neighborhood often. These streets were paved for Mercedes and BMWs and Lexuses.

Outside, a semi pulling a huge trailer that said Hendrix Hauling had stopped outside. A beefy guy was getting out and looking up at David's house. As David watched, he circled to the passenger side of the truck.

By the time David had reached the front door and opened it, the man had escorted Claire to the porch.

"Found something that might belong to you," he said.

Despite his daughter's sulky mouth and hateful stare, David felt relief so intense, he squeezed his eyes shut for a moment.

"Claire." He stepped aside, controlling his voice with an effort. "You go up to your room. I'll talk to you in a minute."

She shook off the trucker's grip and stalked past her father, racing up the stairs. Her bedroom door slammed, vibrating the lone etching that hung on the vestibule wall.

David said roughly, "I don't know who you are or where you found her, but…thank you."

"She was hitching just south of Renton." He shook his head. "She tried to tell me she was sixteen, but I didn't buy it."

"Claire is thirteen."

"About what I guessed. I've got kids myself. I thought about finding a police station, but I figured it wasn't so far I couldn't come back. When I said it was the cops or home, she chose home."

"I'm surprised," David said with a hint of bitterness. "We're having our problems."

"She told me. Said her mom wants her, but the courts gave custody to you." The trucker wasn't asking a question, but he was wondering all the same.

David didn't usually talk about personal business with strangers, but this one had earned an answer.

"Her mother is an alcoholic. She wants Claire only to lean on. Claire was paying the bills, doing the grocery shopping and cooking, calling work to cover when her mom was too sick to go."

"Being the adult," the other man said slowly.

"She thinks her mother needs her. The truth is—" he grimaced "—her mother has found a new man and isn't very interested. But I can't tell her that."

The trucker nodded. After an awkward moment, he stuck out his hand. "Make sure you tell her you were worried about her."

David shook the man's hand. "Thank you," he said again, inadequately.

He watched his savior retrace his steps, climb back

in the cab and laboriously back the truck into the cul-de-sac to turn it around. Claire had gotten lucky.

This time, David thought grimly.

Upstairs, music pounded from beneath Claire's bedroom door, a deep throb that pulsed through the house. David braced himself and opened her door without knocking.

When she saw him, Claire flipped onto her stomach on the bed, as if the sight of her father was unbearable.

David headed straight for the CD player and turned the music off. Usually she would have protested. Today she knew better.

To her back, he said, "You scared me. Do you have any idea what can happen to a girl who gets into cars with strangers?"

She hugged her pillow and remained silent.

His hand itched to whack her bottom, although he'd never believed in spanking.

"We've talked about this, Claire. You live here now. If you'd made it to San Francisco, your mother would have shipped you right back to me."

"No, she wouldn't!" In a flash, the thirteen-year-old launched herself to her knees and faced him furiously. Her face was wet and swollen with tears. "Mom wants me!" she sobbed. "And you don't! I can tell you don't! Why won't you let me go?"

"I do want you." Hell, no, he didn't, not anymore. But he loved her. Or at least the memory of the sweet sprite who had adored her daddy. It was that child he was determined to save from the alcoholic mother who used her as a crutch.

"You don't!" Claire's face crumpled and she flung herself back onto her belly. Her shoulders shook with sobs.

David made himself sit on the edge of the bed. He'd forgotten how to say *I love you.* She wouldn't have believed him anyway. His hand made an abortive move toward her, but he knew damn well she would have knocked it away.

"I'm sorry you miss your mother." His every word sounded wooden, and he swore inwardly. "She's an alcoholic. She can't take care of you. She can't even take care of herself."

"We were doing fine!"

"You weren't doing fine." He knew he was wasting his breath. Logic never penetrated with her. But he had no other weapon, so he tried, anyway. "You were missing school, getting Ds on your report card. You were terrified of being alone at night." And her mother didn't want to stay home with her.

"So what if I'm not good at school!" she flared. "Mom says she wasn't, either!"

"You have the ability to do fine," he said grimly. "If you'd turn in all your assignments."

She threw one miserable, furious look at him over her shoulder. "That's all you care about! That I be some perfect daughter. Well, I'm not!"

He'd thought enviously of Grace Blanchet's daughter today. The memory stung. Did he resent Claire, because she wasn't a model daughter he could brag about?

Wearily he said, "All I ask is that we be able to hold conversations without them blowing up in my face. That I not be dragged away from work because you've taken off again. Is that too much to hope for?''

"I hate you!" she screamed, though the words were muffled in her pillow.

David jerked. Pain engulfed his chest. He stood and started to leave the room, forcing himself to stop in the doorway. "Fine. But you will live with me, like it or not." He didn't—quite—slam the door when he left the room.

"I HATE HIM," Claire repeated gloomily.

She and her best friend, Linnet Blanchet, ignored their school lunches. The salad bar wasn't that good, anyway. Linnet had wanted to know everything about yesterday. About Claire running away, and whether it had been scary, and what had happened. Claire told her the truth except for the scary part. She'd shrugged and said it was no big deal when really she hated hitchhiking. The cars and trucks would rush by, the wind sucking her toward the tires, and sometimes gravel would pepper her painfully. She'd be there praying someone would stop, but afraid at the same time of who it might be. She was always hoping some nice old couple would pull up, and then they'd offer to drive her all the way to her mother's front door even if it was two states away, because they felt sorry for her.

Linnet's brow crinkled. "Why can't you live with your mom if you want?''

She gave her pat answer. She didn't want to tell

even Linnet the truth. "Because Mom couldn't afford really good lawyers. Not like Dad's."

Linnet was stubborn. "But why does he want you so much?"

"I don't know!" Seeing the way Linnet flinched at her quick, furious response, Claire touched her arm. "I'm sorry. I didn't mean to yell at you. It's just, he's never home. When he is, all we do is fight. I think he got custody just so Mom couldn't have me. You know?"

"That's really mean," her friend marveled.

She nodded. Her misery burst out of her. "I won't stay with him. I won't!"

"But even if you get to your mom, he'll know where to find you and then you'll have to come back anyway. Unless your mom is willing to go into hiding with you." Her face brightened. "She could. If you moved to, like, Idaho or Missouri or something, and she was really careful and didn't use credit cards or anything, he'd never find you."

Linnet was used to thinking practically. "Mom is talking about getting married. It's this guy who I think is really rich. He'd have to come with us, and then how could he get to his money? If you use a bank machine or something, they find you."

Linnet had seen the same movies. She nodded thoughtfully. "Maybe your mom could forget about him. If she knew how unhappy you are." The gaze she gave Claire held a hint of a question.

The bell rang, making both girls jump. Claire hadn't noticed how the cafeteria was emptying out. She stood with Linnet and they carried their untouched trays to the busing station, where they dumped the food and put the utensils in the right tubs.

On the way out, Claire said reluctantly, "My mom isn't that good at taking care of herself. I do a lot of stuff for her. She gets alimony from my dad, and child support when I lived with her." Claire knew, because she'd gotten her mother to sign the checks, her hand wavering when she'd had too much to drink, and then Claire had deposited them and bought groceries with the cash. "She'd lose all that money."

"But she'd have *you*," Linnet pointed out inescapably.

Claire didn't want to say that she had asked her mother. Just a couple of weeks ago. She'd called on a Saturday, about noon, which was the best time. Her mom would be up, but she wouldn't have had her first drink yet.

"Clairabelle!" Mom had cried, her voice lilting with pleasure. "Oh, I miss you so much."

"I hate it here," Claire said with quiet intensity. "I want to come home."

"Just a minute, honey." A few clicks and thumps later, her mother sighed. "Coffee. I desperately need that first cup."

Just as she desperately needed that first drink a few hours later. She was always saying she'd quit, or cut back, but it was hard. At school, Claire had learned that alcoholism was a disease. Her mother couldn't help herself.

"Now, what were you saying?" Mom asked.

Claire repeated herself.

"You know your father has custody now. The judge decided you have to live with him. I tried."

"What if we ran away?" Claire had been thinking about it. "If we just moved, and didn't tell him. You could get a job, and I could baby-sit, and we could start all over."

"Honey…" Her mother paused. "What would I do for a living?"

"Well…" That took her aback. "What you do now." Mom was a bookkeeper. Wouldn't it be easy to do that anywhere?

"I'd need references. About the only kind of job you can get without any is to be waitress or work at a fast-food restaurant. Can you picture me behind the counter at The Burger Quickie?"

"I could help! Besides baby-sitting, I could maybe mow lawns or clean houses or something." She'd trailed off, knowing already that her mother wouldn't do it.

"I love you, too," Mom said sadly. "But what you're suggesting is impossible. Maybe, if your father was abusive, but he's not a bad man. I know he'll take good care of you."

"But I hate it here!" she'd said again. Tears were running down her cheeks, and she was hunched around the telephone as if it were a magic talisman, her only hope.

"You know, I'm not the world's best mother."

"I like you just the way you are!" Claire said fiercely. She had to swipe away tears.

"I'm flattered," her mother said lightly, "but I need to go now. Pete's picking me up in…gracious, less than half an hour! You know me. Noon, and I still look a mess.''

Claire sniffed. "Have you...have you had breakfast?"

"Oh, just coffee." She laughed. "Well, you heard me pouring it, didn't you? I've always told you, I'm not a breakfast eater, but you never believed me, did you?"

If Claire didn't make it, she wouldn't bother. In fact, she hardly ate at all if Claire didn't put a meal on the table.

"I'll get a bite while I'm out," she'd say airily. She went out a lot, most evenings, and came home after midnight even on weeknights. Claire would hear her fumbling at the door, the key missing the lock, until finally Mom got it open. Then a whispered goodbye to whoever had brought her, and then thumps as she knocked into furniture on her way to the bedroom. Sometimes she would pause in the hall outside Claire's room, a dark silhouette that swayed unsteadily.

It was Claire's job to get her up in the morning. Sometimes she'd miss her bus when Mom groaned and put the pillow over her head and wouldn't get up at all, or had to run to the bathroom to throw up. Her mother had a delicate stomach. She was always better if she'd had a real dinner the evening before. Claire wondered if Mom was sick every morning now.

"Is everything okay at work?" she asked, not wanting to say *Have you been fired again?*

"Oh, they're being the usual poops, but I'm fine.

They need me,'' Mom declared. She had noticed the clock again and said a hasty goodbye.

Today, the last thing Claire said to Linnet before they separated to go to class was, ''Well, I won't stay with Dad, no matter what! Even if I have to live on the street in Seattle.''

In her math class, the teacher handed out a quiz. They were doing graphing, and Claire didn't get it. She hadn't even opened her book in three days. She stared at the paper and decided not to bother scribbling any answers at all. Instead she stood up and said, ''Mr. Wilson, I don't feel good. I need to go to the nurse's office.''

His eyes narrowed. ''Fine, Ms. Whitcomb, I'll write you a pass, but I'll expect you after school to make up the quiz.''

She ignored the whispers. ''I have to take the bus.''

''Then tomorrow during the lunch hour.''

''Um…sure.'' She didn't quite curl her lip. Yeah, *right.*

The nurse bought her story of an upset stomach, since she didn't often use it. She spent the rest of the afternoon lying down in the nurse's office, only leaving when it was time to catch the bus.

She was hurrying out, trying to ignore all the creeps who went to this school, when a girl she really hated named Alicia called out from a bus line, ''I heard you ran away.'' Her expression was avid. ''Did you sell yourself?''

Claire looked her up and down and said coolly, ''Is that what you would have done?'' Amid laughter, she continued toward the bus.

"Claire!"

She turned at the sound of her friend's voice. Linnet was tall and skinny, but she took dance classes, which made her graceful. Her light brown hair hung all the way to her waist. Right now, she looked pretty with her cheeks flushed as she rushed up to Claire.

"I've got to go, but I had this idea," she said, the words tumbling out. "Maybe you could live with *me*."

"You?"

"I'll bet my mom would agree. I'll ask her, if you think you'd want to."

Dumbfounded, Claire stared at her. "You really think she'd say yes?"

"I know she likes you." Linnet glanced toward her bus line. "I really, *really* have to go. Do you want me to ask?"

Little fizzes that might have been excitement or hope rose in Claire's chest. What she wanted most was to live with her mom, but until she could figure out a way to do that...

Somebody bumped her from behind, and she was being pushed away from Linnet toward the yawning door of the bus. "Yes!" she called.

"I'll phone, okay?" Grinning, Linnet ran.

In a daze, Claire found a seat and didn't even care that it was next to some seventh grader who had opened her notebook and was actually doing homework—homework! Claire was just glad not to be bugged.

Claire didn't know why Linnet's mother would take in somebody else's kid, but Linnet had sounded so sure. Was there any chance at all that Mrs. Blanchet really would agree?

If she did, what would Dad say? Claire frowned. He had all kinds of reasons why she couldn't go home to Mom, but none of them applied to Mrs. Blanchet. *She* didn't drink, and Linnet went to school every day—in fact, she was almost a straight A student, which was an argument Claire could use in her favor. But Mrs. Blanchet didn't seem to *make* Linnet do stuff. When Claire was spending the night, she'd ask for help sometimes, but nicely.

"Any chance you girls could empty the dishwasher?" she'd say with a smile.

Linnet was never grounded, like Claire seemed to be half the time.

It *had* to be better than Dad's.

She hugged her day pack to her chest and stared out the window past the seventh grader.

If Mrs. Blanchet said yes, and Claire's father said no, she'd never forgive him.

Never.

CHAPTER TWO

DINNER WAS BUBBLING on the stove when the doorbell rang. Surprised, Grace wiped her hands on a dish towel and hurried to answer it. No clatter of feet from upstairs; Linnet must have her headphones on, or else she'd be racing to beat Grace, sure one of her friends was here.

Grace opened her front door and was immediately sorry that the caller *wasn't* Erica from down the street, wanting to share a new music CD. Because, instead, a very angry man stood on her doorstep.

Claire's father was a devastatingly attractive man with dark brown hair, hooded eyes and bulky shoulders that belonged on a construction worker, not an executive. If he would just once smile… But on those few occasions when they'd met while exchanging daughters, his expression ranged from preoccupied to tense.

Today, he didn't bother with a hello or a "we need to talk." He glowered. "How dare you tell Claire she could move in with you!"

A spurt of anger surprised Grace, who rarely let herself be bothered by other people's foul tempers. Suppressing it, she gripped the open door. She didn't want the neighbors to hear a brawl on her front doorstep.

"I did not," she said very carefully, "say that your daughter could live here. What I told *my* daughter is that I would *discuss* with you having Claire stay here on a temporary basis and with stipulations. *If* you agreed."

"Really." David Whitcomb's voice was soft and yet icy. "Claire announced to me that you had given permission and she was ready to pack."

Thank goodness for the headphones that kept Linnet deaf while she did her homework. Grace had tried to give this man the benefit of the doubt and to convince Linnet to do the same, despite all of Claire's complaints. If Linnet saw him in a towering rage once, she'd be ready to do anything to aid her friend. Which, given their age, might be something very foolish.

Trying to lighten the mood, Grace said, "Surely you know better than to take every word a thirteen-year-old says at face value."

If anything, his voice hardened. "And yet, you professed to be shocked when I questioned whether Linnet was telling the truth."

This time, she let herself be offended. "My daughter knows when it's important to be honest." If she spoke crisply, she didn't care. "Which doesn't mean I don't sometimes have to delve for the real truth, not the truth as she sees it."

He swore and shoved his fingers through his disheveled hair. "Why in the hell should there be a difference?"

For the first time, Grace felt a pang of sympathy. The lines in his face were carved deeper today than on the other occasions when she'd met him. Genuine bafflement was tangled with the anger in his eyes. He wore a beautifully cut dark suit, but the silk tie was yanked askew and the top button of his shirt was undone. He'd probably come home from work and hoped to pour a martini, put on dinner—although she had difficulty picturing him cooking—read the newspaper. Instead, his daughter had hit him with this, using all the subtlety of a jackhammer.

"Would you like to come in?" Grace suggested. "Probably we should talk about this."

He grimaced. "I can't imagine why you would want to."

"I like Claire." At his open disbelief, she smiled ruefully. "Okay. I feel sorry for Claire. And I like my daughter, who has faith that I will extend a generous hand to her best friend. How can I fail her?"

His expression closed, became stony. "Let me count the ways."

"What?" she asked, startled.

"I seem to be failing my daughter on a regular basis. The only trouble is, I'm not quite sure how. Or why. When I figure it out, I'll tell you."

"Oh, dear," she said on a rush of real compassion. "You do care, don't you?"

He rocked back, that same hard stare not disguising the faint shock in his eyes. "You thought I didn't?"

"Some parents don't, you know," Grace said gently. "How was I supposed to know?"

He frowned. "I was hunting for her."

"That didn't mean you loved her."

David Whitcomb made a guttural sound. "It's hard as hell to love her."

"But you do." Why she was so certain, she couldn't have said, but she would have bet her paycheck that this man was hurting right now. "Please." She stepped back. "Come in."

He hesitated, then gave an abrupt nod and stepped over the threshold, the glance he gave toward her living room wary.

Grace took a guess at the reason. "Linnet's upstairs."

Another nod was the only response, but he seemed marginally less tense when she led him into the kitchen of the compact town house. "I was working on dinner," she explained.

She had gradually and completely remodeled since buying the place after Roger's death. The pale colors that seemed to be standard issue these days had struck her as cold, echoing too much the bleakness of grief. Now the floor of the kitchen was tiled in terra-cotta, the countertops in peach. She'd stripped and stained the cherry cabinets herself, until they glowed to match the antique table in the small dining room. Touches of copper, baskets and rough-textured stoneware all added to the warmth of her kitchen.

As she went to the stove, she covertly watched her guest. His expression showed surprise and, she thought, reluctant admiration.

"Can I pour you some wine?" she asked.

He stood by the table looking awkward, a state that

was probably rare for a man with his presence. "Thank you," he said.

When she handed him the glass, she was careful not to let their fingers touch. Why, she couldn't have said.

He took a deep swallow, then met her eyes. "This isn't a good time. Why don't I come back?"

"And what are you going to say to Claire in the meantime?" Grace stirred the sauce simmering on the stove top. "No. Actually, right now is fine. Dinner won't be ready for fifteen or twenty minutes, and Linnet is occupied with homework. Let me say my piece."

His frowning gaze continued to hold hers. She kept stirring to give herself something to do.

"Linnet tells me Claire has run away several times."

He gave another of those sharp nods that seemed to be his speciality.

"Apparently going to live with her mother is not an option?"

"No." For a moment it seemed he would say nothing more, but finally he added grudgingly, "My ex-wife is an alcoholic. She is also seeing a new man who is apparently not interested in being a stepfather."

"Oh." Poor Claire, Grace thought sadly. She'd been wrenched from a drunken mother who had lost interest in her into the care of this remote, uncommunicative man who admitted it was hard to love her.

"Claire is convinced her mother needs her."

Grace stirred, processing the information. "I see."

"Do you?" His gaze was ironic.

"Well, no." She hesitated, knowing she was crossing an invisible line but choosing to do it anyway. "What I don't understand is why she is so determined *not* to live with you."

"You haven't been fed stories of abuse?"

"No-o, not exactly."

He gave a rough laugh that held no humor and turned from her to stare out the window at her tiny brick patio. "Do you want to know the honest-to-God truth?"

She felt unforgivably nosy, but... "If I'm to become involved...yes. Yes, I do."

"Then here it is. I don't know. I have no idea why my own daughter hates my guts." He faced her, expression raw. "I wouldn't blame you if you can't buy that."

Did she? Was it possible to be genuinely ignorant of where you had taken such a monumental misstep?

"I don't want to ask," Grace said slowly, "but will you tell me more of the background? How long you've been divorced, for example?"

He picked up the wineglass from the table, looked at it, set it down. "Six years. Claire was seven. Miranda's drinking was a problem between us, but she didn't drink and drive, and I thought Claire was better with her. I thought, for a girl, that her mother was important."

At last Grace put down the spoon. "And Claire?"

He shook his head. "There was so much tumult, I just don't know. I assumed she'd rather stay with her mother.'' Sounding stiff, he added, ''Obviously now she wants to be with her, so I guess I was right.''

Or very, very wrong, Grace thought but didn't say. ''I assume you continued to see her.''

He began rubbing the back of his neck. ''Not as often as I should have. I was transferred up here from the Bay Area. I talked to her on the phone, but when you're not living with someone it gets harder and harder to think of anything to say. She was supposed to spend summers, but Miranda had her in swimming lessons and an arts program, and I work long hours, so—'' his eyes closed briefly ''—I took the easy road.''

''She never came?'' Grace couldn't help sounding shocked.

''Oh, two weeks here and there. It was...not comfortable.'' His eyes met hers, his hooded. ''I'd take time off, but she didn't want to do anything. She was always sullen. I thought it was her age. Or later I figured it was me. I wasn't real life for her. Eventually—'' he grimaced ''—I realized that real life was doing the grocery shopping and coaxing her hungover mother out of bed in the morning and making excuses to the boss if she couldn't. The first couple of years, Claire would show off her report card. This past couple, she stopped. I found out that's because she had so many tardies and unexcused absences, she was flunking. I flew down for a visit at the end of the last school year and talked to teachers and Miranda. Claire threw a fit, but I packed her up and brought her home with me. She's been trying to run away ever since. And that," he said, "is the whole pathetic story."

"I'm sorry." She stirred uselessly again. "This must be very difficult."

"Being her father?" he asked ironically. "Or admitting to you how inadequate I am?"

"Well, both."

He said something under his breath that she suspected was profane, and then took a swallow of the wine. The stare he gave her held a challenge. "You were the one who was going to say your piece, as I recall. Somehow, I seem to have done all the talking instead."

"Yes." She made a business of turning off the stove, setting the pan to one side. "Well, here it is." She lifted her chin. "If it would help you and Claire, if you need some space to work out your problems, she is welcome to stay here for the time being." Here was the hard part. "But only if you both make some promises. And keep them."

His eyes narrowed. "These being the stipulations."

She nodded, mute.

"And they are?"

"Claire has to promise not to run away. And to go to school every day. No cutting classes. Plus to, well, follow my house rules." She gestured vaguely. "You know. Help clean the kitchen. That kind of thing."

David Whitcomb inclined his head, his watchful gaze never leaving hers. "And what do you expect from me, aside from support money?"

"That you become *very* involved in her life. Take

her places, join us for dinner, call her, look over her schoolwork...be her father.''

He scrutinized her for the longest time. ''I'd be over here constantly.''

''That's okay.'' Was it? she asked herself, with a faint, fluttering sense of panic. Too late.

''Claire won't want me here.''

''But that's the deal,'' Grace said firmly. ''She, too, has to promise to work at being your daughter. And one of my house rules is that we are all polite to each other and to guests.''

''Guests.'' He tasted the word as though it was questionable wine.

And who could blame him? His position would be awkward, to say the least. His daughter was choosing to live with someone else because she detested him. He would feel constantly as if he was foisting his company on strangers—and on Claire, who would be civil, if at all, simply because her foster mother insisted on it.

Not a palatable option. Except that his only other one was to go on the way he had been—with his thirteen-year-old daughter determined to hitchhike to her mother in California.

The struggle, visible on his face, was severe but short. She had to give him that much credit.

Jaw muscles flexed, and then he gave one of those brief, off-putting nods. ''I'll talk to Claire.''

Grace pressed her lips together. ''If you think I'm presuming—''

''What?'' Irony edged into his tone. ''That I can't cope with my daughter? You'd be right.''

"I'm trying to help," she said gently.

He looked at her with a disquieting lack of expression. "I know you are."

"Mr. Whitcomb..."

"Hadn't you better make it David?" he suggested sardonically. "Since we're going to be one big happy family?"

A gasp from behind him startled them both. Linnet stood in the doorway, Lemieux draped in her arms. The big snowshoe Siamese struggled as she squeezed him.

"Claire's going to live with us?" Linnet's face glowed with hope.

"Her dad will talk to her," Grace said repressively. "And, you know, if Claire does come to stay, it won't be one long sleepover. You'll both have to do homework and chores."

"But it'll be like having a sister." She hugged the cat again, so hard he uttered a cry that sounded very much like "no-o-o!"

"Sisters," her mother said dryly, "often get tired of each other." Grace was very conscious of Claire's father, silent and stiff.

"Not us. We never will." Linnet set poor Lemieux down and twirled into the kitchen. The cat shot a look at David and bolted. "Can I call her?" Linnet begged.

"No. Dinner is almost ready. And Mr. Whitcomb and I haven't made a decision. He and Claire need to talk. This is between them."

"Oh." She halted her pirouette and showed the

whites of her eyes as she rolled them toward her friend's father. "I didn't mean…that is…I mean…"

"I think he knows what you mean." Grace held out two plates with silverware piled atop. "In the meantime, please set the table while I show him out."

"No need." His face and voice were wooden. "I'm sure we'll be talking."

She'd hardly had time to set one foot in front of another when she heard the soft sound of the front door opening and closing behind him. She was left with the horrifying realization that she'd gotten herself into something she wasn't at all sure she wanted to do.

It should have been Claire she was thinking about. Unsettled, Grace had to admit, if only to herself, that she was far more worried about dealing with the grim father than with the sulky teenage girl.

DAVID HEAVED CLAIRE'S SUITCASE out of the trunk of his Mercedes and found his daughter was already hurrying up the brick steps to the front door of the condo. Her step was light; he could feel her joy as she raced toward liberation from her father. The door was swinging open even before she reached it, the two girls squealing, vanishing inside with their arms around each other's waists.

He was left with a lump of heavy, rough concrete where his heart should have been and with the certain knowledge that, once again, he had taken the low road.

He was her father, damn it. He'd walked away once, and here he was essentially doing it again. He wasn't tough enough to see his own child through a bad patch. Despising himself, David thought, *Hell, no, hand her over to someone else. Let them deal with her.*

He wondered how sternly Claire's foster mom would hold him to his part of the bargain. Would Claire meld gradually, naturally, into Grace Blanchet's family? Or did she really expect him to somehow become the father Claire needed?

Grunting at the thought, David picked up the suitcase and started after his daughter. The woman was a legal secretary, for Pete's sake! How the hell could he think she would do for him—and Claire—what licensed psychologists couldn't?

But did it matter? his mocking inner voice asked. So what if he failed, again? At least Claire was out of his hair. He didn't have to come home from work every day to the deep, obscene beat of rap music, to a kid who'd rather sneer "I'm not hungry" and starve than sit down to dinner with him.

Grace was waiting for him in the open doorway. This being a Saturday, she had her hair in a ponytail and she wore jeans and a blue flannel shirt tucked into them. Casual, but her loafers gleamed like her warm brown hair. A classy lady who invariably left him feeling unsettled for reasons he didn't understand.

And wasn't in any hurry to identify.

"Why don't you take that right up?" she suggested. "The girls wanted to share a bedroom, but for now I'm giving Claire our spare." She lowered her voice. "I'm guessing that they will eventually want their privacy, even if they don't believe me."

Now, how did she know that? The way those two had hugged and squealed had him guessing the opposite. But then, his insight into a thirteen-year-old girl's mind had been skewed from the get-go. Grace Blanchet had the advantage, at least, of having *been* a thirteen-year-old girl once upon a time.

"Sure," he said, and started up the stairs behind her.

Even burdened with his daughter's possessions and his own foul mood, he found his gaze lingering on Grace's tiny waist and gently curved rear end. In her usual conservative suits, she looked skinnier than he found appealing in a woman. Snug jeans and the soft flannel of her shirt made plain that she was more womanly than he'd guessed. Half memory, half imagination stirred, and his palms briefly tingled with the knowledge of how her bottom would feel gripped in his hands.

He was grateful to reach the top of the stairs and be distracted by her gesture as she stood aside.

"Second door on the left."

Although she'd said it was for guests, this bedroom had as much personality as the downstairs. A puffy denim comforter covered the antique bed. The maple bedside stand with spooled legs matched the bed. On the wall above the bed hung a small quilt, beautifully hand-stitched even to his uneducated eye, and old, he thought. A lacy valance matched a doily on the carved oak bureau.

The girls had flung open the closet doors and

pounced on the suitcase the moment he walked in. Ignoring him, Claire unzipped it while he headed back downstairs for another load.

He was carrying her CD player in when he heard Linnet say, "You can do whatever you want to this room. You can put posters everywhere and—"

"I don't think so," David said. "Claire, you're a guest. You can't punch holes in the walls."

She gave him a spiteful look.

Behind him, Grace intervened, her voice easy. "Of course, you can put up posters, Claire. Just use the sticky stuff that peels off, if you don't mind. Do you want me to take down the quilt?"

Claire held the blistering look for one more moment, then turned her back. "I don't mind it, Mrs. Blanchet."

Grace laughed. "Somehow it doesn't look right for a teenage girl. You need a poster of…who, Freddie Prinze, Jr. there?"

He doubted very much that his daughter would choose anyone so innocuous to emblazon on the walls. She preferred men with multiple body parts pierced, lank greasy hair and foul mouths.

"Dad had me bring my posters," she said. Her tone suggested he'd ripped them off the wall and shoved them down her throat. Where, in fact, *she* was the one to strip her bedroom bare, as if she never intended to come back.

He turned to fetch them. That was, apparently, his only acceptable role in this handoff. He couldn't imagine coming back tomorrow or the next day and knocking on this bedroom door, going in for a chat.

How, he wondered, would Grace deal with it when Claire refused to sit down at the dinner table if he was there?

"You'll stay for lunch, won't you?" Grace asked, when he came back with the roll of posters.

He sensed Claire's sharp movement without looking at her. "Thanks, but I have to go into the office. Another time."

"Then dinner tomorrow," she said with an air of satisfaction. "Claire, what's your favorite dinner? I cook a lot of pastas. Do you both like Italian?"

He had no idea what Claire ate besides the microwave meals she'd pop in when he wasn't around. "I do," he said. "But maybe I should let Claire settle in before I start hanging around."

The stubborn woman didn't know when to let up. "No, the sooner the better," she said. "We'll expect you tomorrow. About six?"

His daughter's eyes narrowed.

"Fine." He made himself look at her. "Claire…"

It was hard not to flinch at the hatred blazing in her eyes.

Without expression, he said, "I hope you'll be happy here," and walked away.

His specialty.

SHE WAS *SO* HAPPY when he left without bothering with some fakey goodbye scene. She didn't even know why she'd been worried about that. Look how glad he was to get rid of her.

Well, he wasn't any gladder than she was to be

gone! Claire told herself for the fiftieth time today that anything had to be better than his house.

Mrs. Blanchet had made him promise he'd come over all the time and play daddy. Yeah. Right. They'd see how long *that* lasted, she thought bitterly. He might come a couple of times, but then he'd cancel at the last minute and say he had to work, and finally weeks would go by without anything but a check from him. He'd pay whatever he promised. Why not? Like he wasn't loaded. And if he didn't pay, Claire might be dumped back in his lap. Which he wouldn't want.

What she figured was, once he'd forgotten all about her existence, she'd get Mrs. Blanchet talking to her mom. That way, once they got tired of her here, she could just quietly go home again.

Daddy might never even notice.

She wished, Claire thought viciously, hating the sadness that squeezed her chest like the asthma she'd had as a little kid. So what if he didn't love her? She had her mother. Mom was all she needed.

"What CDs do you have?" Linnet was digging in her bag. "You have hardly any!"

"I left most of mine at Mom's house. I just brought a few." She didn't have that many there, either, because Mom didn't make much money. If she'd asked *him* for money, he probably would have given it to her, but she wasn't going to.

"Oh." Linnet gave up looking and flopped on the bed. "You can just borrow any of mine you want."

Like she'd want to listen to Britney Spears or 'N

Sync. Music was one thing she and Linnet did *not* agree about.

"This is going to be so cool," Linnet said dreamily. "We can talk whenever we want. And do our homework together, and borrow each other's clothes, and…" She rolled onto her side and propped her head on her hand. "Hey! Would you like to take dance with me?"

"Me?" Claire scrunched up her face. "I am so-o clumsy. I'd fall on my face."

"Yeah, but see, dance makes you *less* clumsy," Linnet said earnestly.

"*And* I'd be in a beginner class. Not with you."

"Well…" Linnet frowned. "Yeah, but there's one at the same time as my jazz dance. I think it's ballet, but that's okay, because you should get training in ballet first."

Claire pictured herself in a pink leotard, standing with heels together and toes pointing out in that dorky position, slowly bending her knees and straightening all to the tinkle of a piano. No, thank you.

"Dance isn't my thing."

"What *is* your thing?"

Claire jumped to her feet and yanked open a drawer. She wasn't going to hang those posters, she wouldn't be here that long, but she might as well put her clothes in the drawers.

"What do you mean, what's my thing? I like music and hanging out. It's not like everybody has to dance." She knew she sounded disagreeable and was mad at herself. She didn't have to take her bad mood out on Linnet, who had rescued her from *purgatory*.

"I'm sorry." Her friend flushed. "I mean, I just thought you'd want…"

"To be like you." She still sounded weird. Abrupt. "I can't be."

"I'm nothing so great! I just think dancing is fun." Linnet was starting to look ticked. "Is that so bad?"

Collapsing onto the floor cross-legged, Claire wrinkled her nose in apology. "I'm really sorry! I'm just jealous because I know you're really good at dance, and I don't want to be the only beginner over eight years old. Besides, your mom shouldn't have to pay for stuff like that."

"No, but I'll bet your father would."

"I don't want to take his money!"

Her friend rolled onto her stomach and hung her arms off the bed, her chin resting on the edge. "Why not?"

"Because I don't want to owe him anything!" she said fiercely.

"Who says you owe him?" Linnet asked logically. "I mean, parents don't expect to be paid back. He's already giving Mom money for your food, right? Mom says he is. So why not lessons? Isn't there something you've always wanted to do? Skiing? Windsurfing?"

"Horseback riding." Where had that come from? It just popped out, a little kid dream. She had those plastic horse statues, now sitting on a shelf in her bedroom at home. She used to play with them for hours. Sometimes, with her eyes closed, she'd imagine herself on horseback, galloping like the wind.

"See?" Linnet crowed. "I knew there was something! That's it! Ask to take horseback riding lessons.''

Part of her balked at the idea. But another part started thinking, why not? The temptation nibbled at her resolve. She could spend his money. Lots of his money. Maybe she could ride English. Learn to show-jump.

Uh-huh. Sure. Let *him* think he'd done something for her. Tell everyone he was a good daddy because he'd paid for horseback riding lessons.

''No!'' She shoved the roll of posters in the closet, in her haste denting it. ''No. I don't want his money. I don't want *anything* from him.''

''Wow.'' Linnet sounded awed. ''You must really hate your dad.''

''I told you I did.'' And she didn't want to think about him, not anymore. One of the Blanchets' two cats gave her an excuse, poking his head into the bedroom. ''Hey, Lemieux,'' Claire coaxed, holding out her hand. ''Here kitty-kitty. Maybe he'll sleep with me.'' She trailed her fingers down the big Siamese's taupe back. ''Listen,'' she said to Linnet, ''why don't you set up my stereo while I put away my clothes? Okay?''

Linnet slid nose first off the bed, like a seal going into the water. As she hit the floor, the cat erupted under Claire's hand and fled, thundering down the hall.

Both girls laughed, and Claire's mood improved for the first time. This wasn't home, but it would be okay.

For now.

CHAPTER THREE

DAVID HAD NEVER SO BADLY wanted to make an excuse as he did Sunday. But he wouldn't—couldn't—let himself. Leaving Claire with her mother, believing she'd be better off there, was one thing. Deserting her on a stranger's doorstep was another. He might be a coward, but not that big a one.

Besides which, damn it, he'd promised.

What the hell, he thought with grim humor as he rang the doorbell, Grace Blanchet might as well find out now what her Good Samaritan plans would come to.

She was the one to open the door. She wore an apron again, like the other day. From inside her home wafted the smell of garlic and baking bread and a whiff of something sweeter. Apple pie? Behind her, on the stairs, lay a different cat from the other day, this one a fluffy brown Maine coon type with a white bib. It paused in the midst of some intricate grooming ritual and stared at him, unblinking and distinctly unfriendly.

He tore his gaze away from the cat and looked at Grace Blanchet, who was smiling like any good hostess should, even one entertaining this particular guest only because she felt she had to.

"I'm glad you made it." That smoky voice completely belied her prim exterior. "Claire wasn't so sure you would."

Yeah. More likely, Claire had hoped.

When Grace turned, his gaze flicked to her jean-clad rear. The white bow of the apron was a saucy accent to her slender curves.

Hating himself for ogling, feeling the cat's stare between his shoulder blades, David followed Grace back to the kitchen, into déjà vu. There she was, behind the tiled counter, the apron protecting her clothes from the marinara sauce bubbling on the stove, which she stirred. He stood in exactly the same spot, beside the sliding door, feeling as socially inept as he had that day. He hadn't stuck his foot in his mouth yet, but he knew damn well what was to come and hadn't warned this perfectly nice woman.

"If you want to go up and say hi to Claire," she began.

"I was hoping to talk to you first," David said truthfully. "Is she, uh…"

"Behaving herself? You bet. She's very polite." A faintly troubled look crossed Grace's face. "She hasn't exactly settled in, though. She doesn't want to put up her posters, for example. I wish you hadn't said that."

He shook his head. "Usually, my opening my mouth would guarantee that she'd do whatever I suggested she not do."

"That bad, huh?"

"Worse."

She set a wine bottle and corkscrew on the counter. "Would you open this?"

He automatically began turning the screw into the cork. "In all fairness," he said gruffly, "I should warn you that Claire and I haven't sat down for a meal together in a month or more. She's bound to make an excuse tonight."

For an apparently gentle, pleasant woman, Grace had a steely core. "She can try."

With a pop, the cork came out. David poured two glasses, held his up, and said, "To a very brave woman."

She lifted hers in turn. "Courage is in the eye of the beholder."

They both swallowed.

David leaned one hip against the cabinet and watched her run water into a big pot for the pasta.

"I want you to know that I'm grateful to you for trying this," he said abruptly.

She clapped a lid on the pot. "All I'm doing is giving your daughter a safe place to stay while you two work out your problems."

He took another gulp of wine. "I have a bad feeling that you're underestimating our problems. We don't have father-daughter tension. Claire hates my guts."

Her eyes were drenched with compassion. "And loves you, too."

His laugh hurt. "Sure she does. So much so, she'd rather hitch a ride across three states than stay with me."

"Thirteen-year-olds don't think anything bad can happen to them."

He wasn't so sure about that. Claire knew that divorce happened, that mothers became drunks, that fathers disappeared from their daughters' lives.

"Maybe. Just remember," David said, "if you have trouble with her, you're not stuck with her."

"If she doesn't keep her word, you'll be the first to know." She gave him an odd, crooked smile. "Now, would you go yell up the stairs? Tell the girls dinner is ready."

She made it sound so easy, so casual. Bemused by the idea of being able to call, "Dinner's ready," and have his daughter come running in good humor, David went to the foot of the stairs and braced himself for the customary rejection.

"Claire? Linnet? Time for dinner."

"Okay!" Linnet's voice floated cheerfully down from above.

David didn't wait. The less obvious his presence was to Claire, the better.

Back in the kitchen, he discovered Grace had the phone tucked between her shoulder and ear as she took a strainer out of the cupboard and set it in the sink.

"Mom, Claire is a very nice girl." There was a pause as she lifted the huge steaming pan of pasta to the sink and dumped the spaghetti into the strainer. "No, she won't be here forever." Seeing David, she rolled her eyes although her tone was very patient. "Mom, I really can't talk right now. Claire's father is here to see his daughter, and I'm putting dinner on the table.''

He mouthed, ''Can I help?''

Covering the receiver, she whispered, ''Will you put this on the table? Are they coming?''

''Linnet answered me,'' he said noncommittally.

''Oh, good. Here.'' Grace handed him a heaping bowl of sauce. Then, into the receiver, she said, ''No, I wasn't talking to you, Mom. Listen, I'll call tomorrow. Say hi to Dad, okay?'' She listened for another minute, repeated goodbye and set down the phone, shaking her head. ''Maybe we forever feel like teenagers in the presence of our parents.'' Her gusty sigh told him she did not look forward to speaking to her mother again. ''Oh, well. Okay, here's the spaghetti.'' She handed him this bowl in turn, although clearly she was murmuring to herself now. He could all but see her ticking items off on her fingers. ''The garlic bread is on the table and all I have to do is dish up the green beans.''

''Smells good.''

So did she. Close to her, he caught a whiff of an elusive, flowery scent. His gaze lingered on the slender, elegant line of her neck, on tiny wisps of hair against the cream of her skin.

Thank heavens, she didn't seem to notice his momentary reverie…oh, hell, call a spade a spade—what he'd felt was yet another spark of sexual awareness that was, to put it mildly, highly inconvenient. For crying out loud, this situation was complicated enough without her becoming self-conscious around him, or him having to stonewall yet another emotion.

As it was, he couldn't figure out why he hadn't developed an ulcer.

"Why don't you sit down?" Grace suggested, smiling at him. "Pick any place."

The talking-to he'd just given himself didn't keep him from noticing how pretty that smile made a face he'd labeled plain.

His daughter's timing was, as always, impeccable. She chose that moment to slouch into the dining room, Linnet at her heels. She had a gift for killing any good mood of his.

"Oh, girls." Grace bustled from the kitchen. "I hope you're hungry. I made tons. Sit, sit!"

"Hello, Claire," David said quietly.

She rolled her eyes and dropped into a chair.

Grace cleared her throat meaningfully.

Claire stirred, shot him a resentful look and mumbled reluctantly, "Hi." *And I wish it was goodbye,* her tone seemed to say.

He was too surprised by getting a semi-civil response to take offense.

"Well…" Grace smiled at them all from her place at one end of the table. "Linnet, why don't you start the pasta? Claire, would you like garlic bread?"

David's sense of unreality grew as the meal progressed. An outsider would guess this to be a family—Mom, Pop and kids. Grace, with help from her daughter, maintained a cheerful stream of chatter that disguised Claire's sullenness and David's monosyllabic responses to his hostess's occasional questions. He had the queasy feeling that he was delicately balanced over a deadly precipice.

Claire had come to the table. She was keeping her head bent, but she was eating. She even laughed once at something her friend said. She wasn't refusing to break bread with her father. She wasn't shooting him dagger looks. She was following Grace Blanchet's first rule of basic civility.

It stung, of course, to know that she was trying this hard only because she was so desperate to stay here, to *not* have to go home with him.

But she was trying.

And David knew damn well it would take only the smallest misstep on his part to fuel one of her explosions. So he couldn't make that misstep. Unfortunately, his care made him a lousy guest. Not by glance or tone did Grace acknowledge that this meal was anything but a pleasure.

The girls were done and looking restless when she said, as casually as when she asked him to summon their daughters to dinner, "David, Linnet's thinking about trying out for the middle school play on Wednesday. Claire is considering the idea, too. At the very least, she wants to stay and watch the audition. Unfortunately, I have a meeting that might run until almost six. PTA board. We're planning the autumn dance and carnival. I hate to have the girls hanging around waiting too long. Any chance you could pick them up?"

"A play?" He couldn't help sounding startled. Claire? On stage? And taking direction from someone in a position of authority?

"I told you he'd be busy," Claire said, not looking at him.

"No. Of course I can pick them up." He ventured a toe in the waters, speaking directly to his daughter. "I just didn't realize you were interested in theater, Claire."

She slouched lower in the chair and twirled her hair on her finger. "I don't know if I am."

Grace was looking at him with obvious appeal. *Persuade her,* those extraordinary eyes begged. *Be a father.*

What a joke. If he said a single damned word in favor of the idea, Claire would...

Whoa.

He gave his idea a lightning assessment and deemed it sound.

"It would mean a lot of reading and memorization." He sipped his wine, shrugged. "And it's no fun to try out and not get a part."

Claire's eyes flashed at him. "That figures! You're so sure I wouldn't!"

"I didn't say that," he argued mildly. "What's the play?"

"Much Ado About Nothing," Linnet contributed, her anxiety about the new-sprung tension evident in the way she hastened to fill the silence. "You know. Shakespeare."

Grace made a sound that might have been a suppressed laugh, buried in her napkin.

"I know that one," David said, straight-faced. "Beatrice and Benedick. The wimpy Hero and the jerk...what's his name?"

"Claudio," Linnet supplied. She frowned. "You think Hero is a wimp?"

He saw the error of his ways. Hero was undoubtedly her dream part, and with reason: she was no
Beatrice. "Actually," he said hastily, "she is probably a realistic product of her time and class. She
didn't have much choice but to marry the man her
father chose." Not an idea Claire would embrace, he
realized belatedly, and not a good idea as a topic at
this dinner table. Turning to her, he asked, "Which
part were you thinking about?"

Her chin shot up. "Beatrice."

She had the fire, in a preteen sort of way. He found
that he badly wanted her to go out on a limb and try
for this.

He nodded, managing to make his expression sub-
tly doubtful.

Fury on her face, Claire said to Grace, "I am going
to try out."

"Oh, good." She smiled warmly. "Darn. I wish I
could see the audition. Except Linnet would be embarrassed if her mom was there. For which I don't
blame her. Listen, do you want me to be an audience
tonight when you practice?"

"Yeah, cool," they said almost in tandem.

"Then I'll clean the kitchen if you two want to go
take your showers and get ready for school."

Silverware clattered and chairs scraped on the
wood floor as they raced for the door. David watched
them go, then braced himself yet again. He hated this
feeling, as though he was a high school kid in trouble
waiting outside the principal's office. He resented the
fact that this woman, a stranger, was able to sit in
judgment of him.

Grace said not a word until the thunder on the stairs was followed by a slammed door upstairs. Then she grinned. "Well done."

Some of the tension in his neck eased. "I expected you to chew me out."

"It's hardly my place." She laughed. "Well, maybe I would, in my bossy way. But I could tell what you were doing. You won't get away with it very many times. She'll start to catch on."

David grimaced. "I just hope she actually gets a part. If not Beatrice, at least the maid who plays footsie with the scumbag. What's his name. Don John." He got back to the point. "Her ego is delicate right now, to put it mildly."

"Mmm," she agreed. "I hope they *both* get parts. They're getting along great right now, and we don't need any jealousy to interfere."

Another horrifying possibility.

Slowly he said, "Maybe I should have kept my mouth shut."

"Heavens, no!" Grace stood. "Would you like a cup of coffee? I'll just clear the table and—"

"I'll help."

Against her protests, he gathered dishes and even insisted on rinsing them and loading the dishwasher while she put leftovers in the refrigerator and got out cream and sugar for the coffee.

There seemed to be no polite way to excuse himself although he guessed she was no more excited about a further tête-à-tête than he was.

He felt raw in her presence. She knew more about him than anyone but his closest friend. Not many people knew even the basic facts: that his ex-wife was an alcoholic, that he'd sloughed off responsibility for his daughter, that she'd come to live with him because she was in trouble at school. Never mind that she had run away three times.

But this woman had seen how desperate Claire was to escape him, how pathetic he was as a parent and had been, presumably, as a husband. She had a clear gaze that seemed to see right through what few pretenses he still possessed to wear as protection. She must despise him, but unless she wanted to be saddled with Claire permanently, it was smart of her to encourage his effort to build some kind of decent relationship with his daughter.

He gave a soft grunt of rueful amusement. No, Grace Blanchet would not want his sulky daughter permanently.

In the interest of speeding up this obligatory social interlude, he took a gulp of his coffee.

Grace sat back down at her place at the table. "Tell me, what do you do for a living?" she asked, her gaze inquiring, interested, all that a good hostess's should be.

"Didn't Claire tell you?"

"She said you're a businessman." Enunciating the one word with a hint of distaste, Grace suggested the sneer his daughter had worn when she spoke it.

"I'm a vice president with International Parcel Service. We focus primarily on quick service for businesses, versus the birthday gift to Tulsa."

She nodded. "The law firm where I work uses IPS."

"I'm in charge of day-to-day operations as well as some long-term planning. If an airplane is grounded in Boston because of ice, it's my problem."

"That sounds stressful."

"I like problem solving. I don't find the job stressful in the sense that it's affecting my blood pressure." He made a sound. "If I'm getting high blood pressure, it's this thing with Claire doing it to me."

"Do you work really long hours?" She sounded tentative.

He realized with a start of irritation that she was, in a sense, interviewing him. He was being judged again. The counselor had asked him the same question. Was he supposed to quit his job? Claire was a teenager! It wasn't as if he was leaving a two-year-old in day care fourteen hours a day.

"Sometimes," he said tersely. After a moment, he decided reluctantly that she deserved better. Shrugging, he expanded. "Long days—and sometimes nights—goes with the territory. On the other hand, when the weather is good, the pilots aren't threatening a strike, and we haven't committed some PR faux pas, my schedule isn't too bad. When a crisis threatens, sometimes whether I can get home for dinner or not is out of my hands. That's a drawback when you're a single parent."

Grace made a face. "No kidding. I may be the only parent of a teenager in this town who can't wait until her kid gets a driver's license."

Claire behind the wheel…he shuddered.

Almost apologetically, she said, "Linnet has common sense. Knock on wood. It's always scary, I imagine, but she's not the kind to drink and drive or speed.''

He could live without hearing about the perfect kid. The way Claire was going, by the time she was sixteen, she'd have her eyebrows and nose pierced, be pregnant by a nineteen-year-old boyfriend who played drums in band, and be a high school dropout.

Unless this woman, Saint Grace, could pull Claire's bacon out of the fire.

He did hate having to be grateful.

Physically aching to be gone, he took another sip of coffee and said, ''I understand you're a legal secretary.''

''That's right. Nine to five. The girls, by the way, should be done by four.''

Four. He hadn't left the office that early in years, except for once when he had come down with the stomach flu and for the three times Claire had hit the road.

Hell, he was entitled. If it would make a difference to Claire…

He came back to the present to realize that Grace was studying him with crinkled brow.

''Is that a problem?''

''No.'' David shook his head. ''No. Of course not.'' He took a last swallow of coffee. ''Listen, you must have things you need to get done, and I have some paperwork waiting. I'll pick up Claire and Linnet on Wednesday. Why don't I take you all out for pizza afterward? You must hate to cook when you don't walk in the door until six-fifteen or later.''

"What a nice idea." She looked pleased—and surprised, which stung.

Apparently he wasn't expected to be considerate. Which made him wonder what Claire *had* told her foster mother about him.

"Oh, I wanted to mention that Claire and I have an appointment with the counselor on Thursday. For what it's worth," he added sardonically.

"She seems to be making an effort."

For you, he thought. Resentful yet again, he was then angry at himself for his pettiness. Grace Blanchet had generously taken on a difficult teenager. He had no business blaming her for what was his fault.

She walked him to the door, courtesy worn like skillfully applied makeup, making her hard to read, somehow remote despite her unfailing friendliness and warmth. An unworthy part of him would have liked to see her veneer crack. Surely she got mad sometimes, had moments of being spiteful, passionate, tired. He wouldn't mind seeing one.

If for an instant he chose to imagine her not angry but passionate, her cheeks flushed, mouth soft, hair tangled, well, it wasn't a picture he let linger in his mind.

"Thank you," he made himself say again. "Not just for dinner, but for—"

"No." A sharper note entered her voice. She closed her eyes, opened them again, said more quietly, "Please. We'll both get sick of it if you feel you have to thank me every time you come. Let's just consider it said, okay? I'm doing this for Claire's sake, and for Linnet's. I like kids, I'm comfortable with them. Having her is really no problem.''

"Then good night."

He felt no less guilt, no less relief when he walked away this time.

SLUMPED LOW IN HER SEAT in the darkened auditorium, Claire chewed on her fingernail and pretended to listen to the guy auditioning for Benedick.

"'Hath not the world,' um—" he frowned at his script "'—one man but he will wear his cap with sus…suspicion.'" He sounded it out carefully, then continued in the same monotone, one word at a time.

Totally tuning him out, Claire focused on her terror. This was worse than hitchhiking. *Way* worse. Not that she couldn't do better than all these morons who'd already gone. But still. There must be forty kids trying out for parts, and half of them had friends hanging out, too. They were all listening. She'd have to stand up there on the stage and face not only the two teachers sitting in the front row who were going to be director and assistant director, but half the school, too.

So far nobody had been mean when someone screwed up, but probably they were all, like, buds. Everybody hated her. Claire knew they did. What if they laughed? Or *booed?*

Her stomach cramped and she had to scramble out of her seat, whispering, "Excuse me, excuse me," six times to get to the aisle and race to the bathroom.

When she got back, a totally cute ninth-grade guy who was also—wouldn't you know—president of the student body was reading Benedick. Josh Mc-Kendrick was really good. You could tell he actually understood what he was saying.

"'I can see yet without spectacles and I see no such matter,'" he declared. And then, with a scowl, he demanded of Claudio, "'But I hope you have no intent to turn husband, have you?'"

Please, please, please, she whispered to herself. It would be *so* cool to play Beatrice to his Benedick. People would look at her differently. Like *she* was cool.

This was taking *forever*. Finally they finished with the guys and started on girls reading for Hero. Linnet went sixth. Her voice was too soft, but she stood straight, without fidgeting, and read, "'But nature never fram'd a woman's heart, Of prouder stuff than that of Beatrice.'"

Claire thought she was the best. Hero was sweet. Well, wimpy. Claire hated to agree with her father, but he was right; that's why she didn't want to be Hero. This guy treats her really badly, and then she falls into his arms when he realizes he was wrong about her? Yeah, right.

"We'll start with those reading for Beatrice now," the director said. "Jessica Wisniewski? You go first, please."

Jessica was one of the popular girls. She grabbed the script and sauntered out on stage in her flare jeans and peasant blouse, tiny crystal butterflies sparkling in her hair. The scene Mrs. Hinchen was having them read was from near the end, when Claudio had spurned Hero and Beatrice was mad.

"'I cannot be a man with wishing, therefore I will die a woman with grieving.'" Jessica sounded like she was gossiping with her friends. She kept giggling.

"Thank you," Mrs. Hinchen said hastily, interrupting before Jessica could go on to Beatrice's next speech. "Lacy Parker, you're up next."

Claire's hands were sweating. She couldn't do this, she thought desperately. She didn't have to! This wasn't her thing, it was Linnet's. The only reason she'd opened her big mouth and agreed to audition was...

Her father.

"I didn't bother to try out," she'd have to tell him. Which was exactly what he expected.

No. She'd go up there if it killed her.

Which it might.

"Claire Whitcomb?"

Her knees were jelly when she stood up and started down the aisle. She stumbled over somebody's book bag and heard a whispered sorry. It seemed to take forever to get to the front row. She took the script in stiff fingers, then tripped again on the stairs going up to the stage. If anybody laughed... Claire turned and faced the audience with a glare.

Silence.

She could see faces better than she'd expected. Linnet had moved up closer to the front and was smiling encouragement. Josh McKendrick was whispering something to Jessica Wisniewski. The door at the back opened and a man came in, letting it ease shut behind him.

Claire gaped. Her father. What was *he* doing here?

She stole a glance at the clock. Five o'clock. This *was* taking forever. He must have sat in the car for ages and then decided to hunt for them.

But, oh wow. Wasn't he lucky, arriving just in time to watch his darling daughter? He stood unmoving at the back, waiting for her to make a fool of herself.

"Claire?" Mrs. Hinchen prompted.

Claire moistened her lips and looked at the script. For a moment the words on it were all a blur. She absolutely could not do this.

You can! she told herself. *Deep breath. Show everybody. Especially* him.

Mrs. Hinchen had highlighted Beatrice's speeches with a hot pink marker. Another deep breath, and Claire focused on the opening lines. She'd already heard them over and over.

You can.

"'Is he not approved in the height a villain, that hath slandered, scorned, dishonoured my kinswoman! O! that I were a man.'"

Mom had always complained that even her whisper could be heard two blocks away. Now Claire let her scathing voice soar to the back, to her father. She let her bitterness be Beatrice's.

"'O God, that I were a man! I would eat his heart in the market-place.'"

It came more easily. A sense of power flooded her veins and made her giddy. She was better than Jessica Wisniewski. Better than anyone. She was dazzling her father, who had been so sure she couldn't do it.

Still facing the audience proudly, Claire finished at last, a heartfelt, anguished cry, "'I cannot be a man with wishing, therefore I will die a woman with grieving.'''

Her voice seemed to linger in her ears, if not the air. In the long moment of silence that followed, her confidence drained from her with a whoosh, and heat rose in her cheeks.

She'd made a fool of herself. Nobody else had acted. If you were cool, you didn't.

But then, suddenly, kids were clapping. As she stared, incredulous, somebody—Josh McKendrick—stood. Others joined him. They were giving her—*her*—a standing ovation. Dazed, she kept standing there.

Mrs. Hinchen's smile was broad, approving. And her father—Claire's gaze sought the back of the auditorium.

Her father was gone.

He probably hadn't even stayed to watch. Unexpected anger gave her the courage to grin, wave and walk nonchalantly off the stage.

Without tripping.

CHAPTER FOUR

DAVID WHITCOMB'S MERCEDES BENZ was parked at the curb in front of the condo. Grace had known he would be here, of course, but still the awareness that he must be inside gave her an odd start. He was not a *comfortable* man, the kind she could easily imagine grabbing something to drink and the newspaper and making himself at home. She wasn't sure she liked the idea of him at home in her place. She wanted him at arm's length.

And yet she'd insisted he come often, feel at ease. Claire needed him. As long as Claire lived here, Grace had to try to do what was best for the girl.

But when she let herself in from the garage, Grace couldn't let go of the day's tension the way she usually did the moment she stepped into her home, her refuge. Instead she felt a wariness almost as great as if she suspected an intruder. *He* was here, somewhere.

A muffled shriek of laughter from upstairs told her where the girls were. They wouldn't be giggling like that if he were up there with them. She glanced briefly at the telephone, but messages could wait. Going out to dinner gave her a good excuse not to think about plans for the annual fall school carnival, which she, ever ready to wave her hand in the air, had volunteered to organize.

Pausing only to pet Lemieux, who was curled in a too-small cardboard box she had left out just for him, Grace set down her purse and moved quietly through the dining room.

She found David in the living room reading the newspaper she'd left on the table that morning. He didn't hear her coming, and for a moment she was able to observe him unseen.

He'd tossed his suit jacket on the ottoman and loosened his tie. His face showed weariness he hadn't yet let her see. She had the sense that the newspaper was a time filler, that he wasn't really concentrating. As she watched, he let out a soft sigh and rubbed his thumb and forefinger over his eyes.

Grace felt a quiver under her breastbone. What would this guarded man look like if he smiled? His laughs to this point had been bitter, more a rough sound than a genuine curve of the mouth. Was he stern in the office? Did he *have* a sense of humor? Was he capable of tenderness?

She hoped so, for Claire's sake. For hers…well, it hardly mattered, Grace had to remind herself, as long as he was civil. If he ever were to smile at her with devastating charm…the flutter in her chest at the image her mind conjured was enough to scare her. She should be grateful that he was uninterested in her as a woman. If he were…face it, she'd be in trouble.

She must have moved, because he turned his head in that contained way he had, in the same instant assuming a mask of distant civility.

Donning her own, Grace strolled into the living room. "You made it."

"Eventually. The audition ran until five-thirty."

"So you haven't had to wait long." Oh, she was a fount of brilliance tonight.

"No." He appraised her, a lightning-quick glance that made her flush with a sudden, desperate desire to be beautiful, shapely, to provoke a spark of hunger in those hooded eyes.

Praying her cheeks hadn't turned pink, Grace kicked off her heels and sank onto the couch. "So, did the girls say how the audition went?"

"Aside from long?" A hint of a rueful smile quirked one corner of his mouth so fleetingly she'd have missed it if she blinked. It was enough to steal her breath.

"Um..." Focus. "Aside from long," she agreed.

Lemieux, the snowshoe Siamese cross, strolled into the living room, having abandoned his beloved box, and leaped to her lap. Grace couldn't help a small "oomph," when his muscular body landed. He circled, settled and began happily purring when she petted him.

David shook his head in seeming bemusement at the drool from the contented cat forming a puddle on her skirt.

"What did your daughter say the cat's name is?"

She explained that he was named after the hockey star, Mario Lemieux. Then, feeling David's still fascinated stare, she prodded, "The audition?"

He tore his gaze from the cat. "I missed Linnet's reading, but I saw Claire's." The oddest expression crossed his face. "She was incredible. She got a standing ovation."

Pride. That's what she saw in his expression. Pride he hadn't known he felt, didn't quite know what to do with.

"Does she know you saw her read?"

His face shuttered. "I told her on the way home."

"And?"

"I said she was great. Talented." The soft voice was emotionless.

Grace wanted to shake him. "And?" she prompted again, less patiently.

"For a moment I'd swear she looked pleased. She asked, 'Do you really think so?' Linnet jumped in with how great she was, and how many people stopped them on the way out to tell her that. I asked when they'd find out whether they got the parts. My daughter had remembered by then that she has to be invariably negative with me. She shrugged and said it didn't matter, that some popular ninth grader would get any good one." Furrows formed in his forehead. "I tried to tell her they'd be crazy not to cast her. She went for the rude 'Like *you* know anything about it.'"

"But she was pleased. Just remember that."

He shook his head. "Claire doesn't believe me."

"Maybe not this time, but if you say it often enough…" She stopped, realizing how preachy she sounded. "I don't know why I'm lecturing you. I'm certainly no expert."

"And yet, you're raising a great kid yourself. You must be doing something right."

"I'd like to think so," she admitted. "But my two cents is hardly needed when you're seeing a counselor."

"Oh, yeah. We're seeing one. Have seen." His grimace carved a groove in one cheek. "Heck, make it plural. We're on number three now. I figured Claire didn't like the first one. Or the second one. Maybe she'd respond to someone else, I told myself. Now, I'm beginning to wonder. But do you know, plenty of these people don't have kids themselves. I asked number one. Well, no, she admitted. She's never had children."

Grace's hand paused on Lemieux's sleek tan-colored back. "But she's studied them."

"Is that the same thing?" He sounded deeply cynical. "Claire isn't mentally ill. How the hell does somebody learn from books how to raise a normal kid to be happy, self-confident and productive?"

Lemieux protested the lack of fingernails, and Grace automatically resumed scratching.

"I doubt anyone believes there's a magic formula. And think about it. You can be knowledgeable about something you've never done yourself. Just remember all the coaches and movie directors and teachers, for example."

"Maybe." David's eyes, clear and intelligent, pinned her. "Tell me what you were going to say earlier. Your two cents."

Her cheeks warmed again. Wishing passionately that she had never opened her big mouth, Grace said diffidently, "Only that I believe the most important thing we can do is praise our children often, and tell them just as often that we love them.''

"Love and praise,'' he repeated, deadpan.

He wanted some secret, and she had offered the equivalent of the ABCs. Something stupidly obvious. Her chest burned. *She* felt stupid.

"I'm sorry,'' Grace began. "I'm sure the answer for you and Claire is far more complex.''

David let out a sound that might have been anything: a sigh, a grunt of wry laughter, self-disgust. She realized he hadn't even heard her hasty apology.

"Love and praise,'' he repeated. "Neither of which I have any talent whatsoever at expressing.''

Appalled, she began, "Oh, but…''

"My personal life, Ms. Blanchet, has not been an overwhelming success. Chances are, you're right about why.'' He looked at her without expression. "Perhaps we should go for dinner now.''

She couldn't leave it at that. "Rebellious teenagers can happen to anyone.''

His eyes were opaque. "Can they?''

"And divorce sure as heck can. *You* weren't the alcoholic.''

"Maybe I drove Miranda to drink.'' He seemed to be musing, as though the subject were of merely academic interest.

"Did you?'' she dared to ask, and then instantly wished she hadn't. She already knew as much as she had to know to help Claire. The rest of this wasn't her business. This man did not want her help, assuming she would have the slightest idea how to give it.

With sudden and ill-concealed impatience, he

shrugged. "Who knows? That disaster is long past mending. Let's stick to Claire, if you don't mind."

Translation: *Keep your nose where it belongs.* He might as well have waved a sign.

And he was absolutely right. She'd been nosy. Worse—although mercifully he couldn't know—she had let herself be intrigued by David Whitcomb himself. Big mistake.

"I'll go call the girls," she said, rising hastily enough that she scared Lemieux, who shot out of the room. To top it off, Grace stepped carelessly on one of her shoes and lurched into the coffee table.

David started to rise. "Are you all right?"

"Oh, yeah." Just being her usual graceful, elegant, self. Why, she mourned, had *her* mother not insisted on ballet lessons? Pretending she didn't feel ridiculously self-conscious, she said, "I'll tell you what. If you don't mind waiting about three minutes, I'd like to change clothes. If we're really going out for pizza, jeans sound more comfortable." Besides, poor Lemieux had dampened a goodly portion of her skirt.

"No hurry."

"Right." She ducked behind the coffee table and grabbed her navy pumps. Aware of his gaze on her back, she clutched at her dignity and strolled out. Only when she was out of his sight did she race up the stairs, banging her knuckles against Linnet's bedroom door as she passed.

"Girls! We're leaving for dinner in about two minutes."

She stripped off her panty hose and suit with record speed, sighed over the skirt, which would now have to be dry-cleaned, and pulled on jeans. At least a full minute was wasted by her agonizing over which shirt to choose. Finally, annoyed with herself, Grace grabbed a vee-neck cotton sweater in a luscious shade of soft coral, brushed her hair firmly and slipped on a pair of clogs.

Linnet's door was still closed. Grace rapped again. "Girls?"

"Can't we just phone in an order?" her daughter called. "We have homework."

Now, why did that sound canned? Could it be that someone else had planted the words in Linnet's mouth?

Without asking permission, Grace opened the door. Both girls were sprawled on the rug with a teen magazine open in front of them. Linnet made a jerky motion as though to push the magazine out of sight under the bed and then blushed when she realized she was too late.

"We do," she said hurriedly. "Have homework, I mean. It's just that my *YM* came today, and we were only looking."

"That's fine," Grace said equably. "You'll have plenty of time to do your homework later. But right now, Claire's dad is waiting to take us out for pizza. And *I'm* waiting to hear all about the audition."

"Oh!" Linnet's face lit and then clouded as quickly. She jumped up. "It was *so* scary. Wasn't it, Claire?"

Before the other girl could answer, Grace smiled at her. "I hear you were fabulous. Your dad says you're a natural."

The pretty dark-haired girl squirmed. "It, um, went okay. But it was scary."

"I would never, in a million years, have gone out on stage in front of an audience at your age," Grace admitted. "I'm amazed at you two."

They blushed and mumbled something, not protesting again as she hustled them downstairs where David waited. He opened the rear passenger door of the sedan. Linnet climbed in with a smile of thanks. Claire, of course, sauntered to the other side and got in on her own, refusing to accept even a routine courtesy from her father.

Once in herself, Grace repeated her praise. "What about you?" she asked David. "Did you ever do any acting?"

"Actually, I did," he stunned her by saying. "I even played Benedick in *Much Ado,* once upon a time."

"*You* did?" his daughter exclaimed from the backseat. She sounded as if he'd admitted to having flown to the moon or served time for murder one.

"Uh-huh." He was smart enough to keep his response low-key. Starting the car and pulling on to the street, David continued, "I acted in both high school and college. Not during football season—I was a wide receiver. But the rest of the year…heck, I did *A Streetcar Named Desire, Inherit the Wind*…probably a dozen plays."

"Well." Grace tried very hard not to sound as poleaxed as Claire had. "I can see you as Benedick," she heard herself saying, and realized it was true.

He shot her a glance. "Flailing against the inevitable?"

Marriage and love, he meant. Benedick had been determined never to take a wife. To his horror, his friends fell one by one to the lure of gentle women— or, perhaps more accurately, to the lure of the manors and acres with which fathers were willing to dower daughters of marriageable age. And Benedick, poor Benedick, loved a sharp-tongued spinster without even knowing it, until she taunted him into admitting to his weakness. And until *she* admitted to needing him.

Grace wondered if Benedick had tried marriage once before, and failed. Shakespeare hadn't said, not that she recalled. Benedick might well have been a man who didn't know how to tell his daughter he loved her. He was rather clumsy about expressing affection.

She could hardly say that, however. "I was thinking more of his cynicism."

Could a man's eyes smile when his mouth hadn't curved?

"So you think I'm a cynic," he murmured.

"What's a cynic?" Linnet piped up.

"Somebody who thinks everything is going to turn out bad," Claire said.

"Not exactly." Grace smiled over her shoulder at the two girls. "That's a pessimist. A cynic is more somebody who thinks everyone is really behaving selfishly no matter how it appears on the surface."

"You mean, like saying Mother Teresa was only in it for the press?" Claire suggested.

"Uh...I have a feeling that even a cynic would have a tough time with her." A laugh bubbling in her throat, Grace took a shy look at David. "Shall we ask our resident expert?"

She had expected wolfish charm if he ever genuinely smiled. What she got was clear eyes momentarily lit by humor and a smile that pierced her to the heart with a kind of sweetness, as though it were a gift meant only for her.

"You're right. Cynics don't take on saints." He switched on the turn signal. "Ah. Here we are."

"Oh, cool." Linnet bounced. "Bernardino's has the best pizza!"

Inside, they ordered. Then Grace asked the girls to tell her all about the audition before she gave them any money for the arcade.

Claire insisted Linnet had been great, Linnet said Claire was *so* fabulous, and then David offered a five-dollar bill to his daughter while Grace dug in her purse. She watched out of the corner of her eye as Claire hesitated, then took the money.

"Thanks, Mom!" Linnet gave her a flying hug.

Claire gave Grace a quick, sidelong look, before hunching her shoulders and mumbling, "Um, yeah, thanks." The girls took off, their chatter high-pitched and carefree.

Watching them go, Grace was surprised by how hopeful she felt. This might work. Perhaps she was foolish to be optimistic so soon, but it *was* going well. "Isn't it?"

She hadn't realized she'd spoken aloud until the

man across the table from her raised his brows and said, "Depends what 'it' should be."

"It? Oh." She laughed self-consciously. "I'm sorry. I was just thinking that Claire is really trying. That's good, isn't it?"

"Maybe." He nodded his thanks to the waitress who brought two mugs of beer.

"Why so dubious?" Grace asked when they were alone again in their corner booth.

"The calm before the storm. Or, hell, maybe this is the eye of the storm. You should have seen her a week ago."

"But maybe this is giving her the space she needs to realize she was overreacting."

David gave another of those quick, startling smiles. "Do you ever think badly of anyone?"

"Actually, quite often," Grace said with dignity. "In this case, I'm just pleased with how Claire is doing."

He seemed to give himself a shake. "You're right. She is making an effort, and that's all I can ask."

"Oh-oh." Grace nodded toward the arcade room. "Cute boys coming."

His eyes smiled. "Should I go play the heavy?"

"Are you kidding?" She fell back in mock horror. "Now, *that* would be a way to kill all hope of rec-onciliation." When his forehead furrowed, she said quickly, "I'm sorry. I shouldn't joke about something so important."

"It's okay." His gaze caught hers. "Really. I think maybe it helps." Now he looked and sounded awkward. "Claire and I have been letting high drama rule our lives. Could be we're both taking ourselves too seriously.''

''She was trying to hitchhike to California. How could you *not* take that seriously?''

The furrows deepened. ''She scared the hell out of me.''

Grace searched his face. ''How could you suggest, even for a minute, that you don't love her?'' she asked in real puzzlement.

''She makes it hard.''

''I know she does,'' Grace said quietly. ''But tonight, she's speaking to you.''

A trace of a smile returned to his eyes. ''Yeah. Tonight she's speaking to me. Thanks to you.''

''I haven't done—''

''Don't argue,'' he interrupted. ''I won't say thanks every time I see you, but once in a while I've got to slip it in.''

She couldn't look away. Her pulse was sprinting, making her momentarily light-headed. How did he do that, suggest a smile without so much as a twitch of the lips? And why did the slightest softening on his part make her so giddy?

''Your daughter,'' he said abruptly. ''She's never mentioned her father. Neither have you. Do you mind my asking about him?''

Grace had to pull herself back from wherever she'd been. Dreamland. *Not* somewhere even minutely grounded in reality.

Did she mind? With a near physical wrench, she produced a mental snapshot of her husband. As so often, she saw him frowning, preoccupied. He was opening his briefcase and telling her with suppressed irritation that no, he couldn't go out to dinner or rent a movie or talk—he had work to do.

There were days and even weeks where she scarcely thought about Philip anymore. Grace found that she *didn't* like the idea of talking about him with David Whitcomb, but for obscure reasons. The closest she could come to pinning down her discomfiture was the fact that he occasionally reminded her of her husband. The well-cut suits, the thinly disguised impatience and drive, the fact that neither had had time for their daughters.

But David, at least, was trying. Something Philip hadn't been interested enough to do.

And what could she say, anyway? *No, I won't tell you anything about my husband?* Heaven knows, she'd asked David enough nosy questions about *his* personal affairs. What went around, came around.

"No, of course I don't mind," she lied.

"How did he die?"

Three years had elapsed and she'd told the tale often enough that she could speak with more wryness than grief or anger. "Philip dropped dead of a heart attack. No warning. He was a criminal attorney, in court that day. He was almost done with his closing argument when he collapsed. I got a call."

David watched her with such complete stillness, it was as though he feared spooking her. "How old was he?"

"Forty-two. He played racquetball, watched what he ate." She gestured helplessly. "But his father had a heart attack in his forties, too, and the one thing

Philip didn't do was keep his stress level low. He worked long hours, was ambitious, never thought of himself as mortal.''

David gave a brief, thoughtful nod. "How did Linnet take it?''

"Hard. Harder than I expected, considering that my husband worked seventy-hour weeks and couldn't possibly take the time for any of Linnet's trivial activities.'' Some acid had crept into her voice. "Maybe in a way that made it worse. She didn't have many memories to comfort her. I think fathers are terribly important to girls. Linnet had dreams of him waking up one morning and noticing what a wonderful young woman she was becoming. She imagined him…caring. Approving of her. Only then, just like that, he was gone forever, and none of her dreams about him would ever come true.''

"Yes. I see.'' His lashes veiled his eyes.

What did he see? she wondered. That she was telling him a cautionary tale? That Linnet was not the only girl who'd grow to be a woman who regretted never knowing her father's love and approval?

She hoped he did. Once upon a time, she had loved Philip, but now when she thought about him at night, on the edges of sleep, it was with anger rather than hunger for his arms around her. She was the one who should have counted to him—she and Linnet. Not the awards or whatever case he was working on or the fact that the Democratic Party was grooming him for office.

The politicians and the attorneys had bowed their heads at his funeral and given solemn quotes to the newspapers. But not a one of them genuinely mourned his passing. She and Linnet were the people who had really cared, and because they hadn't been as important to him as they should have been, neither of them felt uncomplicated grief.

David Whitcomb was not a man to beat around the bush. "This is why you were willing to go out on a limb for Claire," he said flatly.

"I suppose, partly." Over his shoulder, she saw Linnet and Claire wending between tables. Drawing in a breath, she warned, "Here they come."

He stiffened. Grace felt as much as saw it happen, as if the air suddenly was charged with tension although he hadn't moved, still sat on the other side of the table, one hand wrapped around the mug of beer he'd scarcely sipped.

"Wasn't that our number?" Linnet asked.

"Number?" Grace looked for the slip of paper. She had been deaf and dumb, lost in past and future.

"Yep." David handed it to Linnet, who reached them first. "Will you go get it?"

She snatched the ticket from his hand. "Come on," she said to Claire. "You can get the plates."

He watched them go. "They're getting along really well, aren't they?"

"So far, so good," she agreed.

"The audition…"

"Disappointments happen. From what you tell me, Claire's a shoo-in. If Linnet doesn't get a part—" Grace shrugged "—she has dance."

She didn't have a chance to say more. The girls arrived with the pizza. Claire handed out plates and even slipped into the booth next to her father and across from her friend. In between bites, conversation was general: a drug bust at the high school, a plane crash in Frankfurt, the thunderstorms over Chicago that were playing major havoc with airplane flights, and therefore parcel deliveries, and a sad child-custody case Grace's boss was working on pro bono.

She continued the chatter on the way home with reasonable cooperation from everyone else, and by the time David dropped them at home her sense of optimism was mushrooming.

Okay, call her a Pollyanna, but Claire *was* being less moody and hostile, David was relaxing around her a little bit more, and when he said, "Let me know when you hear about parts in *Much Ado,*" Claire's shrug was only slightly sulky and definitely pleased.

"I'll pick you up at six-thirty tomorrow night for our appointment," he reminded Claire, and her rolled eyes were typical teenager, not hateful.

Grace handed Linnet her key and, as they raced to the front door, bent to say good-night. "That was nice. Thanks for dinner, David."

"You're welcome."

"Maybe you'd take the girls to a movie this weekend."

"Only if you'll go." His grin gave her a fleeting glimpse of the man he might be if Claire abandoned her animosity. "You don't think I'm going to see *Scream 5* without moral support, do you?"

"I think they stopped after three."

"Did they?" he said dryly. "I'm sure Linnet and

Claire will come up with an alternative that appeals to me just as much.''

"A teenage romance.'' She laughed at him. ''Just think, a whole theater full of squealing teenage girls.''

"Oh, I'm thinking.'' His eyes were heavy lidded, the smile lingering. ''That's why you're not sticking me with it all by myself.''

"Dang.'' She pretended to regret she didn't feel. Not even close. Popcorn, previews, a sense of camaraderie…oh, who was she kidding? His thigh near hers in the dark, his hand brushing hers as he reached for popcorn, a touch on the small of her back as he guided her into the aisle.

"Unless—'' a small frown furrowed his forehead ''—you had plans and wanted me to take the girls off your hands. I'm sorry. Am I being dense?''

Do you have a date? was what he was really asking, she realized.

"No. Oh, no.'' She blushed at hearing herself— honestly, she sounded as if the whole idea of dating was foreign to her. If she went on like this, he'd think no man had ever asked her out. And, for reasons she didn't want to examine, it was very important that he *not* think of her as some pitiful spinster. Chuckling, she said, ''Hey, I'm a single parent. I wouldn't dream of planning an honest-to-goodness social life without knowing well in advance that my daughter would be safely occupied. Which—'' she sighed elaborately ''—is all too seldom.''

His forehead smoothed. ''Ah. Then are we on?''

"Why not?'' Telling herself he couldn't possibly

have been pleased that she had no date—she was imagining things, of course—Grace managed to sound no more than a little breathless. "How about if we talk later in the week. See what's playing and whether those thunderstorms let up. Good night, David."

His voice was soft and stayed with her. "Good night, Grace."

She followed the two thirteen-year-olds into the house, feeling more teenage than they did. The stern lecture she tried to give herself helped not at all.

Yes, probably this crush she seemed to be developing was an indication that she'd been living like a nun for too long. Certainly, dating would be a good idea.

It was just too bad that the first man she'd met who she *wanted* to go out with happened to be troubled Claire's father.

CHAPTER FIVE

CLAIRE JUST *KNEW* THAT going out for pizza had made her miss a call from her mom. On the way home, she'd suddenly thought, *Oh, no!* The minute they got in the house, she made Linnet check the messages.

Her friend set down the phone, shaking her head. "Just a bunch of PTA stuff for Mom."

"I'm going to call her." Claire felt sick, thinking of Mom trying and trying to reach her. She'd been so busy pigging out and playing dumb arcade games and even, for a minute, imagining her father had his nice side, she hadn't even thought about Mom for almost two hours!

"Do you want to use the phone in my room?"

"Thanks." She took the stairs so fast she banged into the wall at the top and pushed off to race down the hall. She knew her mother wasn't going to be home. She'd have gone out for the evening already. But Claire flopped down on Linnet's bed and dialed anyway. She hadn't talked to Mom all week. Not since she'd come here.

It was starting to scare her. Tonight was the first time she'd let the worry go for even a while. She'd left messages, at least one every day. Maybe Mom just didn't want to leave a message in return on some stranger's voice mail. Or maybe she hadn't gotten Claire's for some reason. She could be taking a vacation, or working really, really long hours, or be sick in bed with the flu.

Listening to the first ring, Claire knew she was lying to herself. Maybe Mom had married Pete. Or she could be in jail because she'd been driving drunk. Or maybe she was sick, but not with the flu. Claire had read about cirrhosis of the liver, which could kill alcoholics. Mom could even have been in a car accident, because she did drive sometimes when she shouldn't.

"You know how careful I am," she always claimed. "If I've had a drink or two, I drive like a little old lady. If I get pulled over, it'll be for going too slow."

The phone rang four times and then Claire got the answering machine, just as she had all week.

"Mom…" She took a deep breath, but panic squeaked in her voice anyway. "Please call me." She gave Linnet's phone number again and then repeated, "Please. I'm worried about you."

Afterward she lay facedown on the bed, her hands curled into fists, and thought over and over, *I shouldn't have left tonight, I shouldn't have left.* Her mother *always* called around six. Claire *had* to be here.

And now tomorrow night she had that stupid counseling appointment. She hated them. Every one of the counselors had started with tests to see whether she was dumb or crazy or something, and then they wanted to talk. They'd have this sympathetic "I know how you feel'' tone and they expected her to fall for it.

Sometimes she just wanted to yell "Why don't you talk to *him?*" *He* was the problem, not her. She wasn't the one who'd walked out on his wife and child when they needed him. The one who was too busy for visits and whose secretary probably picked out the birthday presents, the one who was keeping Claire and Mom apart just because… She pounded her fists on the mattress. She didn't know why!

Somehow she'd ended up curled in a fetal position, and she was crying big, fat sloppy tears that were soaking Linnet's coverlet. It made her mad to cry, but she couldn't seem to stop herself.

She was so scared. What if Mom was in the hospital? Or… Claire shuddered, a sob rattling in her throat. What if Mom had even died? Did *he* know? Would he tell her?

What if Mom had cancer, and *that's* why her father had taken Claire, and why Mom hadn't really argued, because she knew she wouldn't be around to take care of Claire? She could be in the hospital right now, wishing like anything that Claire was at her bedside and they were playing cards like they used to do before Mom started going out every night.

Claire's chest hurt. Imagining all the possibilities was making her even more scared. She remembered suddenly a family vacation when she was…like, six or seven. She saw it with this weird clarity. They'd gone to the Grand Canyon, and at one of the viewpoints her father had swung her up to look over this stone wall right down into the canyon. She'd de-

manded he lift her up, but when she saw this night-
marishly huge chasm, she was terrified. Claire had
screamed and screamed, even after Dad backed away
and lowered her to the ground and held her tight.

That's what she felt like right now. As if she was
falling and falling into this huge hole, and she was
so tiny nobody would even see her tumbling downward or hear her cries. She was being swallowed by
fear and emptiness, and all she wanted was to go
home.

She balled up covers and shoved them against her
mouth to smother her moan.

Mommy, Mommy, Mommy.

DAVID KNEW, from the moment he arrived to pick up
Claire, that yesterday's détente had not held. When
he rang the doorbell, Grace answered it, her smile
forced as she called, "Claire! Your dad's here." She
lowered her voice. "I told her to get ready. I don't
think she's had a very good day."

"Did she not get a part?"

"They didn't hear." She stopped when she realized Claire was coming down the stairs, moving as
slowly as she could, her hair loose and lank around
her sulky face.

Grace shook her head in warning, presumably
thinking he was stupid enough to say *We're going to
be late. Can you hurry?* His charming daughter had
cured him of such parental admonitions months ago.
It was part of what had made living with her such
hell. He'd say something casual, like "Have you had
breakfast yet?" and she'd blow up. He could never

relax, never let his guard down. The grinding frustration and anger of being married to an alcoholic had been bad enough, but this was worse. He couldn't say, *Enough!* He couldn't wake up one day and realize he didn't give a damn anymore, that she'd killed his love.

Claire was a child. His daughter. Marriage was a simple business compared to this tangle of guilt and love and memories. Claire's first joyful smile, her first word, *Dada.* ''Upsy,'' she would demand, raising her arms to Daddy in complete faith that he would swoop her onto his shoulders. The sight of her terrified, tearstained face as he stomped out of the house after an ugly fight with Miranda. And always, always, the convulsive way she'd hugged him after he packed his suitcase and threw it in his car, the way he'd had to peel her arms from around him.

Most of all, it was the memory of her absolute faith in him, her father, that made him the victim now of her raging pain and anger. She had trusted him; he'd let her down. How could he expect her faith again?

In his more rational moments, David knew better, of course. He hadn't been that bad a father. He'd paid generous child support. He'd called, sent gifts. Maybe he hadn't always known what to say, or chosen the right gifts for a girl her age, but he'd tried. He'd had her to stay with him on a regular basis, if not as often as he should. He had genuinely believed Claire would be better off with her mother, who, although an alcoholic, had loved her child fiercely. Or so he thought.

What parent couldn't look back and repent choices

made? He was doing his best now, wasn't he? Didn't all the damn books on child rearing say that, no matter what, every child longed for her parents' love?

He stood aside and let Claire pass him. She walked to the car without looking back, got in, slammed the door and sat there without so much as turning her head to see if he had followed.

"What happened?" he asked.

"Linnet says she's worried because she hasn't heard from her mother, but I don't know whether there's something else going on." Grace's gaze was worried and apologetic. "I'm sorry."

"Not your fault." That familiar tension gripped him. "Well. Here goes nothing."

She touched his arm. "Good luck."

"Yeah. Thanks." *Come with us,* he wanted to beg. He only nodded and turned away.

During the few steps to the car, he rotated his shoulders, trying to loosen them but without success.

The moment he got in behind the wheel, Claire shot him a look full of defiance and anguish. "I don't want to go. Mom's supposed to call."

Six forty-five. Miranda would be plastered by now. He knew it, Claire knew it.

He buckled his seat belt. "Why didn't you call her earlier?"

"I did! She wasn't home."

"Then what makes you think she's going to call now?"

"Because!" she spat. "I just know!"

Pain throbbed behind his eyes. "Claire, your

mother isn't going to give up on you because you're out of the house for an hour.''

"You know where she is, don't you?" Strung so tight she quivered, Claire glared at him.

Damn it, he knew better than to get involved in a pointless argument with her, but how could he help it? If they didn't talk, they got nowhere. He had to ask. "What do you mean, *where* she is?"

His daughter's head whipped away from him. "Nothing!"

"It's not nothing. You're upset."

She hunched her shoulders and didn't answer. David decided that, for the moment, retreat was the better part of valor. Perhaps the counselor could get Claire to open up.

A small thundercloud, she got out of the car when they arrived and trailed him in at a pointed distance. *I do not want to be with him,* she made sure any observer knew. David checked them in and then pretended to thumb through a *Newsweek* magazine while Claire sat on the other side of the waiting room and glared at a toddler who was making engine sounds as he crashed two toy trucks into each other in the play area. The mother laughed and David smiled to avoid looking rude despite the pain now splitting his skull.

"Claire? David?"

The current counselor, Meg Holm, was a young woman. This time, David was shooting for someone with whom Claire could identify. They'd seen her a couple of times without noticeable success, but he hadn't expected miracles.

David stood and shook hands. Claire rolled her

eyes and pointedly ignored Ms. Holm's outstretched hand. The counselor only smiled and led them back to her office. The colorful childlike illustrations on the walls and the corner set up for play therapy elicited another curl of the mouth from his daughter, just as they had the two preceding weeks.

"Well!" Ms. Holm said brightly, as soon as they were all sitting. "How did this week go?"

Claire slouched low, eyes downcast, and twirled a lock of hair on one finger.

David waited through a silence that became uncomfortable before saying, "As we discussed last time, Claire has gone to stay at her friend's house. The...foster mother tells me things are going fine."

"Oh, great." Claire slumped lower. "She reports on me."

"No. I asked how you'd settled in."

She jerked her shoulders as if to register indifference.

"Claire, how do *you* feel about the change?"

The silence was just long enough to be insolent. "I wanted to go somewhere. Anywhere."

"Yet you're here tonight with your father. I'm really glad to see that."

"Like I had a choice," she mumbled.

David gripped the wooden arms of the chair. Hard. He should have taken something for the headache but hadn't wanted Claire to spot a weakness. He imagined her scenting it like drops of blood.

"Is there anything you want to talk about this week?" the counselor asked her.

"No."

Ms. Holm raised her eyebrows at him. "David? How do you feel about having Claire living with these friends?"

"We needed the break," he said. "I've been over there a couple of times this week, and things have gone better. Claire tried out for a school play, and I saw her audition. She was incredible."

"Oh!" Ms. Holm was all smiles. And who could blame her? At last, something positive to pounce on. "Did you get the part?"

Another jerk of the shoulders. "I probably won't."

"Were you pleased with how you did?"

"It was okay," she said without expression.

"Well! I'll keep my fingers crossed for you. I think that would be exciting."

No reaction. David surreptitiously massaged his temple.

"Have you spoken to your mother this week?"

"She probably called tonight while I'm *here*." Claire shoved back her hair and, without looking at him, said bitterly, "My *father* probably knows why she hasn't called."

He gritted his teeth. "Your mom and I don't talk, except when it concerns you. I haven't spoken to her since the last time you ran away. Why would I?"

Claire turned her blazing fear and hatred on him. "Then where is she?"

Wearily David said, "I don't know. For all that I was aware, you two were talking every day. She hasn't called our house."

"*Your* house!"

"Claire, it's yours, too. You cannot go back to your mother."

Her hands knotted into fists in her lap. "Maybe she'll quit drinking. *Then* what will your excuse be?"

David said very quietly, "I gave your mother the option of going into alcohol treatment before I took you. She wasn't ready. She couldn't do it, even for you." Couldn't. Wouldn't. He didn't know. "Claire, it's not going to happen, not soon enough for you. I'm sorry."

She shot to her feet, eyes glittering with tears. "You're not sorry! You want to ruin my life!"

"Sometimes decisions that parents make seem hard to understand," Ms. Holm began.

He talked right over her. "I love you."

Although tears tracked her cheeks, his daughter's voice vibrated with hostility and shocking intensity. "Well, I don't love you. I will never live with you again! You can't make me. I'll keep running away until sometime you don't find me."

This shouldn't still hurt, David thought distantly. He shouldn't feel as if she'd just gutted him.

"Claire!" Ms. Holm spoke sharply enough to make Claire's head turn. "You miss your mother and you're angry at your father for taking you away. But think—if you were him, what would you do?"

The pain in his child's eyes was what was ripping him open. She looked back at him as she said flatly, "You don't know him. You weren't there when he left. I was so scared. Now he wants me to say it's okay, but it's not. I wanted him to be my father then, but now I don't."

Ms. Holm leaned forward. "The past can't be changed. Your dad is trying to focus on the future. I hope you can discover that you don't really mean—"

"No." He hadn't realized he was going to speak; heard his voice from far away. He sounded controlled, utterly emotionless. "Claire deserves to be listened to. Because she's not an adult doesn't mean that she shouldn't be taken seriously."

Claire and the counselor both were staring. David stood up. "Claire, I'll take you home."

Ms. Holm scrambled to her feet. "David…Mr. Whitcomb. We've opened a dialogue here. Hurtful things get said in the heat of the moment. That's part of the process. You can't…"

She was speaking to his back. He had waited only for Claire to realize, wide-eyed, that he meant what he said and to scoot ahead of him out of the office. He strode down the hall, the counselor scuttling after them with her voice rising as she realized he wasn't listening.

The agonizing pain in his head almost drowned out the emotional pain of understanding, once and for all, that he'd lost his daughter.

Wordlessly he unlocked the car and let Claire get in by herself as he circled to his side. In silence he started the engine, pulled out of the parking lot onto the road. *Get her home. You can survive that long.*

Claire darted looks at him during the short drive to Grace Blanchet's. He drove grimly, the pain in his head and heart excruciating. In front of the town house, he put the gearshift into park, set the emergency break and then said, "Going home to your mother is not an option. However much you love her, you must accept that she's an alcoholic and incapable of being a responsible parent. I'll talk to Grace about making your stay here permanent. If that's not possible, we'll think of something. Don't worry."

She spoke softly, hesitantly. "We, um, aren't going to do counseling anymore?"

"No."

"But you kept saying..."

"You're old enough to know your mind. And you're right. I wasn't there when you needed me."

"So...are you, like, never going to come over?" She sounded terribly young.

David turned his head and looked into his daughter's face. Saw the child and the teenager as if they were color overlays, the one, shy and confused, dimly seen through the distortion of the other.

"We'll talk another time, okay?"

She gave a quick nod and got out, hesitated for an instant, then slammed the car door. He waited as she ran across the tiny lawn, the flare bottoms of her jeans frayed and her hooded, army-green sweatshirt baggy.

Some things were past mending. Perhaps, he thought painfully, the counseling sessions had always been for his sake and not hers. Had he just wanted to prove to her and himself that he was doing everything a good daddy should? Was he seeking forgiveness?

On instinct he put the car in gear, drove home. He could make it. Only inside his house where no one could see would he be able to rage at the heavens, drink until anesthetized.

Cry.

FROM THE MINUTE Claire came home early from the counseling session, Grace suspected something was wrong. She heard the front door open and close, the pound of feet on the stairs and a moment later the slam of the bedroom door. Going to the bottom of the staircase, Grace called up, "Claire? Is that you?"

"Yes!" came her muffled voice.

"Is everything all right?"

"Yes! I just have cramps. I'm going to bed."

She hesitated, her hand on the newel post. "If you need anything, just yell."

Not until she'd gone to bed herself did she hear Claire come out and use the bathroom. The next morning, the teenager was quiet at breakfast, her eyes puffy, but she claimed again that nothing was wrong. The fact that she was, at that moment, squeezing poor Lemieux in her arms so hard that he let out a baritone cry made Grace doubt her brave claim. But she couldn't force even her own daughter to talk when she didn't want to, never mind Claire, who was still something of a stranger.

Although Claire continued to be subdued and David neither called nor stopped by that weekend, Grace nearly convinced herself everything was fine. He must be busy with work, or he was out of town for the weekend and hadn't thought to let her know. Perhaps Claire *did* know, and just wasn't saying. He wouldn't just vanish. They'd all been getting along so well.

Hadn't they?

Monday she called him, but got no answer and

wasn't quite sure what to say to his voice mail. Tuesday, feeling more assertive, she left a message.

Wednesday, when she walked in the door from school, the two girls pounced.

"We both got parts!" Linnet said joyously.

"Really?" Her tiredness magically dropped from her. "That's great! Who got what part?"

Claire hung back a little, but her pleasure was palpable. "I'm Beatrice."

Linnet's happiness briefly dimmed. "I didn't get Hero. I'm Ursula, the maid. It's a really small part." She brightened. "But that's okay. I won't have to memorize as much. And I won't have to be so terrified on opening night!" She suddenly clutched her stomach. "Oh. I'm already getting scared."

"Don't worry. You'll be great. Girls, that is such fabulous news!" Grace held out her arms. "You've got to let me hug you."

Linnet came gladly, Claire with hesitation, but she gave them both a big squeeze.

"Did you let your dad know, Claire?"

Her face and tone both went blank. "He won't care."

The worry that had niggled all weekend gave a twinge. "He was thrilled by how well you read! Of course he'll want to know!"

His daughter gave a shrug meant to look uncaring. "If he calls and asks, I'll tell him."

Grace's apprehension sharpened and took focus. She said straight out, "Claire, something did happen between the two of you, didn't it? Will you tell me?"

"He said he'd find me someplace permanent to live."

Her voice rose. *"What?"*

"He said if that's what I want, then it was okay with him." Her elaborate nonchalance was woefully unconvincing. Grace's diagnosis was that Claire didn't want to care but was failing miserably.

"Linnet," Grace said, "will you please leave Claire and me alone to talk for a minute?"

Wide-eyed, Linnet nodded, backed clumsily away and left the kitchen.

Grace gently touched Claire's arm. "Sit down, honey."

The girl bit her lip, then scrambled up on a stool and seemed to brace herself. Claire had huge, melting brown eyes, almost too big for her pixie face. She tended to wear oversize clothes rather than the tight baby tees popular right now. Grace suspected Claire could be stunning if she could be made to feel confident. She'd assumed that Claire was sensitive about her changing body, imagining that her breasts were too big or too small, her hips fat or skinny. Whatever. But looking at her now, Grace wondered instead if she wasn't hiding out, not just physically but emotionally, inside sacky clothes and a lank curtain of hair that she seemed to deliberately shake over her face.

"You'll be beautiful in a long gown with a snug waist," she said thoughtfully. "With your hair in a snood."

Claire looked startled, presumably at the unexpected subject, and then perplexed. "A...what?"

"You know." Grace's hand fluttered at her nape. "One of those net bags that women wore over a chignon in the nineteenth century. Pretty."

"Oh. I, um, don't know what kind of costumes we'll wear."

"Maybe the director would like help with costumes. I'm a whiz with the sewing machine, and I'll bet I could organize some other parents to help." Grace stopped herself with an effort. "That is, unless it would embarrass you. Or Linnet. Maybe you'd rather I weren't around."

"No!" Claire's prettiness shone through for an instant. "No, I'd like that. If you have time."

Grace gave fleeting thought to the prizes she had to pick out for the fall carnival, the lists of parents she had to call to enlist volunteers to help out with games and the dance, to the baby shower she was organizing for a young attorney at her firm, to the extra hours she'd promised to work next week so that a paralegal could go on a business trip to London with her husband. But the girls needed her to be involved, Claire even more than her own daughter.

She gave Claire another quick hug and then sat on a stool herself, one foot hooked on the leg. "You wouldn't catch me dead on stage, but I'd love to help behind the scenes."

Claire nodded.

Grace hesitated, then sighed. "Okay. I'd like if you would tell me about your counseling session."

The story was brief and of course one-sided. Claire had been upset because her mom hadn't called, and she was sure for some unknown reason that her father had something to do with that. Or maybe it was just his fault that she'd missed her mother's call, because he'd insisted on taking them all out for pizza and then made her go to the stupid appointment the next night.

"And I said I wouldn't live with him, and he just suddenly said that was fine, I was old enough to make up my own mind. And we stood up and left right in the middle of the appointment." She gave another of her shrugs that were supposed to say *See, I don't care*. But at the same time her face worked, as if she were struggling to prevent tears. She bowed her head and the hair swung down to hide her expression. "It was okay with me."

"You didn't say anything to him that you haven't before?" Grace asked carefully.

The thirteen-year-old shook her head without looking up. "*He* wanted to claim he loved me, and it made me mad. Like, now he wants to be daddy and so everything should be cool. But we argue all the time. This wasn't any different. And then he, just, like, changed his mind."

During the conversation her entire posture had changed, from straight back and head held high as she felt a dawning of hope that she could be beautiful on stage, to this: hunched shoulders, head pulled in like a turtle's, hair veiling her face.

Grace felt a burst of pure rage. Clearly David Whitcomb was either a complete crud or a coward. Either way, this girl deserved better from her father.

And Grace was damn well going to see that she got it. He had made both her and his daughter promises, and he would keep them or she would personally fight for Claire to be able to go home to her mother. Miranda Whitcomb might be an alcoholic but at least loved her daughter, if Claire was to be believed.

Grace reached out, not knowing if Claire would hate to be touched but unable to help herself. Smoothing the hair back from the girl's face, feeling the delicacy of her bone structure, Grace said very gently, "I can't believe your father meant what you think he did. He's obviously out of practice at being a parent. He and I need to have a serious talk."

"He said he wanted to talk to you, about you keeping me. But..." She faltered, didn't finish.

"But he hasn't called." Which meant what? That he'd spoken in anger and now didn't know how to backtrack? That he couldn't be bothered to pick up the phone to discuss his daughter's welfare?

Grace preferred the first alternative. She hated to think she could be quite so deceived by anyone. David had admitted himself that he had a hard time expressing love. But he *had* taken the trouble to regain custody, to go to counseling with Claire, to bare his life to an uncomfortable degree for Grace's scrutiny. Surely, surely, he wouldn't have done any of that if he hadn't cared at all.

But then, she had been wrong in painful ways about her husband. And whatever his reasoning, David Whitcomb's behavior was inexcusable.

It was high time somebody told him so. And she had just elected herself as the voice of his conscience.

"Well, guess what?" she said to Claire. "*I* can call him. We'll figure all this out. I promise."

Nodding, Claire swiped her forearm angrily at her tears.

Grace had to blink against the sting of dampness in her own eyes. Throat tight, she said, ''In the meantime, we're your family as long as you need us. Okay?''

Claire's face crumpled. With one more nod, she gulped and fled, the stool rocking in her wake and then settling back on all four legs.

Grace grabbed a paper towel and blew her nose firmly.

Oh, yes. She would indeed be calling Mr. David Whitcomb.

CHAPTER SIX

HE SHOULD HAVE CALLED Claire, little though she would want to hear from him. The trip to Atlanta had been unexpected and urgent, but he should at least have left her a message. Hell, he could have called any one of the past three evenings, but had found it all too easy to put off speaking to his own daughter, or justifying himself to Grace. When he got home, he had told himself.

Feeling unutterably weary, David dropped his suitcase onto his bed and unzipped it, extracting his toiletry kit and carrying it into the bathroom. The sight of his own face in the mirror was unwelcome and he turned away. Pretty damn sad, when a man couldn't meet his own eyes in the mirror.

In the office, he was hard-assed, blunt, unwilling to hear an excuse twice. To some extent, in his marriage he'd been the same. Miranda's acute denial about her drinking problem bothered him more than the boozing itself. Her dad had been an alcoholic, too. Hell, for all he knew, it was a hereditary disease, like they said. What he couldn't stand was her unwillingness to look him in the eye and say "Yes. I have a drink before breakfast. Yes. I was drunk at the dinner party. Yes. I have a problem."

But, no. She had an excuse for everything. That wasn't alcohol on her breath, it was mouthwash. It was her new high heels that made her fall down at the party. Don't be silly. Just because she enjoyed an occasional drink didn't mean she was an alcoholic. He was a Puritan, she'd tease.

Maybe he was, David thought now, grimly. But he had never been a coward. He had never been childish, sulking when he got his feelings hurt, refusing to say why, stomping out without resolving a problem.

So why, as a father, was he both? Damn it, he was the adult here!

It was past time he start acting like one.

David had emptied his suitcase and was putting it in the closet under the stairs when the doorbell rang. Surprised—not many people stopped by unexpectedly—he opened the door to find Grace Blanchet on his doorstep.

Shining hair tugged into a severe bun, her shoes sensible and her suit brown, she had the look of a nun on a mission. A nun from a martial order; pink flagged her cheeks and her eyes sparkled.

Given his mood, her mood, and the sorry state of his relationship with his daughter, it dismayed David to have his body respond as if she were a stripper teasing the audience with a prim costume she'd be dramatically shedding with the next beat of music. Damn it, she wasn't even pretty!

Fortunately, it would never enter her head to suspect him of lust unbecoming to the moment. "Mr. Whitcomb," she said formally, not a trace of her former friendliness in her voice, "I need to talk to you."

"Have you been trying to call?" he asked. "I've been out of town on business." *Excuses, excuses,* his inner voice taunted.

"Really?" She was not impressed. Her tone was appropriately tart. "Up the Amazon, perhaps? Surely someplace with no phone, fax or e-mail."

"I should have called," he admitted stiffly. After a moment, he stood back. "Please. Come in. You're right. We do need to talk."

Grace marched past him, a soldier on her way to war. Despite its drab color, the straight skirt nicely outlined her rear.

David wrenched his gaze from his visitor's curves to the tight knot of hair at her nape. Voice grainy, he said, "The living room is to your right."

He followed her, seeing it through her eyes—assuming, that is, that she wasn't too angry to notice her surroundings at all.

With no interest in haunting antique stores or mulling over fabrics, he'd hired a decorator when he bought this place. She had asked him a million questions and done her best to create a home, not just a showplace. Somehow—he'd never quite put his finger on how—she had failed. Or he'd failed. Every grouping of objets d'art appeared staged, the leather furniture self-consciously grouped, the rag-rolled walls trendy. David entertained in this room; he didn't sit down with the evening newspaper and put his feet up in here. Grace Blanchet's living room settled around its occupants with a sigh of relief and pleasure. His waited to be admired.

"Have a seat," he said.

She hesitated, then chose a chair with a linen slip-cover that the decorator had assured him provided an effective contrast of textures. As if he gave a damn.

"Can I get you a cup of coffee?"

"No." After the tiniest of pauses, Grace added a polite if grudging thank-you.

He realized he'd been hoping for a reprieve. Maybe also for the sense of conviviality that having coffee together suggested.

"All right." He sat on the leather couch, rotated his shoulders, then said straight out, "I suppose Claire told you about our last, disastrous counseling session."

"Yes. Finally." She bit off each word as if she'd have rather sunk her teeth into him. "Last night, *after* spending the week either hiding in her room or plastered with makeup to hide her puffy eyes."

Stunned, he asked, "She cried?"

"Of course she cried!" Grace looked at him with dislike. "She is a child whose father just announced that he'd had enough and would find somebody else to take her in."

Momentarily he closed his eyes. "That's not how it was."

"Then how was it?" *And you'd better make it good,* was the subtext.

David rubbed his hands on his thighs. Through a tight throat, he said, "She told me that I'd blown it as daddy long ago, and my scrambling now to be a full-time parent was futile. She repeated that she'd never live with me. Said she'd keep running away until one time I wouldn't find her."

"And you believed her." She sounded stunned and exasperated.

"The counselor started to tell her why she didn't really mean what she was saying. That's when I lost it."

"Why were you paying a psychologist if you were unwilling to listen to her?"

Agitated, he stood. "Because I've been trying too damn hard to believe that Claire doesn't really hate me no matter what she says. And it suddenly occurred to me that, hey, maybe she does. Isn't she old enough to be listened to?"

"She's a *child,*" Grace said again.

He spun to face her. "You didn't hold any sincere beliefs at thirteen?"

"At thirteen, I was quite sure my parents were abusive because they wouldn't let me go out on a date with Johnny Hines, who was sixteen and had his driver's license. I sincerely believed I was plenty mature to date. When my parents said no anyway, I screamed that I hated them and sobbed into my pillow until I fell asleep."

He gestured impatiently. "Overrating your maturity isn't the same thing as knowing what people are really important in your life. If Miranda and I were fighting for custody again, the judge would ask Claire who she'd rather live with, and he'd listen to her. How can I do less?"

"And yet, you're not willing to let her go back to her mother."

"She uses Claire."

"Who is deliberately blinding herself to the flaws

of someone she loves.'' Grace suddenly spoke with a gentleness that had been missing earlier; her eyes held the compassion that unmanned him. "If she can do that, is it really so unlikely that she's also, out of long-stored hurt, blinding herself to her need for her father's love?''

David opened his mouth. Closed it. Stood in the middle of his living room, hands dangling uselessly at his sides, and felt foolish. Thunderstruck. Was it really so simple?

"I don't know what more I can do." He hardly recognized his own voice, blurred by bewilderment and helplessness.

"I believe with all my heart that Claire needs you." Grace stood, too, and came to him. "Don't give up on her. I don't know what you should do. Just...don't give up."

He tried to smile and felt it twist into a grimace. "Contrary to appearances, I wasn't going to. She hit me hard that night. By the next morning, I knew I'd been an idiot. I just didn't know what in hell to do next. And then I had to fly to Atlanta.''

"I wish you'd called me.''

He could tell her this much about himself. "I don't like admitting to my failings.''

The edge returned to her voice. "You know, the problems are Claire's more than yours. Plenty has happened in her life that didn't involve you.''

"In other words, I'm being self-centered." He discovered that he didn't much like being criticized, even if he deserved every word.

She didn't flinch. "Maybe. Do you really think

about what Claire is feeling instead of what you feel?''

"I thought I'd tried."

Clearly irritated, Grace shook her head. "No. I'm not talking about what she *says* she feels. Isn't that camouflage for most of us? I'm talking about putting yourself in her shoes, imagining how a girl her age would have viewed your divorce, your occasional visits, her mother's dependence."

Stung, he said, "I admitted the failing was mine."

"But not all of it is. And not all the solution can come at your hands. Your daughter, Mr. Whitcomb, is not a scheduling problem that you can solve with some deft rerouting or hand off to your assistant."

He hadn't wanted to look at himself in the bathroom mirror. Well, thanks to Grace Blanchet, he was seeing himself now. And the very fact that she was the one holding up the mirror made him feel like an even lower life form than he already had.

"You don't think much of me, do you, Ms. Blanchet?" he asked.

Her face was more expressive than she probably knew. Startlement dilated her pupils, self-consciousness pinkened her cheeks, and some unidentifiable emotion caused her gaze to slide from his.

"I wouldn't exactly say that." Her tongue touched her lip. "Until this past week, I would have said—" She stopped herself abruptly.

She was only a few feet away, her eyes vivid as she stole a glance at him. Her face was too long for beauty; her nose was high on the bridge and lightly freckled. She lacked the sultry mouth of a model, hers instead being as uncompromising as her character. But her skin was pale and almost translucent, her bone structure fine.

Although his hands remained curled at his sides, his fingertips *felt* the smooth texture of her skin. He imagined her eyes closing as she tilted her head back, her lashes fanning against the faint smudges beneath them. Her mouth would soften, tremble, as his thumb played across the fullness of her lower lip.

"Would you have dinner with me?" he asked hoarsely.

She blinked, willing to look at him again. "You mean, to talk about Claire? Well, I suppose, if you think it's necessary. We sure as heck don't want to say anything where she or Linnet could overhear."

"No. That isn't what I meant." Was he crazy? David wondered. But some force drove him on. "I shouldn't ask. All you have to do is say no. But I would like to get to know you, leaving my daughter out of it." *I'd like to kiss you.*

She fell back a step, renewed wariness in her amazing eyes. "You're asking me for a *date?*"

He found himself tensing, felt his expression becoming stiff, at the way she said it. *A date?*

"I'm sorry," he said impassively. "It would appear I'm being self-centered again. I seem to be shouldering Claire aside. No wonder you dislike me." He rubbed the back of his neck. "I'm out of line. Forget I asked."

"No!" Grace twined her fingers together and squeezed so hard her knuckles showed white. The freckles on her nose stood out, as if she'd paled. "No, I don't dislike you."

"I'm still out of line." To put it mildly. He didn't usually speak before reason had a chance to kick in. "Everything else aside, us dating is a complication we don't need. Like I said, forget I asked."

A small silence fell. She cocked her head to one side, her forehead puckering. "I've never heard anyone backpedal so fast. If you don't mind telling me, why *did* you ask?"

Because I want you. "I find you attractive." She sure as hell wouldn't return the compliment, as suavely as he'd behaved.

Her doubt was plain. "Really."

"You don't believe me."

"I am not a beautiful woman. What's more, I've never seen the slightest indication you were interested. You haven't even been very friendly."

Truth? Instinct told him yes.

"The fact that I wanted to kiss you didn't keep me from resenting like hell the fact that, as a single parent, you'd still somehow managed to raise a great kid while my daughter had her thumb out on some freeway entrance." He gave a grunt that wasn't quite a laugh. "No, let me be completely petty. My kid liked you better than she liked me. I could see in your eyes that you were judging me, and finding me wanting."

Now those same eyes were enormous. "I didn't…"

"And I deserved it," he said, jaw muscles knotted, "which didn't make me enjoy the experience any more."

She took a deep breath. "You wanted to kiss me?"

His voice always became softer, less emphatic, the more serious he was. "Oh, yeah," he agreed.

Her brow crinkled again in gentle perplexity. "But I'm not…"

"Not what?"

"Beautiful. Or…or…" Her hands shaped curves that would have left Marilyn Monroe lacking.

For the first time, David's tension abated and some sense of humor returned. "You were married. Your husband must have found you sexy."

"Sometimes I wond—" The word ended in a strangled gasp, and pink flooded her cheeks.

Just like that, he was uncomfortably hard. He gritted his teeth against a desire to close the distance between them and kiss her senseless. Just because she was amazed that he found her attractive didn't mean that she felt any reciprocal tug.

"Take my word for it," he said dryly. "You have enough curves. I like you in tight jeans."

"Oh." Blushing, her freckles standing out, Grace Blanchet looked very young and vulnerable. "Why did you tell me to forget it, then?"

She'd lost him. "Forget it?"

"You asked me to have dinner with you. Then you said to forget it."

"Because I realized that you were right. I was back to me, me, me." One more thing he hated admitting. And here was another one. "Because Claire has mauled my ego badly enough, and I also realized I'd set myself up for another pummeling from you."

Grace seemed to marvel at the idea. Perhaps she

liked the notion of having such power over him. "You thought I'd say no?"

"You had just finished expressing your disdain for my character." He let out a breath. "Ms. Blanchet, can we just go with my first suggestion and forget I asked? I should be concentrating on my daughter right now."

"It wouldn't hurt her to see that someone else likes you," she said thoughtfully.

"What?"

She nodded, as if to herself. "We could try dinner just once. See how she reacts. And whether we have anything whatsoever to talk about besides our daughters."

He stared at her, wondering if they'd gone in circles so many times he'd become dizzy.

"You'll have dinner with me."

"Well..." A faint blush touched her cheeks again. "Unless you're sorry you asked in the first place."

He had to shake his head, which failed to clear it. "I'd like to have dinner with you."

"Oh dear." She rolled her eyes. "I didn't leave you much alternative, did I?"

A laugh slipped out of him. Damn, he did want to kiss her. "I could say I really do want to concentrate on Claire. But the truth is, I keep thinking about you. I'm...only hoping you've given me some passing thought. Beyond my shortcomings as a parent."

"I gave you a passing thought." She was still blushing. "You know, I really should go."

"Tomorrow night?" He named a Bellevue restaurant well-known for its Mediterranean cuisine.

"Tomorrow?"

"It is Friday," he said persuasively. "If I come over at six, I could talk to Claire for a few minutes before we go."

"Yes." She hesitated. "Okay. But what should I tell Claire about tonight?"

"She knows you're here?"

Grace nodded.

"Tell her this is still her home, and that her father is going to be an irksome presence in her life forever more."

Her smile was reward enough. "That will do very nicely."

"Then I'll see you at six."

Their goodbyes were awkward. He wondered if they'd be any less so tomorrow night.

But to hell with it. He'd kiss her either way.

Just like he'd tell Claire that he wasn't going away, however much she wished he would.

And then he'd try to figure out how she *really* felt about that.

"WHY ARE YOU GETTING so dressed up?" Linnet asked with deep suspicion.

Claire was wondering the same thing. Did Mrs. Blanchet *like* Claire's father?

The two girls sat cross-legged on the bed watching Linnet's mother put the finishing touches on her appearance. Stanzi lay between them, watching with as much interest and a certain degree of suspicion, too, which was in character for her. She didn't like anything out of the ordinary, Claire had discovered. *Es-*

pecially anything that might prevent her meals being served on time.

Mrs. Blanchet turned from side to side, scrutinizing her reflection in the full-length mirror on the closet door and plucking at the neckline as if she was worrying about whether it was too low.

It was a really pretty dress, although Claire couldn't figure out why. There were hardly any seams. Royal-blue silk just hugged her body without being tight, like something Christina Aguilera would wear. It made Mrs. Blanchet look as if she had a real cleavage, which Claire knew she didn't. And her neck was so slim and graceful and white, Claire thought about swans.

Mrs. Blanchet gave a last tug. "I will never be beautiful," she said with a sigh.

"No," Claire said without thinking. She blushed fiercely. "I mean, you do look pretty, but really you're more..." She frowned, trying to think of the right word. "Elegant," she said triumphantly. That was it. Linnet's mom was really classy.

"Why, thank you."

Mrs. Blanchet smiled and bent to give her a quick hug, something she did easily and often. Claire wasn't used to it. Her mom only leaned on her when she needed help getting to her bedroom.

"You do look nice." Linnet scowled. "But why do you *want* to look nice?"

"For two reasons. Number one," Grace held up a finger, "Scalzo is a four-star restaurant. You don't go in jeans. Number two, Claire's dad is a handsome, well-dressed man. Have you seen those suits he wears? I refuse to look dowdy in comparison. There,'' she said lightly. ''Does that satisfy you?''

Claire couldn't say, *Not really.* Anyway, the doorbell chimed just then and she jumped.

Mrs. Blanchet gave her a significant look. ''Claire, your father wants to talk to you before he and I go out. So why don't you go answer that and I'll be down in a minute.''

She gave a tight nod. She'd been dreading this since Mrs. Blanchet came home last night and said that Claire's father *hadn't* wanted to talk about finding a permanent place for her to live.

She descended the stairs more slowly than she should have, considering he must be standing on the porch wondering if anyone was going to come to the door. She didn't know why she was so nervous. It would be the same old same old.

Wouldn't it?

Still, her palms were sweating when she turned the knob. Last time she'd seen him, he had looked so…grim. Like he meant it about never wanting to see her again. The confusing part was, she should have been happy and wasn't.

''Hello, Claire,'' he said now.

As usual, she couldn't tell what he was thinking. ''Um…hi.'' She stood back. ''Mrs. Blanchet says she'll be down in a minute.''

''Okay.'' He came in. ''Can we talk?''

Claire gave a brief, jerky nod.

They went into the living room, her noticing because of what Mrs. Blanchet had said how well his suit did fit. It was true that he was hot as fathers went,

Claire had to admit, not without some pride. Maybe she didn't want to live with him, but he was her father, and at least she didn't have to be embarrassed about how he looked. He wasn't going gray at all, and he had broad shoulders and no pot belly, and he had a great smile.

Only, she never saw it anymore, except in memories of him coming home from work, his face lighting when he saw her, just before he tossed her in the air and crushed her to him for a hug.

"Will you sit down?" he asked her.

She only hesitated a second before curling her feet under her on one of the big squishy chairs. He sat, too.

Then he looked at her steadily. "I didn't mean what I said last time. You aren't getting rid of me that easily. I had a hell...a heck of a migraine headache, and you got to me. Probably you will again, but parents don't give up on their children even when everyone is angry. And hurt."

She opened her mouth, but he lifted a hand to stop her.

"No. Just let me finish. Then it will be your turn. For now, I'm going to drop the counseling sessions. Neither of us was comfortable talking in front of someone else. I think the sessions were just putting pressure on us. Later, that might be something we'll want to do again. For now, I'm just going to see you here. Maybe take you places sometimes."

A funny feeling spread in her chest. Relief? she wondered in shock. And then, for no reason, she was crying, these huge, humiliating sobs. Big fat tears poured down her cheeks and her nose was running and she was still just sitting there in front of him, the enemy.

Her father.

His face spasmed and he came to her so fast she didn't have a chance to ward him off. He sat on the arm of her chair and wrapped her in strong arms and let her cry against his chest even though he was all dressed up.

When she quieted and wiped her nose, he smoothed her hair back from her face.

"I've been a real jerk, haven't I?"

She tried to shake her head.

He didn't seem to notice. "You haven't been hearing from your mom, have you?"

Forehead against his tie, Claire shook her head again.

"I know you don't want to believe I understand, but I do. I loved your mom, and it hurt when I realized one day that the next drink meant more to her than I did. She's...not very reliable. From everything I've read about alcoholism, it's not her fault, and it doesn't mean she doesn't love you. Addiction is a powerful thing."

"She does love me!" Claire said fiercely, jerking away. "If you hadn't taken me away..."

"She'd still be leaving you alone all evening while she went out to bars. She'd be letting you lie about why she can't go to work, letting you miss school." He looked so sad, Claire didn't interrupt. "Your mom is too much in the grip of her disease to be able to take care of you. It's no different than her having cancer or heart disease. None of this is fair to you, Claire, but it's reality.''

"But she always called me." Her voice came out all blubbery.

"Maybe she lost her job again and is drinking from the minute she gets up in the morning. Or maybe she thinks that you'll be better off if you quit depending on her.''

Claire knew he'd offered the second alternative because he felt sorry for her. The fact that he bothered almost made her cry again.

He reached out and gave the back of her neck a gentle squeeze. "Claire, we need to start over again. This time, I'm going to set one ground rule."

She wiped her nose on her sleeve and asked warily, "What?''

"You can't say you hate me. Maybe you do. I don't know. But you and I are stuck with each other for the long haul. I will always be your father. It...really gets to me when you say that. So do me a favor and tell me you're mad or don't like something I've done without saying 'I hate you.' Can you do that?''

Claire nodded and said in a creaky voice, "I'm sorry."

"I'm sorry, too." His smile was painful, not the one she remembered from when she was little. "But I do love you, Claire."

She opened her mouth but she couldn't say it. She was too confused. Memories were all jumbled. Sitting on her daddy's shoulders with her fingers gripping his hair and her heels drumming his chest as she urged him to gallop, Daddy, gallop. Her creeping down the stairs when she heard her mother screaming and throwing things, and him turning to order her back to bad, his eyes so icy it terrified her. The murmur of his voice and the comfort of his big, strong presence when she had nightmares and the horror of waking frightened in the night after he was gone, because she knew nobody would come. The gentle way he'd tease and the joy in his smile, just for her.

That last, painfully tight hug and the sight of him walking away, getting into the car despite her sobbing pleas.

I love you.

He kissed the top of her head and said softly, "We can do better."

Footsteps on the stairs warned that Mrs. Blanchet was coming. Claire gave a jerky nod but didn't look up. He rose to his feet and she felt him looking down at her for a moment before he walked away.

"We'll only be gone a few hours, girls," Mrs. Blanchet called. "The restaurant's number is by the phone."

Then the front door opened and closed. Claire buried her face in her arms and let the hot tears come.

CHAPTER SEVEN

WHATEVER HAD HAPPENED in there with his daughter had shaken David; he emerged from the living room with his eyes blank, stunned. He might have been a man walking away from a traffic accident. He looked at Grace, but not as if he really saw her.

"Shall we go?" he asked, in that quiet voice with the subtle burr.

"I'm ready," she agreed.

David waited politely while she checked to be sure the front door was locked, then walked behind her to the curb and held open the passenger door on his Mercedes. She had buckled herself in by the time he got in on the driver's side. He put the key in the ignition, but instead of turning it he suddenly gripped the steering wheel, bowed his head and swore softly.

"David!" Grace said in alarm. She touched his arm and found it rigid with tension. "What's wrong?"

He took long, slow breaths as if fighting for control. "She cried. Claire cried."

"You mean you two fought?"

David shook his head. "She listened to me. We talked about her mother. For the first time, I somehow tapped into how sad she is.'' He swore again. "I haven't given her what she needs, have I?''

She laid her hand on his arm again. "You've tried.''

He grunted. "Do you know how half-assed that sounds? Should be engraved on my tombstone. 'He tried.'''

"But you're not dead. Which means it isn't too late to try harder.'' Grace heard herself and made a face. "I'm sorry. That was repulsive. I sound like a cheerleader.''

He turned his head, a genuine smile glimmering in his eyes. "You often do, you know.''

"I can't help it,'' she admitted. "My mother called me her little sunshine. I can't seem to outgrow expecting the best of everyone.''

The smile in his eyes was replaced by something more intense, something that sent her pulse into overdrive.

"I'm only grateful you chose to include me with 'everyone.'''

Time to lighten this, Grace told herself. Her pulse was bouncing as erratically as a misweighted rubber ball.

"You're venturing into forbidden territory,'' she reminded him.

He raised his eyebrows. "Forbidden?'' Then his face cleared. "Ah. Okay, no more thanks. Not today, anyway.'' He finally reached for the key and turned on the engine. "You're a remarkable woman, Ms. Blanchet.''

She basked in the compliment for a moment before

the self-congratulations became uncomfortable. She didn't want anyone, and especially David Whitcomb, to decide she was some kind of saint. The truth was, she had as many unworthy thoughts as anyone else. She hadn't taken in Claire just for the girl's sake, and certainly not for her father's. Grace had the niggling suspicion she'd agreed so that she would glow in her daughter's eyes. *See, forget your father. He wasn't half the parent I am anyway.*

There were moments already when she half wished she hadn't agreed, moments when she missed the lost closeness with her daughter, who no longer wanted to do stuff with Mom now that she had a friend who was cooler to hang with.

"No." She sounded harsh. "No, I'm a very ordinary woman, I promise you."

He shot her a surprised glance. "You're supposed to blush modestly and say 'Thank you.'"

Now she did flush, embarrassed at her vehemence. "I just don't want you to think I'm something I'm not."

"I doubt," he said thoughtfully, "that I do."

Grace drew in a frustrated breath, then expelled it. Protesting made it worse, made it look as if she was begging for more compliments. She wasn't even sure why she'd been so disturbed by the one.

"Here's an idea." David signaled and made a turn into busy downtown traffic. "Let's make a pact not to talk about Claire tonight. You know more about me than I do about you. I think it's only fair that we even the playing field."

"Even it? All you've ever said is that your ex-wife

is an alcoholic and you have problems with your teenage daughter. Oh, and that you're some kind of executive. You know at least as much about me! What do you do for fun? Where'd you grow up? Do you have family? You tell and I will too.''

His half smile was enough to make her pulse leap again. "Fair enough. And here we are."

After he parked and as he escorted her into the high-rise, he gently laid a hand on the small of her back to guide her into the elevator. Grace's inner tremor at even such a meaningless, courtesy touch scared her.

He didn't know her, not really. He thought she was some kind of Pollyanna and was grateful to her. Whatever interested him in her wouldn't outlast the day she had to say, "Your daughter can't live with me anymore."

She hoped that day wouldn't come, that Claire would continue to be cooperative and not start identifying Grace as the enemy, too, her father's stand-in. And she hoped, if the day did come, that she had the guts to risk her standing in Linnet's eyes to have their privacy and formerly quiet life back again.

The restaurant was at the top floor, its rustic, warm decor welcoming. Ceiling-hung copper lamps shed a golden glow, candlelight flickered, a rich meaty aroma and the sound of sizzling drifted from the open kitchen where white-hatted chefs worked. At the window-side table where David and Grace were seated, they looked across the dark expanse of Lake Washington to the lights of Seattle. Grace felt enclosed in a warm cocoon with David alone, the other diners and waiters somehow distant, their voices muted.

After ordering drinks, David inclined his head. "You first. Do you have family around here? Where did you grow up?"

Grace talked about her childhood on a wheat farm in eastern Washington, the long school bus rides and drives on the combine with her father, carving furrows in great arcs up and over hills that were warm brown and sometimes purple in the right light and pale gold when the wheat matured.

"The nearest house was two miles away, my best friend twenty miles. We hardly ever saw each other outside of school. She finished high school and married a local boy and they're farming his father's land. But it's getting harder and harder to make it. My parents finally sold their acreage to a conglomerate that owns half the wheat farms in the Palouse country. They moved to a development in Arizona."

"You don't miss it?"

She couldn't give a simple yes or no; wasn't childhood always more complicated than that? Her mother had been—and still was—difficult. She and her sister had been loved, but home had often been filled with tension.

But other bits and pieces of childhood—oh, yes. Grace often thought reminiscently about the quiet and the incredible spangle of stars across the night sky, so far from city lights, about the subtle shades of color as dusk crept over the rolling hills and sharp gullies, the hot summer sun and the vast silence. She remembered fondly the small town where they'd done their shopping and gone swimming at the city pool and bought school clothes at the one emporium, where everyone knew everyone else and life had an old-fashioned rhythm utterly unlike her present life. But she also recalled the loneliness and the endless dust and the way she'd yearned as she watched television, glimpsing a world that seemed so colorful compared to her own.

"No," she said. "There are things I miss, of course. Doesn't everyone feel that way about their childhood?"

Shadows harshened David's face as he said with a singular lack of emotion, "No. Some of us don't miss a single thing about it."

Her heartbeat hit a bump, and she knew she wouldn't like his answer. Still, she needed to ask. "What do you mean?"

"This is about you. My turn will come."

"Tell me," Grace demanded.

"Nothing so terrible. My father was never around—he'd wandered away by the time I was two or three—and my mom died when I was eight. Her brother took me in and kept me, I've got to give him that, but I was part of the reason his wife and he split, and he never let me forget it." He sounded as if he were talking about someone else, a story heard at work. "He was basically a son of a bitch."

"Oh, dear," Grace said inadequately.

His big shoulders moved in a shrug. "It could have been worse. The foster care system stinks."

"Yes." She moistened her lips. "No wonder you don't know how to..."

"Hug people the way you do?" His eyes, unfathomable and dark in here, held hers. "The way I was raised, men don't hug." His tone became caustic, unlike his own, as if he unconsciously mimicked. "They sure as hell don't cry or murmur sentimental crap unless they want something from a woman. Or so my uncle would have it."

"I hope," Grace said softly, "your mother had already taught you differently."

Another, nearly indifferent shrug. "Not well enough, apparently. Anyway, you've heard my story. I want to know what you did when you left home."

So she told him that, too, as they ate roasted chicken that melted from the bones and tender new potatoes sprinkled with herbs she couldn't identify and sipped white wine nothing like the kinds she bought at the grocery store.

She had gone to college, not to Washington State University in Pullman or Eastern Washington up in Cheney near Spokane, because that's what was expected—those were the destinations for her classmates. She'd headed for the University of Washington in Seattle, eager for urban bustle and a mix of races and languages, for rain instead of a blazing sun, for the chance to study abroad for a year and to be with other people who weren't content with solitude.

After her year in Madrid, she had met Philip, in his last year of law school at the U.W. Older, charismatic, handsome, brilliant, he had instantly altered her dreams. Marriage, children, supporting *his* dreams had become her priorities. In retrospect, she was disgusted with herself. She hadn't worked because he hadn't wanted her to. She had become a stereotypical corporate wife who created an elegant home, entertained skillfully, drove their daughter to the best preschools and filled her time with volunteer work. In the end, she was lonelier than she had ever been in the midst of miles of wheat fields and tumbleweed.

But to David, she embroidered only slightly on the bare facts he already knew. It was easy to talk about some of her charitable work as well as Philip's rising star. She made no mention of the fact that she would have been a divorcée if her husband hadn't had a heart attack when he did.

"After Philip died," she concluded, "I realized his life insurance and investments would put Linnet through college and provide a living of sorts, but that I would need to supplement it. A colleague of his offered me a job in his firm, and here I am." Ironically, she sometimes thought, doing the same thing during her workday that she'd done in her marriage: providing nearly invisible, little-appreciated support for a high-profile attorney.

David was a wonderful listener, his gaze intent, his few comments encouraging. Most people really wanted to talk about themselves and tried to trump every story with one of their own. He didn't. By not interjecting, he had allowed her space to say more than she'd intended. He'd understood implications; by the flicker in his eyes, she saw that he had read unerringly her brief hesitations.

Grace couldn't decide if she minded. Tonight she felt rash. Perhaps the glass of wine on top of the earlier drink explained her light-headedness, the warm glow in her chest, the way she just kept talking.

Or perhaps the explanation had more to do with David Whitcomb. Not just the fact that he was a quiet man who listened well, but also with her increasingly distracting sexual awareness of him. Those hooded eyes that sometimes held a faint smile, the strong neck and powerful shoulders, the large hands that seemed more made for manual labor than for wielding a computer mouse or cell phone, that controlled, gentle voice. For some reason this man who guarded his emotions with a barbed-wire-topped wall was making her imagine how deep those emotions ran. Would he make love as carefully, as deliberately, as he did everything else? Or could he be goaded into losing control?

And if he loved a woman, what expression would she see in his eyes, just for her?

How had his Miranda thrown him away, for what she found in a bottle?

Grace was grateful that David had been momentarily distracted by the waiter, who suggested desserts. She was all too afraid of what her own eyes would have shown him, had he chanced to be looking before she could hide yearning that shocked her with its intensity.

She dated sometimes, and had never been even slightly tempted to take any one of the men into her bed, far less imagine him there forever, till death do us part.

"Just coffee for me," she said, while issuing herself a stern lecture.

Okay, he pushed her buttons sexually, but she still knew next to nothing about him, and what she did know should make her wary. He'd had a tough upbringing that had taught him emotions were to be suppressed if not despised. His marriage had ended badly, he had all but abandoned his daughter, if not financially in every other way, and a week ago he had been willing to do the same thing all over again. He worked ridiculously long hours, and his personal life came a distant second to the demands of the job.

A chill doused the warm glow Grace had been feeling. Oh, yes, she should be wary. Because what she'd just done was describe Philip in all but the end of his marriage, which death had severed before she could find the courage to present him with an ultimatum.

Was she one of those idiotic women who was only attracted to one kind of man—the worst kind for her?

David stirred, bringing her sharply back to the moment. "What are you thinking about?" he asked.

"Oh…" *You.* "Just realizing that we've progressed to coffee and I've monopolized the entire conversation. It's your turn."

"I did tell you the basics," he reminded her, eyes shuttered. "No, I have no family to speak of. My uncle and I haven't bothered to stay in touch. I grew up in the Bay Area in California. San Jose. Tract house that looked just like all the neighbors'." He shrugged. "What do you want to know?"

Everything. The worst sign of infatuation. "Did your uncle encourage you to go to college?"

"Not if he had to pay for it," David said dryly. "No, I was lucky in my best friend. Guy named Nick

Sanchez. His dad was a professor at San Francisco State University, his mom was a librarian. They assumed their kids would go on to college, and I spent so much time there they treated me like one of theirs. They hunted for scholarships for Nick, and copied the information on every one that fit me. I was a good student, and I got a full ride to Stanford." Humor showed briefly in his eyes. "Nick had to pay part of his way. We roomed together. We each served as best man at the other's wedding."

So he did know what family should be like, Grace thought in relief. She wondered if Nick Sanchez and his parents were aware of what they'd meant to him.

"Your friend Nick. What did he end up doing?"

Definitely a smile now. "He's a philosophy professor, beard, tweed jacket, pipe, the whole bit. I don't even understand the titles of the papers he writes for academic journals." Abruptly the amusement left his voice. "Nick and his wife have three kids. Under other circumstances I might have sent Claire to them, but their youngest has leukemia. He's undergoing chemotherapy. I haven't even mentioned my latest troubles. In comparison to theirs, mine is a blip on the screen."

"Yes, I see," she said slowly. How sad that when he needed his friends, he couldn't turn to them. No wonder he'd ended up at the mercy of a total stranger—her.

He wrapped his hand on his coffee cup but didn't lift it. "Their son is doing well. Medical science accomplishes miracles these days. His odds are good, but it's been scary as hell."

Grace shuddered. "Any parent's worst nightmare."

He grunted agreement. After a moment, David said, "I shut Nick and Laura out, too, for a while after my divorce. I regret that. I should have taken Claire to visit them."

She opened her mouth to utter another platitude—*Hindsight is easy. Don't waste regrets on what can't be changed.* At the last second, she caught herself. Unable to think of a substitute, she closed her mouth again.

David smiled, the melting sweetness and wicked amusement and devastating sexiness combining to strip her of any last defenses. For all her caution, if he did but ask, she'd be his.

"Let me guess," he said contemplatively. "You were going to try to convince me not to punish myself, but you talked yourself out of it. Did you decide I deserved to suffer?"

She sounded—almost—as if she too were amused, instead of breathless with love. Or perhaps just lust.

"No, I'm trying to cure myself of this ridiculous desire to smooth the waters, to make everyone happy. I sound so saccharine! I repulse myself."

His gaze seemed to caress her. "You know, I find that very quality in you rather endearing. Why is it a flaw?"

His eyes couldn't possibly hold all the messages she wanted to imagine they did. He was just looking at her, probably thinking she was being foolish.

And he was more right than he knew.

"It makes me some kind of enabler." Grace let

out a puff of air and decided to go for broke. "There I am, patting people's backs and saying, 'It's okay. You don't have to feel guilty.' Well, maybe they should. Maybe they'd become better people if they genuinely regretted their behavior. But the thing is, I suspect I'm saying all these nice, soothing things not for them, but because I'm more comfortable when everyone is happy. And *that's* why I despise myself for it."

"In other words, you're being really nice to people because you're selfish."

Damn him, he was laughing at her. "Yes!" she declared pugnaciously. "I'm taking credit for being nice when the truth is I just don't know how to respond to real distress."

"You know, I'm just not sure I buy that."

"Why not?"

"Because you have one of those faces that gives away what you're thinking. I see you worry about Claire and Linnet and even me, little though I deserve it. You push me to talk, you don't put me off. You just want to think the best of me. You don't want to believe even I could be the jerk I must sometimes seem."

"Maybe. Partly," she admitted. "I do generally like people. Lately I've just been feeling..."

"What?" he asked when she trailed off.

"Oh, I don't know." Yes, she did: used. That's what she'd been feeling. But she wasn't going to tell him that. Grace shook herself. "Nothing. I've been cranky lately. An early midlife crisis."

"Aren't those the specialty of men?"

"What? I can't have one?" she said with mock outrage. "More discrimination against women?"

He grinned, giving her a glimpse of the man he might be when not under stress. "I think I was issuing a compliment."

"Oh, well, in that case..."

The waiter discreetly presented the tab, and David placed some bills in the leather folder and snapped it shut. He raised his brows at Grace. "Shall we go find out whether the girls have held a wild party in your absence?"

Her pulse sped, and not because of Linnet or Claire, who at worst might have watched an R-rated movie they knew she wouldn't approve of.

No, what she immediately, graphically imagined was the good-night kiss. He would kiss her, she knew, and oh she wanted him to, although she was ridiculously panicked at the idea, as well.

She forced an answering smile. "I'm not that easy to scare."

No? she thought derisively, as she moved ahead of David through the restaurant, his hand occasionally touching her back to guide her between candlelit tables. Tonight, she was all too easy to scare. And she knew why.

Since Philip's death, she'd been on no more than a dozen dates. Kisses had been cool, a dry unemotional touch of lips. Anything warmer or more seeking had sent her into flight. A step back was all it took, a disinterested smile, thanks for a pleasant evening, and her date didn't call again.

Grace had begun to think something was wrong

with her. Did her grief run deeper than she had realized? Or was it the other way around, that she was channeling anger at Philip onto these other men?

Certainly it had been a long time since she had responded to her husband with real passion. Those last years, she had been docile rather than enthusiastic when he reached for her in bed. She had begun to feel like a mannequin, not real at all.

But now...

Was she capable of genuine passion? Of inciting it?

Dark floor-to-ceiling windows cast a fleeting reflection of the tall man with big shoulders and an impassive face as he guided that strange woman through the restaurant. Grace had a moment of disorientation. Why didn't she think *There I am,* when she caught such a glimpse of herself? If she had moments of being a stranger to herself, perhaps there *was* something wrong with her.

What if his kiss, too, failed to touch the part of her that felt so remote, as if her innermost self stood apart and watched critically?

Worse yet, what if the brush of his lips lit her on fire but he kept the kiss brief, impersonal. What if he was the one to step back and say pleasantly, "I enjoyed the evening"?

They rode the elevator in silence, both gazing ahead at the doors as if waiting for release. Socially paralyzed, Grace wondered if this tendency to overanalyze everything was a sign of aging. Everyone thought it was hard being a teenager! They should try dating when they were in their thirties!

At the car he courteously held open the door for her and waited while she tucked in her skirt. When she glanced up, it was to see his gaze resting on her legs. Before she could guess what he was thinking, David said politely, "Ready?" and slammed the door.

Despite the cool evening, Grace's palms were sweaty. Her heart slammed in her chest. By the time they got home, she'd probably be so terrified she would giggle inappropriately or clank her teeth on his or just freeze. *Think of something to say,* she ordered herself.

Claire...no, not Claire. Anything but his daughter. That would kill the mood for sure.

What mood? she thought ruefully. She felt pretty much like she had when Linnet dragged her to *Scream 3* and she had been riveted to the screen waiting for the masked psychotic to leap out and knife the next innocent victim.

The parallel restored her sense of humor and she relaxed enough to say teasingly, when David got in and reached for his seat belt, "So, tell me. Did *you* have wild parties when your uncle was away?"

David went still for a moment. "Uh..."

"You did!" she exclaimed, diverted.

The grin he gave her was unexpectedly boyish. He snapped his seat belt shut. "My uncle never knew."

"This is the kind of thing we *don't* tell our children until they're past the age of danger."

"Wouldn't have occurred to me." He started the car, the grin still lingering around his mouth. His very sexy mouth, she saw, in a stolen glance. Softened from its usual grim line, his mouth was more sensitive than she'd realized.

Her pulse leaped again, but with a fizzy sense of excitement rather than outright fear. She would soon know what that mouth felt like on hers. Those big, strong hands, now wrapped around the steering wheel, would touch more than the small of her back.

She thought of something trivial to say; he responded. Even as she was making conversation she knew she wouldn't remember a thing either had said. His interest wasn't any higher than hers, and all too quickly the pauses became longer, then permanent.

They were passing down a dark street, lamps only at the corners. He broke the silence, his voice soft and a notch huskier than usual. "Now what are you thinking?"

"I…" Her evasion died in her suddenly dry throat. She sought frantically for something to say. Anything. "I…" This time she squeaked to a stop.

"Yeah." He spoke even more quietly. "Me too."

"Oh." Brilliant.

"And here we are."

They were pulling up to the curb in front of her town house. The porch light was on, but the living room was dark as was her bedroom above it.

"No police cars or ambulances," David observed.

Again her sense of humor rescued her. "Watch it, or you're going to have me leaping out of the car and rushing in to check the girls' pulses."

He turned off the engine and in the sudden silence murmured, "Heaven forbid."

Grace turned her head and found him looking at her, his lids heavy.

Without a word, he reached out and cupped her jaw in one hand. His thumb grazed her bottom lip— a sensual sampling.

Her breath caught as intense longing surged through her. She closed her eyes and turned her face into his hand until her lips found his palm. At the feel of her kiss, he drew in a breath sharply. His fingers flexed, and he lifted her chin without the gentleness of an instant before. Grace didn't have time to open her eyes and see him coming. Just like that, his mouth was on hers, harder than she had expected, more demanding. She reached for him and moaned when she came up against the restraint of the seat belt and the bulk of the console between them.

David cursed and pulled away just long enough to unbuckle both of their belts. Then he kissed her again, asking for her lips to part, his fingers kneading her nape, his thumbs pressed against the soft flesh beneath her jaw. Her hands in turn gripped his shoulders, learned the shape of the powerful muscles that gave him bulk. Her mind had fogged the moment he reached out for her; she was melting, eager, a woman rather than a mother or PTA volunteer.

His lips were skillful, tenderness mixed with insistence. The scrape of his jaw as he trailed kisses across her cheek and down her throat was more erotic than anything she'd ever felt. Against her collarbone, he paused, his mouth hot, and a shudder racked him. His fingers bit into her arms for a moment, and then he lifted his head.

Hoarsely he said, "I think this is the moment to say good-night."

She couldn't help herself; she made a small sound of protest.

In the dim light from the nearest street lamp, she saw a muscle jerk in his cheek. His voice was soft, almost slurred. "I don't want to rush you."

Rush me, she wanted to cry. But of course he was right. Already she'd felt too much, too fast. He was a stranger; too much about him reminded her of Philip, who had been so terribly wrong for her.

"Yes." She sounded peculiar, voice faint and die-away. She cleared her throat. "I did enjoy myself tonight, David."

He still hadn't let her go. With one hand he massaged the back of her neck. "If we didn't have kids, I'd ask you to go out with me again tomorrow night. Tomorrow morning, if I thought you were willing."

It was the most romantic thing anyone had said to her in...she couldn't remember. Too long. He was admitting that he didn't want to leave, that he wanted to be with her again as soon as possible. She felt the same. Although they hadn't said good-night yet, the knowledge that any minute he would be driving away gave her a near physical wrench.

"I would have had breakfast with you," she admitted, just above a whisper.

He swore and bent his head, kissing her with fierce passion for no more than a heartbeat before he lifted his head again. His chest rose and fell hard; Grace heard the rasp of his breath.

She swallowed. "We could do something with the girls."

"Yeah." There was that maddeningly sexy voice, so soft and uninflected she couldn't help wondering what cauldrons of roiling emotions it disguised. "I'll call in the morning," he said. "Talk to them about what they'd like to do."

"Okay." Grace didn't move.

The fingers on her neck flexed. Then he let her go, his hand curling into a fist as he withdrew it. Blindly Grace reached for the door handle. By the time she got out, he had come around the car to her. They said nothing more as they walked up to the porch and she let herself in. At the last second she turned back.

David reached out and ran his knuckles softly over her cheek and mouth. In the porch light she saw the glow in his eyes. "In the morning," he murmured, a promise of more than she dared believe.

A second later she closed the door and leaned her forehead against the cool wood, waiting with a kind of agony for the sound of his car engine and the knowledge that he was gone, even if only for twelve hours.

She could not be in love so fast, she thought wretchedly.

She was, and knew it.

CHAPTER EIGHT

WONDERFUL SMELLS MINGLED in the kitchen: bacon frying, scrambled eggs already heaped fluffy and yellow in a bowl, and a fresh loaf right out of the bread machine. Claire and Linnet sat on stools at the breakfast bar watching as Mrs. Blanchet squeezed fresh orange juice. Claire had never seen anyone do it before. The two cats sat on separate windowsills waiting hopefully, Lemieux occasionally uttering plaintive cries. The bacon was driving them crazy.

One minute Claire was paying attention to her growling stomach and the next she watched Linnet's mother without being obvious. Why was she in such a good mood? What had she and Claire's father talked about last night? Claire didn't know which was worse: that they'd spent the whole evening talking about her, or that they hadn't. What if they *liked* each other? she wondered with wrinkled nose.

When the phone rang, Linnet pounced, even though Claire was the only one who desperately hoped somebody would call.

"Blanchet residence." After a moment Linnet said, almost sulkily, "No, this isn't Claire. Just a minute." She handed the cordless to Claire. "It's Josh McKendrick."

Claire almost peed her pants. Josh was calling *her?* She opened her eyes wide in a plea for help, but Linnet had turned her head away. Mrs. Blanchet kept cooking, but Claire could feel her antennae quivering. It was a mom thing.

Claire took a deep breath and said into the phone, "Hello? This is Claire."

"Cool." It really was him. "I was starting to think I might have the wrong number. Was that your sister or something?"

"That was Linnet."

"Linnet?"

"Linnet Blanchet. She plays Ursula?"

"Oh, right." He didn't sound interested. She was glad Linnet couldn't hear him act as though he didn't even know who she was. "Are you stepsisters?"

"No, I'm just living with her right now."

Mrs. Blanchet set a plate with toast and eggs and bacon in front of Claire. She covered the mouthpiece and whispered, "Thanks." Beside her, Linnet started eating and not paying any attention to the fact that the coolest guy in their school was on the phone, *right that minute,* with Claire.

With a thud, Lemieux leaped to the floor and came to sit beside Claire's stool. His cry was piercing enough that Josh asked, "What was that?"

Claire stole a glance at Mrs. Blanchet, who momentarily had her back turned. Crumbling a piece of bacon, Claire dropped part in front of the big cat and tossed part in the general direction of Stanzi.

"Um…a cat. We're eating breakfast and he wants the bacon. It's his favorite food."

"Oh. Well, um, listen," he said, lowering his voice and talking faster as if someone was in the background. "I was thinking maybe we could go to the public library a couple of days this week after school and work on our lines together. If you can't take the bus home, my brother has football practice at the high school and he said he could run you home."

"Really? That would be great!" Again she rolled her eyes toward Linnet, but her friend was, like, totally snubbing her.

And Stanzi, good ol' Stanzi, couldn't possibly leap from the windowsill to scarf up her bacon. Instead, she let out a sweet, feminine mew and waited hopefully for Claire to bring it to her. Which she couldn't without Mrs. Blanchet noticing. Claire just hoped Lemieux would notice the second tidbit before Mrs. Blanchet, who strictly forbid feeding table scraps to the cats.

"Is that the cat again?" Josh asked.

"Uh-huh." She shooed him surreptitiously with her foot. "He's mad because I'm not supposed to give him bacon."

"Yeah?" Josh came doggedly back to the point. Claire almost laughed at her pun. "Can we go over our lines on Monday?"

"Sure! I..." She put on the brakes. "That is, let me ask."

Covering the phone, she told Mrs. Blanchet what Josh had suggested. "His brother said he'd give me a ride home," she finished.

Linnet's mom lifted one eyebrow. "Josh's brother is how old?"

Lemieux had found the bacon at last and was crunching it loudly. As if he *ever* chewed his food!

Claire raised her voice. "All I know is he's in high school. He must be a junior or senior."

"That's what I was afraid of," Mrs. Blanchet said dryly. "How about if your father or I pick you up the first time, at least?"

Her heart buoyed. "Then it's okay?"

"I don't know why not. You do have a ton of lines to memorize."

"Thanks!" she exclaimed, and uncovered the phone. "Monday's okay, except my dad or somebody is going to pick me up."

"Cool!" After a brief, awkward pause he said, "Well, I guess I'll see you at school then."

"Sure." She tried to be low-key. It wasn't like he'd asked her out or anything; maybe he was just having trouble memorizing his lines. But still... She said goodbye, pushed End on the phone and squealed.

Mrs. Blanchet laughed. "I take it he's cute? Eat your breakfast before it gets cold."

Linnet pushed her plate away and looked coolly at Claire. "I guess he likes you."

What was *her* problem? But Claire knew. She'd have been jealous, too, if Linnet had gotten the bigger part and now Josh McKendrick was calling to ask her to meet him.

"I doubt it." She wrinkled her nose. "We do both have lots of lines." Oops. That sounded like bragging. "I mean, it'll be easier to memorize them if we practice together. I'm not nearly as good at remembering mine as you are."

Linnet made a face. "I just don't have very many to learn."

"The next play, you'll probably have more."

Behind her daughter, Mrs. Blanchet smiled approvingly at Claire.

"I'm not as good as you are." Linnet was trying hard to sound as if she didn't care, but Claire could tell she did.

"Mrs. Wilson was saying how next fall we might put on *The Tempest.* Our high school in California did it, and they did this special performance during the day so a bunch of the classes from the elementary school could see it. The girl who played Ariel, the spirit, was this *incredible* dancer. She was the star. You would be so-o perfect," she said generously.

"Really?" Linnet bounced. "I'd like to be Ariel. Whoever she is."

"Read the play," her mother suggested, laughing and shaking her head. "Oh, heck, there's the phone again."

Linnet snatched up the phone by the second ring. Like she got that many phone calls. Once again, she extended it to Claire. "I think it's your mom," she said in a stage whisper.

"Really?" This time, her voice cracked and her stomach turned over. Where had Mom *been?* Was she sick or dying or... "Um, hello?"

"Claire!" Mom said gaily. "Is that you? Are you all right? You sound funny."

Was *she* all right?

"Why haven't you called?" Claire asked. Now she did sound weird—mad and whiny and pathetic all at the same time. "I've left messages practically every day!"

Mom's voice went vague. "Have you? My answering machine is hopeless. Half the time it doesn't record messages. Besides, you know me. I come home and that red light is blinking over and over and I just can't bear to listen to a whole string of messages, so I delete them all."

Which meant Mom didn't have the money to pay her bills and the credit card companies and her landlord were calling. The same thing had happened a couple of times that Claire could remember. She'd hated having to be careful not to answer the phone or the doorbell.

"I'm so sorry I didn't hear your message." Mom actually did sound contrite. "I've called, but I never seem to catch you at home. It seems silly just to say hi on someone else's answering machine."

Claire glanced up. Linnet had piled the Saturday morning newspaper and was taking it out to the recycling bin in the garage, but Mrs. Blanchet was still cleaning the kitchen within earshot.

"Um, is everything okay with your job?" Claire asked. *Did you lose it?*

"I'm looking for a new one. Pete is being so sweet and helping me. You know they've never appreciated me there."

A fleeting, critical thought passed through Claire's mind. *They just don't like you not coming to work.* Shocked at her disloyalty, she insisted, "They're dumb not to think you're the greatest."

"Oh, thank you, sweetie! What would I do without you to raise my spirits?"

Well, then, why haven't you called? Claire wanted to ask.

"I miss you," her mom said.

Hot tears spurted in Claire's eyes. "I miss you, too."

"Are they being good to you there?"

Claire dashed at her tears. "Yeah, the Blanchets are really nice."

Linnet reappeared from the garage. Her mom smiled at Claire, put an arm around Linnet's shoulders and quietly drew her from the kitchen, leaving Claire alone to talk to her mother.

Mom asked all the right questions. Claire got to tell her about the play and Josh and even the plans for going to the Seattle Science Center today. Mom was excited and said maybe she'd time the visit she'd been thinking about so that she could see the performance of *Much Ado*.

Tears threatened again. "You're coming up?"

"Did you think I'd never come see you?"

"I wasn't sure if you could," she admitted. "I mean, if Dad would let you. Or the judge."

"I do have visitation rights." Mom sounded tart. "Supervised, since your father convinced the court I'm an alcoholic. But I did talk to your dad and he doesn't have any problem with you spending the night with me at a hotel room. He said he'd book me a room at the DoubleTree and you and I could have a fancy dinner and swim in their pool and order breakfast from room service. What do you say?"

"That would be so cool!"

"I guess, if you're going to the Science Center today, I'd better let you get ready."

After they said goodbye, Claire wiped her eyes with a damp dish towel, blew her nose on it, then carried it out to the laundry hamper by the washing machine in the garage. She couldn't believe she'd cried like a baby just because her mother was coming for a visit. But it would be cool, just her and Mom talking and playing games and giggling like they used to.

And Dad was helping her come? He must be intending to pay for the hotel, and maybe he was giving Mom money for the airfare and stuff. He must be, since she'd lost her job and didn't have a new one yet. And he hadn't even said anything. Claire bet he wouldn't have, either; he would have let her think *Mom* was the one paying for the trip. She got a funny feeling inside, thinking about him doing something so nice and not claiming credit.

Upstairs, water was running in one of the bathrooms and somebody was singing. Claire paused in the hall and stared at the closed door to the master suite. Stanzi had beaten her up the stairs and was sitting and staring, too, looking amazingly as if one lip was curled in disdain.

"I could have danced all night," came the muffled caroling.

My Fair Lady. They'd rented it just last weekend. Which *might* be why Mrs. Blanchet was singing a song from it. But why *that* song? Claire's eyes narrowed. Was it because of last night? And because

Mrs. Blanchet was getting to see Claire's dad again today?

Claire felt another funny lurch at the idea, but she couldn't decide whether or not she would really hate it if they dated. She couldn't be jealous; like, who was she jealous *about?* Dad?

Yeah, right.

Shaking herself, she went into her bedroom.

Linnet was sprawled on the bed waiting for her. Her face was bright, as if she'd never sulked downstairs. "Tell me *everything,*" she demanded. "Quick. Your dad will be here any minute, and then we won't get any chance to talk. What did Josh *say?*"

On a whoosh of relief that chased away her confusion, Claire reached for her shoes. "Well!" she began.

"OKAY, SO WHAT'S AT the Science Center?" David asked.

He didn't really give a damn—he was going to be spending the day with Grace and with his daughter, which he was looking forward to more than he wanted to admit even to himself. But he was mildly curious about the choice of destination, given the ages of the girls. He'd expected to be subjected to a slasher flick or an arcade or the mall.

In the backseat, Linnet leaned forward. "It's this exhibit on computer animation. Not just cartoons, but the stuff they put in movies that you know can't be real? Like the ship sinking in *Titanic* or the dinosaurs in *Jurassic Park,*" she kindly explained. "Like that."

"I did see *Jurassic Park,*" he agreed.

"Not *Titanic?*" Grace and both girls asked in si-multaneous incredulity.

"Missed that one."

"You missed *Titanic?*" The two teenagers were begging him to say he was kidding. Apparently he'd committed a social solecism.

"How could you?" asked Grace, with a hint of laughter in her voice.

I-90 crossed Lake Washington, a broad wind-whipped blue expanse today studded with sailboats. Some kind of regatta, he supposed. Sails in crayon colors ballooned and dipped as the boats skimmed the water. Bill Gates, the Microsoft tycoon, had built his high-tech house looking out at this view. David had thought about buying a lakefront place himself, but so far he wasn't home often enough to bother. Besides, that would require moving Claire to the Bellevue schools from the smaller Lakemont district. How could he separate her from Linnet?

To repair his gross omission, his daughter and Grace's took turns telling him the plot to the movie.

A sly smile curling his mouth, he said, "You know, I had read what happened to the *Titanic.*"

In the rearview mirror, he saw the look they gave the back of his head. Clearly they thought he had a screw loose.

"But not to Leo!"

David glanced at Grace. "I take it you went."

"Went?" She laughed. "I saw it three times. And it's a very long movie, you know."

Damn, she was pretty when her eyes sparkled and she shook back her hair so that it shimmered and danced. Maybe not all the time—he could still look at her objectively and realize she was far from beautiful, although he'd come to think of the long oval of her face as elegant at least. With her magnificent deep blue eyes and long white throat, she didn't need a cute nose or rosebud mouth.

"Uh, you don't want to go north, do you?" she murmured.

"What?"

He refocused abruptly on the freeway ahead and realized he was in the lane to head north on I-5, which led ultimately to the Canadian border. Smart. *Drive with your brains above your belt,* he told himself with disgust.

He had no sooner successfully merged onto I-5 and crossed three lines to exit, than he was stealing a glance at Grace's long legs in pressed chinos. Too bad it wasn't summer. She might have worn shorts.

Once he'd exited on Mercer, David let his gaze stray briefly to the rearview mirror again. The two girls were giggling madly, their heads close. The sight drew his brows together.

What was with Claire today? From the minute he'd arrived, she had been in such a good mood she was almost manic. Bouncing in her seat, talking too loudly, too fast, laughing hysterically at everything anybody said. At the same time, with him she seemed almost shy. Yeah, that was it. No dark stares; instead, she'd actually blushed when he said he liked her hair in an off-center braid. Had he missed something?

After he found parking they walked across the Seattle Center, built for the 1960 World's Fair. The

Space Needle leaped toward the blue sky, and in every direction were glimpses of water and mountains. The volcanic cone of Mount Rainier floated to the southeast, Lake Union to the east, the Olympic Mountains across Puget Sound to the west. After a week of rain, the air was crystal clear today, a cold fresh breeze bringing red to everyone's cheeks.

"Can we go up the Space Needle today?" Linnet asked.

"Yeah, yeah! Can we?" Claire begged shrilly.

David shrugged and looked at Grace. "I'll wait at the bottom."

"Why? Is it expensive?" his daughter asked.

Was it remotely possible she was being considerate? he wondered in surprise.

"I don't like heights," he admitted. "Glass-fronted elevators are my least favorite."

"Oh." Claire's forehead crinkled. "I forgot. You didn't go to the top of the TransAmerica building, either, did you?"

He'd waited in the lobby that day she was remembering. "I might go up to rescue you from certain death. Otherwise..." He shook his head.

Grace smiled over her shoulder. "We could let the girls go alone."

He caught the idea right away: And neck while they were gone. Lust stirred.

"Good idea." If his voice had become huskier, the girls didn't seem to notice.

David paid the admission to the Science Center and to the IMAX film currently playing. Grace and her daughter went ahead down the stairs toward the open central courtyard with bronze sculptures rising from shallow ponds. He especially liked the backs of the orca whales.

Claire lingered by his side, for the first time hunching her shoulders, her voice becoming subdued. "Um...Mom called this morning."

"Did she?" About damn time.

"She says she might come up. That you'd talked about it."

What Miranda hadn't said, he was willing to bet, was that he had called her until she had answered the phone in an unwary moment. The offer of an all-expenses-paid trip had got her attention.

"Yep," he said neutrally. "Did she say when she's coming?"

"She thought maybe she would try to see one of the performances of *Much Ado*."

He nodded, hands shoved casually into the pockets of his jeans, just strolling beside his daughter as though they often walked together and talked like this. "I hoped she could make it then."

"You're paying for it, aren't you?" Claire spoke very softly.

Wanting to finish this before they rejoined the others, David stopped at the foot of the staircase. Claire did the same, her gaze fastened on the bronze stegosaurus in one of the pools.

He had hoped not to have to disillusion her any more about her mother. Tempted now to lie, David hesitated a moment. But Claire wouldn't have asked if she didn't have a suspicion. Miranda must have said something.

He chose to answer indirectly. "She's out of a job right now."

In a small painful voice, his daughter said, "I thought so."

"You know, your mother will drink when she's here." He looked at her face in profile.

Claire bit her lip and gave a jerky nod. "But she said I could stay with her at the hotel?"

"I thought it might be fun for you. And I wouldn't have to worry about her driving with you or embarrassing you in front of friends."

He expected her to flare that her mother, unlike him, never embarrassed her. Instead, his daughter nodded again, meekly, took a deep breath and met his eyes. And she said, very politely, "Thank you."

David had to clear his throat before he could say, "You're welcome."

"Josh McKendrick called me today, too." Seeing his uncomprehending expression, she explained, "He's the boy who plays Benedick. He asked me to practice lines together after school a couple of days this week. Mrs. Blanchet said I could."

"Well, good." If the little jerk kept his hands where they belonged. Off David's daughter. He waited, wondering what this had to do with him.

"Mrs. Blanchet didn't want Josh's brother to drive me home. She said maybe you could do it."

"I see." His week's schedule crumbled before his inner vision, but he hid his dismay. "When?"

"Monday?" Her big brown eyes were anxious. "Like four o'clock or something? And Thursday, too?"

He could just picture Grace generously volunteering him. As if a ten-minute drive from the library rated as quality father-daughter time. Ahead, she and Linnet waited by the huge double doors leading into the first of four linked buildings. If he turned his head, she'd give him an encouraging smile.

"Why not?" he said with an inward shrug.

His daughter's elfin face lit up. "Really? Thanks!"

He gave her a lopsided smile in return and nodded toward the others. "Shall we?"

"Sure!" She bounded ahead, but paused briefly and turned a glowing expression on him. "Josh is *so* cute!"

He laughed ruefully. "Fathers would rather think their daughters haven't noticed boys, you know."

That surprised her. She kept walking backward. "Why?"

"Because fathers know what teenage boys are thinking."

They'd rejoined Linnet and Grace, who raised her eyebrows at his comment.

"Oh." Claire struggled with the idea, but her pleasure showed. "Josh probably doesn't like me."

"Uh-huh. Sure."

She flashed him another gamine smile and then darted inside with Linnet.

"Set me up again?" he said in the same dry tone to Grace.

She actually looked puzzled. "Set you up?"

"To chauffeur Claire?"

Her forehead puckered. "Isn't that what parents do?"

Apparently, he didn't know.

"It would seem so." He held open the door for her. "The wonders within await us."

He said it sardonically; the Science Center was for little kids. To David's surprise, the display on computer animation was damned interesting.

He wasn't much of a moviegoer—who had time? Nonetheless, the technical work that had gone into creating astonishing illusions on the silver screen was fascinating. By the time he, Grace and the girls moved on to another building, he was ready to buy stock in one of the companies that employed the youthful geniuses who could bring a T. Rex to apparent life or convincingly recreate the *Titanic*.

Part of his enjoyment came from watching Claire, Linnet and even Grace. The two girls forgot they were teenagers and became children again for a while. They pushed every button, animated their own crude drawings on computer screens, giggled and rushed from display to display. In the tidepool area they dipped their hands into the salt water, in the petting zoo they held a boa constrictor and squealed, and at last they took turns with six-year-olds and climbed into the "rocket" to shoot down a spiral slide.

At their side, Grace was nearly as childish in her pleasure and concentration. She laughed in delight, frowned intently as she took a turn drawing freehand with the mouse on a computer screen, called excitedly when she wanted everyone else to take a look at something. He could picture her easily at the age of their daughters, skinny, self-conscious, perhaps plain, but intelligent, sweet natured, and capable of humor and self-analysis. Her eyes would have been even more extraordinary in a young girl's thin face. He wondered how she had worn her hair. Had she let out childish pigtails so that she could toss her hair flirtatiously? Or was the thirteen- or fourteen-year-old Grace too shy to vie for the attention of boys?

As they watched the girls go down the slide, she said wistfully, "I wish I could still do that."

So she *had* been feeling carefree and consciously young.

He smiled. "We could find a playground."

For a moment she looked wistful. "Will you push me on the swing?"

Letting his gaze rest meaningfully on her hips, he drawled, "Oh, yeah."

She blushed and gave him a little shove. "You have a one-track mind!"

Not habitually, he thought. He worked sixty-, eighty-hour weeks, which didn't leave much time for dating games. But where this rather thin, earnest woman was concerned, he couldn't deny it. Stripping her clothes off, finding out where her curves became ripest, how white her skin was, how tightly she would hold him, whether she would make love silently or with throaty voice, had come to occupy his mind a hell of a lot more often than he liked to admit.

He wasn't required to answer, for Claire dashed up just then. "We're going in the shadow room."

"The what?"

Grace forgot him, her face brightening. "Oh, I love it!"

Curious, he followed. The small room had luminous green walls. The occupants positioned themselves against the walls until a light flashed. Shadows lingered for twenty or thirty seconds on the walls.

Linnet rose *en pointe,* arms gracefully curved. Claire struck a pose with arms and knees akimbo. Grace leaped into the air like a cheerleader, banging nose first into the wall just after the light flashed. All laughed in delight when they saw their silhouettes.

"Come on," Grace urged him. "You, too."

Feeling blockish, David joined them in the shimmering green room.

"Now!" Claire cried.

He pretended to be throwing a football; Claire, seeing him, leaped to catch it. They stayed for another ten minutes. David had to admit that the effects were interesting.

"Must be an ego thing," he commented to Grace, as they went out into the sunny but chilly afternoon. "A chance to see ourselves frozen briefly in time."

"Trying on different roles," she agreed, before elbowing him playfully. "Or, golly, you could just call it having fun."

Fun was not something he could recall having in a hell of a long time, unless his weekly games of racquetball qualified.

"Yeah," he conceded. "You could."

The IMAX film was about flight, and also unexpectedly interesting. The huge screen and wraparound technology allowed for breathtaking scenes—and vertigo inducing plunges.

"For a man who does not like heights," David

murmured on the way out, "that was not a good choice."

"Really? You were scared?" his daughter asked in amazement.

"Not scared." Outside, he began to regain his equilibrium. "Just uncomfortable."

"So I suppose you won't go up the Space Needle."

"Not on your life."

She grinned. "But we can?"

"Okay by me."

Paying for the tickets, he raised his brows at Grace. "Why don't you go, too?" He all but held his breath waiting for her answer. What was he, a randy teenager who couldn't wait to get his hands on his girl?

She wrinkled her nose. "No, I've been. Let them go by themselves. Wave to us, okay?"

"If we can spot you," Linnet agreed, wide-eyed.

David had already chosen a bench tucked in a nook and shaded by a tree, where he hoped like hell they *couldn't* be spotted.

The moment the elevator doors closed on the girls, he gripped Grace's arm and drew her outside and briskly around the corner to his chosen hideaway.

When they reached the bench—from which he was glad to see that, for the moment at least, they had complete privacy—Grace lifted a laughing face to his. "Impatient?"

"I want to kiss you."

She pretended to look solemn. "Don't you think we should talk about Claire instead?"

"Tell me you're kidding."

In answer, Grace stood on tiptoe and twined her arms around his neck. Obediently she said, "I'm kidding."

His hands wrapped around her waist as if they belonged there. "You scared me."

"Um." This smile was mischievous, but not quite in a little-girl way. "It's good for your heart." She paused for a millisecond. "Works instead of exercise."

David's eyes narrowed. Had she intended to scare him again, by suggesting that she thought his heart was engaged? If so, she'd failed. *Love* was a word he used to Claire, and even thought he meant. How else to label the fierce protectiveness he felt toward her?

Otherwise, he wasn't sure he understood the emotion or even completely believed in it. Sex, liking, compatibility…those he understood. But heartfelt words weren't part of what he could offer.

He stroked the long, silky line of Grace's throat and watched her deep blue eyes cloud.

Right this minute, he refused to worry about whether Grace would eventually demand sweet words. He had her to himself for less than a quarter of an hour.

He intended to make use of every moment.

"Here," he said huskily, "is another form of exercise," and his mouth seized hers at the same time as he gripped her hips and pulled her tightly against him.

They had, in his opinion, a very satisfactory and aerobic fifteen minutes.

CHAPTER NINE

WITH LISTS OF computer-generated names and phone numbers spread across the dining room table in front of her, Grace glanced at the clock. Five-thirty in the afternoon. The members of the middle school parent group, primarily mothers, were most accessible now, when they were getting home from work and preparing dinner.

Accessible? Who was she kidding? Grace thought ruefully. *Vulnerable* was more like it.

Now wasn't the time to feel guilty, she lectured herself, not when she had to find thirty volunteers for the big event. Just do it.

She picked up the phone and dialed.

"June, this is Grace Blanchet," she began. "How are you?"

June warily conceded that she was fine. Pans clattered in the background.

"I know you're aware that I'm involved in putting on the autumn dance and carnival at the middle school." She sounded downright gushy, repulsing even herself. "I'm to the stage now where I need to ask parents to volunteer for the evening itself, either to run games, sell food or chaperone the dance. I seem to remember seeing you there last year. It *is* fun, and it's even more fun if you're actively involved. Can you commit to a few hours?''

June was vague about her schedule. Perhaps Grace could call back next week. Figuring June would be careful not to answer her phone for the next two weeks, Grace made a notation on her list, sighed and dialed the next number.

An hour later, Linnet wandered into the kitchen and whined, ''Mom, dinner isn't cooking. Aren't we going to eat?''

''Um…'' Grace surfaced after crossing off a name on her list. Focusing, she saw that, not only was her daughter standing arms akimbo in front of her, Stanzi was sitting in front of her empty food bowl with the air of a cat who has been waiting for years if not centuries. Wrenching her gaze from the puffy brown Maine coon, who was *not* starving to death, Grace said, ''I thought I'd order a pizza. I'll do that now.''

''Could we go out instead?'' Linnet asked hopefully.

''You can see that I'm busy,'' Grace said with scant patience.

''But Mom!'' Her daughter made a sulky face. ''You *said* we could go shopping some night this week. Remember?'' *What kind of idiot are you?* her tone asked. ''My jeans are all too short?''

Grace sighed. ''Sweetheart, I am busy arranging the fall carnival for *your* benefit. Give me a break, okay?''

Linnet kicked a chair. ''I don't even want to go to the carnival! The games are stupid! And no boy ever asks me to dance anyway.''

God give her patience. "One of these days that'll change. You know it will. Maybe one of the boys who is in the play…"

"Oh, yeah, right." She kicked again, hard enough that the chair crashed over. Snatching it up, Linnet thumped it back on its feet. "No boy even knows I'm *alive*. And I'm not going to the dance."

Grace watched, openmouthed, as Linnet stalked out. What was *that* all about? Hormones? Had she and Claire switched personalities?

Instead of following to confront Linnet right now, Grace called and arranged for delivery of a half Canadian bacon, half veggie pizza. Then, although Stanzi had fled when the chair fell over, she also poured dried food in both the cats' bowls.

The pizza didn't arrive for forty-five minutes. In that interval, she called twenty more parents, leaving messages for some, being turned down by more, and signing up three volunteers, one of whom had a tendency to agree to do anything and then fail to show.

Once she'd paid the driver, Grace called up the stairs, "Girls! Dinner!"

Claire arrived first. She peered over Grace's shoulder as she opened the box on the kitchen counter.

"Ooh. Veggie. Cool."

"Will you grab some napkins?" Grace asked, reaching for plates.

Linnet, expression still sulky, came into the kitchen, took a plate and served herself two slices of pizza. "We aren't even having a vegetable?"

"There's some on the pizza."

"Oh, like one whole curl of green pepper." She

rolled her eyes as she grabbed a pop from the refrigerator. "What, a quarter of a serving?"

"As if you care," Grace was driven to mutter.

Linnet's eyes flashed. "Well, I do!"

"Jeez, what's her problem?" Claire asked in an undertone, as Linnet rushed into the dining room and slammed her plate onto the table.

"I have no idea," Grace said wearily.

At the table she was relieved to let Claire's chatter wash over her, although she got a little tired of hearing what Josh said and did and thought.

At one point Linnet interrupted. "I read lines today with Alex Ruiz. He—"

"It's so much cooler to do it with a boy, isn't it?" Claire gestured enthusiastically with a slice of pizza, scattering bits of olives and mushroom across the table. "When Josh reads, he puts so much passion in it. He is really good. You know?"

Foolishly, Linnet assumed this was an actual question and opened her mouth to answer. Before she could say a word, Claire burbled on.

"And he's so funny! I mean, I just kept having to stop because I was laughing so hard my stomach hurt. You know? And then he'd do this *incredible* imitation of Mrs. Hinchen—you know, like she does during rehearsal, when she tells us we're being totally childish and she won't put up with it?"

Eyes glazing, Grace tuned her out. She'd forgotten how self-absorbed an adolescent could be. And how volatile! So angry one minute she was determined to run away, and then the next minute annoyingly cheerful and able to think about nothing but a boy.

Pushing her plate away, Grace ruthlessly interrupted. "Girls, I have to get back to making phone calls. Can you two wrap the rest of the pizza and put it in the fridge and then load the dishwasher?" She reached for the phone and said absently, "Thanks."

"You mean, we can't go shopping?" That annoying whine edged Linnet's voice again.

"Josh said he might call tonight." Claire clasped her hands to her breast. "I've got—I mean, absolutely *got*—to be here."

Linnet whirled in her seat. "He probably won't even call! Anyway, who said you have to come?"

Claire's mouth opened, then closed. "Oh," she said, softly.

"Linnet, that was rude!" Grace stared at her daughter.

"I don't care!" The skinny thirteen-year-old shot to her feet. "Nobody worries about hurting *my* feelings!" With a rush and a momentary tangle of feet, she fled the room.

The two left behind sat in silence for a moment. Then Claire said in a small voice, "Did I do something?"

Grace reached over and squeezed her hand. No way was she going to tell this child that she'd been insensitive.

"No. I think Linnet's wanting more of my attention than she's been getting. Partly because of this wretched carnival. You're planning to go, aren't you?" She couldn't help sounding hopeful.

"To a dance? Are you kidding?" The pretty teenager wriggled in delight. "I can hardly *wait!* I know

Josh is going to ask me to dance.'' Her radiant face fell. ''Oh, no. What am I going to wear? *Can* we go shopping? If I ask Dad for some money?''

Grace forced a smile. ''Sometime before then. But not tonight, okay?''

''Sure.'' Her eyes widened when the phone rang. ''Maybe it's Josh! Can I answer it?'' Without waiting for permission, she snatched it up. ''Blanchet residence, this is Claire?'' She listened for a moment, then sounding crestfallen, said, ''Um, sure. She's right here.''

''Thanks,'' Grace mouthed, and took the phone. ''Judy!'' she said a moment later, assuming her gushy mode. ''Thank you for calling me back. Can you help?''

It was a nearly an hour later when she mounted the stairs and knocked softly on her daughter's bedroom door. After a pause, she heard a muffled, ''Come in.''

Wearing drawstring PJ bottoms and a tank top, Linnet sat on the bed, back to the wall, her knees drawn up to her chest and her arms wrapped around her legs. From the CD player came the voice of one of the teen pop stars singing some perky song about love. Linnet's face was fresh-scrubbed but her eyes were puffy.

Grace closed the door and went to the bed, sitting close enough to her daughter that she was able to give her bare foot a sympathetic squeeze. ''Do you want to tell me what's wrong?''

''Why does something have to be wrong?''

''You've been crying.''

Her thin shoulders jerked.

"Did you like Claire better when she was unhappy than now when she's happy?" Grace asked gently.

Linnet bowed her head.

Grace waited. When the silence drew on, she asked, "Is this Josh everything she says he is?"

Her daughter didn't answer for a moment. Then she mumbled, "He's really popular. And cute."

Grace had a horrible thought. "You didn't like him, did you?"

Linnet rested her chin on her knees. "As if he'd know I'm alive," she said unhappily.

"That doesn't mean you can't like him."

Her daughter released a painfully deep sigh. "Well, I don't. I mean, he's older and I don't have classes with him or anything. It's just..."

"It would be fun to have someone like him wanting to get together with *you.*" Oh, how she remembered that longing!

Linnet lifted her head, her eyes full of an adolescent's anguish. "He's all she ever talks about! It doesn't matter what I say. It's all Josh, Josh, Josh."

"I noticed," Grace murmured.

"And she's got the good part, and I *know* she's better than I am, which is okay, but she's prettier, too, and now Josh likes her, and..." She buried her face in her arms. A muffled wail emerged. "It's so awful to be jealous! I don't want to be jealous, but I can't help it!"

Grace scooted higher on the bed, leaning against the wall, too, so that she and her daughter were shoulder to shoulder. "It's perfectly understandable, you know."

"But I like Claire!" Linnet sniffed. "I don't want anything bad to happen to her, but..."

"You want good stuff to happen to you, too." Grace kissed her daughter's bent head, smelling the flowery scent of her shampoo. "We all feel jealous sometimes."

"Sometimes I wish she didn't live with us," Linnet admitted in a low voice. "It's like, you talk to her, and we never do anything by ourselves."

"I miss that, too." Grace hesitated. "You've had fun with Claire, though."

Linnet burrowed her face against her mom's arm, her nod more felt than seen. "It's just lately..." She trailed off, unable to articulate her resentment and unhappiness.

"She and her dad seem to be getting along better." Grace watched her daughter for a reaction. "I'm thinking she might be ready to try going home pretty soon."

Linnet's tear-streaked face popped up. "But I'd miss her!" Hearing herself, she gave a watery giggle. "It's fun having her here. I just wish, sometimes..."

"She'd go away for a few hours?"

The thirteen-year-old wiped her cheeks and nodded.

"Well, we'll have to figure out a way to do something, just you and me. But I don't know when, with this stupid carnival. I wish I hadn't gotten myself into such a big job."

Wet cheeks, ponytail and all, her daughter suddenly looked disconcertingly adult. "But you always do."

"This is the first year I've chaired."

"Mom, whenever anybody calls and asks you to do anything, you say yes."

Disturbed, Grace pulled back. "What are you talking about? I say no to telephone solicitors, men I'd rather not date, a glass of wine I don't especially want, Mr. Morris wanting me to sign that awful petition about not allowing homosexuals into the condominium association..."

Linnet shook her head impatiently. "Not that kind of stuff. It's people who want you to run some fundraiser or make banana bread for a bake sale or a quilt for a raffle or..."

Ruefully Grace abandoned her indignant defense. She finished the sentence. "Or organize a school carnival my own daughter doesn't even want to go to."

"You know, most of the kids aren't that interested. I mean, we're almost old enough for driver's licenses. School stuff isn't that cool. It's mostly the seventh graders who still think it's fun. Oh, and the sixth graders from Bellwood Elementary."

"Like you did when you were in sixth grade," Grace said, feeling dense. She remembered the evening, when she had supervised the cake walk and refereed mock attempts to shoulder friends from the winning numbers. Meantime, Linnet and her crowd had dashed about the halls of the middle school, all wearing makeup and tossing their hair and giggling madly at every witty word the others said. They'd been so sure they looked as old as the real middle-schoolers, and that some seventh-grade boy would notice them. Last year, Linnet had gone, too, but Grace didn't remember the evening as well.

Maybe, Grace thought, she just hadn't wanted to understand that things changed. Now her daughter was one of the blasé ones. Or perhaps, sometime in the past year, she had become one of the wounded ones who had learned that no boy *would* notice her, that her dreams of popularity were unlikely to come true.

"Any chance *you'd* help out with one of the games, so the sixth and seventh graders can have fun?" she asked tentatively. "Then you could go on to the dance."

Linnet gave her a shrewd look. "You couldn't find anybody to do it?"

Grace sighed. "Oh, a few. No, I'm sure I can round up enough parents. Especially if I get the PTA list from the elementary school." All those sixth graders who'd want to come. "I just thought, well, that you might not mind. And helping other people have fun can be good for your spirits."

Linnet pursed her lips and thought. "Maybe I could get some other kids to help, too. If you need them."

"Oh, bless you! Do you think you can?" she begged. She was already being haunted by nightmarish visions of spending night after night with the telephone to her ear as she left countless cheery messages on answering machines knowing full well none would ever be returned. In the past hour she had even tried to figure out how many games she could single-handedly run.

"I'll try." Linnet appeared to choose her words with care. "Mom? Maybe next year you shouldn't do the carnival."

Grace lifted her hand in all solemnity. "I do swear I will *not* volunteer for *anything* big next year." She let her hand drop. "Hold me to it. Muzzle me if I start to open my big mouth."

Her daughter studied her with perplexity. "Do you enjoy, like, being in charge?"

All she could do was echo, "Enjoy?" For a stunning instant, Grace went completely blank. *Did* she enjoy her volunteer work?

The self-revelation that followed was just as much of a shock. "No," she said slowly. "Not really. I *hate* calling people and trying to con them into doing something they don't want to do. I don't mind giving some hours, but I guess I'm as active as I am because I thought it was important for you. The schools need parents to be involved."

"I did like it a lot when you helped out in my classroom."

In first grade. Second grade. Maybe third grade. Grace had no trouble hearing Linnet's unspoken postscript: *But I don't care anymore.* She only hoped her daughter wasn't really saying, *It embarrasses me when you're around.*

Other parents had been smart enough to guess that their teenagers no longer needed them to be a bustling presence at their school. No wonder they were all making excuses!

"You know what?" Her daughter suddenly gave her a fierce hug. "I think it's cool that you are doing it for me."

Grace was the one to feel a sting of tears in her eyes. Every minute was suddenly worth it. Linnet understood that she was loved, that her mom would do anything for her.

That was what counted.

"I love you," she whispered, cheek to her daughter's hair.

Linnet kept hugging her, arms tight. "I love you, too."

"Help me get through this, and I'll swear off."

In an amused, snotty, teenage way, her daughter said, "Yeah, right."

The brief intimacy was past as they self-consciously disentangled. Nonetheless, Grace felt better about how well she had succeeded as a parent than she had in months. Years. Since Linnet had outgrown the stage when she would fling herself into her mommy's arms for regular hugs, when she would cling and say so sweetly and with such trust, "Mommy, I love you."

The rest of the conversation stayed with Grace in the next few days. She was bothered to discover how much she really did hate and even resent at least some of the volunteer work she had taken on without a murmur of protest. Analysis wasn't difficult. Of course she had been conditioned during her marriage to be the perfect wife of a prominent attorney. Such a wife didn't work for a living, unless she was also an attorney or a doctor or a historian, something worth doing in the eyes of the snobs who composed much of the corporate society Philip had frequented. No, the partners' wives were on the boards of multiple charities. They put on luncheons to raise money for Children's Hospital. They drove their children to piano or horseback riding or dance lessons. They entertained.

After Philip's funeral, Grace remembered most how deep her grief ran despite the problems in her marriage. Fear of the future reared on the periphery of her consciousness like black clouds on the horizon. She had lain in bed and cried until she had no more tears. In her exhaustion, one guiltily relieved thought had finally let her slip into sleep in the small hours of the morning: *At least I don't have to put on any more dinner parties.*

But everything else, well, apparently she had continued to play her role without question, long after everyone stopped looking.

It was past time to refuse any but the kind of volunteer work she did enjoy, the hands-on stuff like sewing costumes for the play.

Tuesday evening was spent working the phones and detesting every minute once again, although she did make sure she put one of Linnet's favorite dinners on the table and ignored incoming calls while they ate and talked about their days.

At almost nine her mother called. "Just thought I'd check in. How goes the play?"

"Oh, fine." Grace chatted about it for a minute without mentioning Linnet's disgruntlement about her lesser part. "And you remember Linnet's friend we have staying with us? I hear she's quite the actress, too.''

''I still don't see how you ended up with her.'' Her mother sounded annoyed. If it wasn't her idea, it had to be a bad one.

Grace felt a familiar tension creep up her neck. ''As I told you at the time, she was having problems at home and I offered to give the family some cooling-off time. That's all.''

''Ridiculous to take on other people's troubles,'' her mother snapped. ''Honestly, Grace, will you never learn?''

She closed her eyes and breathed deeply. ''How is Dad's gout?''

''Oh, he's moaning constantly,'' her mother said irritably, ''but I tell him not to expect any sympathy from me if he won't take his medicine when he's supposed to!''

''He still won't stick to it when the pain goes away?''

With a sniff, she said, ''He says I'm nagging when I remind him.''

Which of course she was, but she would never see it that way. Grace sometimes thought her father did absurd things like not taking his pills as a form of minor rebellion. Mom was a tyrant. She refused to see validity in anybody's viewpoint but her own. Heck, she didn't even acknowledge anyone else's viewpoint!

There had been a time when Grace's parents fought constantly. She remembered family dinnertimes when her mother was shooting furious looks at him and he was eating in mulish silence, when her sister Rosemary had been shrinking beside Grace, quivering in fear that their mother would turn her anger on them.

Not that Mom had ever been physically abusive. Just so critical she ventured into cruelty, rigid about rules, scathing about the girls' friends.

Grace had been the protector, the peacemaker. She would chatter at the dinner table as if she hadn't noticed the tension so thick it was hard to draw breath. She knew how to coax her mother into better moods, how to convince Dad not to dig in his heels, how to deflect Mom when she got on Rosemary's case.

After saying goodbye to her mother, she talked briefly to her father. Tonight he sounded sulky, like a child almost completely under his guardian's thumb but still squirming occasionally in rebellion.

"Your mother just won't let up," he declared. "I don't need the damned pills all the time! She insists on coming with me to the doctor and then she hears just what she wants to hear."

Mom snapped something in the background.

Grace rolled her eyes. "But, Daddy, you are having trouble with the gout. Maybe there's a different medicine?"

"I don't need the damned doctor," he grumbled. "I'll be fine." To punctuate the point, he groaned, apparently having moved his swollen foot. "Damned gout."

Grace was shaking her head by the time she hung up. Thank heavens her parents had chosen to retire as far away as Arizona! Keeping telephone conversations with them on an even keel was hard enough work.

Her hand stilled, the phone almost in the cradle. After a moment she made a rueful sound that wasn't quite a laugh and finished hanging up the telephone.

Maybe she'd given Philip too much credit. Maybe her inability to say no when someone claimed to need her grew from seeds planted much earlier than her marriage. She could almost see the roots plunging deep, tangled and thick.

The little girl who thought it was her job to hold the family together was still trying to fix everyone else's problems.

A little resentment was hardly a surprise.

Going upstairs, she paused in the doorway of the guest bedroom. The door stood half-ajar, light from the hall laying a golden path to the bed. Claire slept curled on her side, her hands tucked almost prayerfully beneath her delicate chin, her dark hair tousled on the pillow like a halo around her face. Her mouth was curved sweetly, as if her dreams were happy ones. Stretched beside her was Lemieux, who seemed to have adopted her. He lifted his head, blinked eyes that glowed red, and uttered a penetrating ''no-oo!'' Which, mercifully, did not wake Claire, who slept with the single-mindedness of the young.

Grace searched her heart and, to her relief, failed to find any resentment toward this child. There were days she came home tired from work and wished everything was back to the way it had been, but not many.

No, if she felt a tiny tug of secret resentment toward anybody, it was Claire's father.

She sighed and went down the hall to her own daughter's room. From here the light didn't quite reach Linnet's bed, but she heard the soft breathing and a few mumbled words. Linnet always had talked in her sleep, although rarely intelligibly. Grace had worried when Linnet outgrew the crib that she would also sleepwalk, but she seldom even stirred, only remarked on who knows what.

Grace brushed her teeth and washed her face, then studied herself unflinchingly in the mirror. The face that stared back at her was thin, bleached pale by the lights, and unalterably ordinary.

Perhaps, she admitted to herself, resentment wasn't quite what she felt toward David Whitcomb.

He was her Josh, the laughing, glowing boy passing by in the halls with his coterie of admirers, never noticing skinny Grace unless he needed help with math. That boy all grown up, David Whitcomb would never have noticed Grace Blanchet in other circumstances.

If he didn't need her.

One of these days—soon—he no longer would.

So, yes, she couldn't help resenting the fact that he was using her. Or despising herself for letting him, for deceiving herself into believing for even a few glorious hours at a time that he actually did want her.

Her feelings for him were, so quickly, becoming almost as tangled as those roots she'd imagined twisting through her psyche. She could so easily fall in love with him. Was maybe already falling, despite herself. Knowing that made her angry. She'd spent years trying to please a man because she continued to be amazed that he had chosen her. Handsome, brilliant, charismatic Philip Blanchet had made her his wife! Of course she would struggle against her shyness and entertain his colleagues. Of course if one of the senior partners' wives wanted her to co-chair a benefit, she would do it. Of course she would put up with his moodiness, his disinterest in his daughter, his equal lack of interest in her, his wife.

Turning back the covers and climbing into bed, the Egyptian cotton sheets Philip had insisted on silky against her skin, Grace wondered if she had learned absolutely nothing. Would she repeat all her mistakes if David Whitcomb, by some miracle, chose her?

IN A PHONE CALL to her at work, David bowed out of dinner Wednesday night, something he'd suggested that weekend. No big deal, Grace told herself. A Mexican restaurant with the kids wasn't that exciting anyway.

"Maybe we can do it tomorrow night," he said. "I'll pick up Claire at the library and then hang around until you get home."

Her disappointment lifted. "Claire will be sorry not to see you tonight."

His voice an intimate rumble, he asked, "What about you?"

All kinds of answers flitted through Grace's head. Every flirtatious response sounded silly and forced coming from her. She just wasn't any good at this kind of thing.

"Hey," she said lightly, "now I have to cook tonight. What do you think?"

He was silent for a moment. "I really was looking forward to it. Takeout at my desk isn't the same. But I'm stuck here, Grace. Tell Claire I'm sorry."

Grace passed on his message as soon as she walked in the door after work.

Hurt flashed across Claire's face, followed by nonchalance that didn't look quite genuine. "He's always having to stay late. Tomorrow's cool." Alarm widened her eyes. "Dad is still picking me up, isn't he?"

"Yep. He hasn't forgotten."

Which did not, Grace discovered the next day, mean he would do it. She was typing and editing a lengthy petition when her telephone rang. Mentally untangling a convoluted sentence that didn't quite work grammatically, she reached for the receiver.

"Forsyth, Wales and Kihlstrom," she said automatically, tucking the phone in the crook of her neck and resting her fingers again on the keyboard. "Grace Blanchet speaking." If she moved that clause…

"Grace, David Whitcomb. I'm sorry to make a habit of this, but I'm not going to be able to pick up Claire today. Unless you can, I'm going to call the school and have the secretary get a message to her to take the bus."

Hands dropping from the keyboard, Grace spun her chair away from the computer monitor. "But you can't do that to her!"

"I have to work." He sounded abrupt; voices in the background suggested he wasn't alone. "Getting together with some boy to read lines is not essential."

Grace gazed unseeing at her cubicle walls. "To Claire it is."

"For Pete's sake!" David exclaimed. "I can do it another day."

"Claire always has been something you can put off until another day, hasn't she?" Grace said quietly, her anger burning bright. "No, don't call the school. I'll find a way to pick her up."

"About dinner…"

"Clearly you won't make that, either." She hadn't known she could sound so cold. "Don't worry, I'll make other plans."

"Damn it, Grace—"

She carefully pressed End and set her telephone back in its cradle.

Her sinuses tingled, but she would not cry. How could she have been so wrong about him?

Oh, he wanted to reconcile with his daughter, Grace thought savagely, but only so long as it—and she—wasn't an inconvenience. Children, apparently, were women's work. Only his ex-wife's gross neglect of Claire had prompted him to step in and assume responsibility.

And, gosh, now he'd found a sucker to be the parent he was incapable of being. Mostly furious with herself, Grace finally understood his thinking. Wine her, dine her, a few kisses, and the homely single mother he was so honoring would be happy to raise his daughter.

The really sad part was, for Claire's sake, Grace couldn't do anything but make excuses for him. Just as she had always made excuses for Philip.

Excuses Claire wouldn't believe any more than Linnet had.

CHAPTER TEN

THE SIGHT OF an angry David Whitcomb on her door-step was familiar. Which didn't mean Grace wasn't just as rattled this time.

The doorbell had startled her at ten o'clock, soon after she had said good-night to the girls and was trying, despite Lemieux's affectionate interference, to finish the newspaper she hadn't had time to read that morning.

Through the peephole in the door she saw that the visitor was David. Not until she unlocked and opened up did she realize he was in a rage.

A man who normally kept his emotions tucked away, tonight he exuded frustration and fury. His hair stuck out every which way as if he'd yanked it, and the knot of his tie hung down by the fourth button of his shirt, which was wrinkled and rolled up at the sleeves. His mouth formed a grim line and his eyes glittered.

"David!" she exclaimed, her voice sounding breathless. And no wonder, since her heart had begun to drum. "It's so late!"

"What in hell was that about this afternoon?" he asked tautly, nostrils flaring. "You've never in your life had to tell Linnet you couldn't drive her somewhere? Can you walk out of the office any goddamn time you feel inclined?''

''I...'' she faltered.

''Well, I don't have that luxury.'' His voice was dangerously soft, faintly burred. ''You think I *like* disappointing my daughter, just when we're getting somewhere?'' He stared at Grace with acute dislike.

Her pulse raced unpleasantly. Now, too late, she realized that she hadn't thought this afternoon, only reacted. She certainly hadn't anticipated a confrontation, which was idiotic of her. Had she assumed he would just go away and suffer guilt in silence? Come crawling to her to apologize?

''I know you don't like disappointing Claire.'' How weak that sounded even to her ears!

''You figured I didn't give a damn? You thought... what?'' Now he was scathing.

I thought you were like my husband. She couldn't say that, but still suspected it was true.

Taking a deep breath, she stood back. ''Please come in. Obviously we need to talk.''

He stalked past her, not stopping until he reached the fireplace in the living room where he swung around to face her. Shoulders held rigidly, he loomed although he was a good ten feet away from her. In the brighter light she was shocked to see how tired he looked, as well as angry. His eyes were bloodshot, every line in his face carved deeper. The faintest of bristle shadowed his jaw.

''All right.'' He bit off each word. ''What's this about?''

''You've canceled on Claire two days in a row.''

And on me, her heart cried, shocking her again with the sharp pang of hurt.

Heaven help her, had she attacked him, not on Claire's behalf at all, but because her feelings were hurt?

His eyes narrowed. "Changing plans automatically makes me a bastard?"

Horrified by how tempted she was to apologize, Grace lifted her chin and said, almost steadily, "It makes you someone who consistently puts your job ahead of family."

He made an incredulous sound. "I am the vice president in charge of operations. How would it look if come hell or high water I folded the tent at five o'clock every day—or earlier, if I have to chauffeur my daughter? A strike is threatening and DuraTech is throwing a temper tantrum because urgently needed computer components didn't show up when and where they were supposed to, but, hey, my kid needs her social hour."

Put that way, *her* temper tantrum sounded incredibly petty. But she wouldn't let him win so easily.

With a snap in her voice, she said, "You have by your own admission neglected your daughter for years. You claim to be determined now to show her how important she is to you." She paused to let that sink in before adding baldly, "If this is how you go about it, let me give you a tip. You're going to fail."

His face darkened. The air fairly crackled with tension as they stared each other down.

If it was a contest, Grace won.

David swore. Abruptly his shoulders sagged and

he ran a hand over his face. "I'm doing my best," he said bleakly. "But you're telling me...what? I should quit my job? Take a sabbatical?"

Her own breath went out with a whoosh. "No," she said softly. "No, of course not. I'm the unreasonable one here, aren't I?"

"I don't know." Complete exhaustion infused his voice. "My daughter hates my guts. Yours loves you. That suggests your priorities are in better shape than mine, doesn't it?"

Grace didn't touch other people casually. But now she went to David without a second thought and hugged him, laying her cheek against his shoulder. For a second, he stood stiff and she started to pull back, appalled at her own boldness. Then he groaned and wrapped his arms around her, holding her so tightly it hurt. She heard the hammer of his heart, felt anguish in every locked muscle.

"I'm sorry, I'm sorry," she murmured.

"No." He rubbed his face against her hair. "Don't be sorry. Clearly I need to be shamed into acting like a human being."

Now she did push back, lifting her face. "No! If you had to stay at work, you had to stay. I was judging you..." The words dried up. She was humiliated to have to voice them.

His eyes searched hers. "Based on your husband," he finished slowly.

Grace ducked her head, mumbling to the loosened knot of his tie, "Yes."

David muttered a profanity and gripped her chin,

lifting her face. "The man was an idiot," he said distinctly, and kissed her.

This time was different. His mouth was achingly tender, brushing hers, tugging at her lip, nipping gently. Her hands went up to frame his face, the bristle on his cheeks sandpaper against her palms. Grace kissed him back with the same sweetness that was sending a rush of heat to pool in her belly even as it brought the sting of tears to the backs of her eyelids.

When David lifted his head at last, the expression on his face brought a hitch to her half-drawn breath. Had Philip ever looked at her with such mingled desire and…oh, not love, surely, but something akin enough to squeeze her heart?

In the next second, David's lashes shuttered his gaze and he stepped back, his hands dropping to his sides. "Maybe that wasn't such a good idea."

Her throat closed. "What?"

"We're getting pretty mixed up here." Gaze holding hers, he ran his hands over his thighs. "You try to give me hell, I kiss you. Probably we should have kept this simple in the first place."

Fear thrust its claws into her. Not until this instant had she realized how very close she was to being deeply, irretrievably in love. "Are you trying to suggest that we shouldn't date?"

He made a raw sound. "I'm saying we probably shouldn't have." Suddenly his eyes were alive, electric with urgency. "As far as I'm concerned, it's too late. I don't know how we can keep the two issues separate, but I can't pretend I don't want you."

One claw at a time, fear loosed its grip. She

sounded—odd—when she said, "I…I can't pretend, either."

David let out a ragged breath, closed the distance between them with one step and yanked her up against him. Her mouth was parted when it met his; his tongue drove into her mouth, his teeth scraped her lips, one hand squeezed her nape while the other gripped her rear and held her hard against him. This kiss was hungry, barely civilized, a presage to ripping off their clothes. She felt the hard bar of his arousal against her belly, and a whimper seemed to be coming from her throat. They were both gasping for air when he broke off, the thunder of his heartbeat echoing in her own chest.

They stared at each other, his lids heavy, a hot light in his eyes, his mouth twisted. Grace moistened her lips and said shakily, "I haven't felt like that in a long time."

"I'm not sure I ever have." A rasp deepened his soft voice.

Grace sucked in her breath. "I…me, either."

He hadn't loosened his hold. She still felt his erection. "I guess we do need to talk."

"Yes."

Briefly he closed his eyes. When he opened them, the desire was banked. Nonetheless, she felt his reluctance in the way his fingers tightened before letting her go.

She let her hands slide from his neck. Almost timidly, she said, "You look awfully tired. Would you like some coffee? Or a drink? Although I don't have very much since I hardly ever…"

David shook his head. "I wouldn't make it home if I had even a beer. And I've had enough coffee today to float me to the sound."

"Did you have dinner?"

"No, but I'm fine."

"Don't be silly." Her hostess instincts, long refined, leaped to life. She was grateful to have something to do. "Come on into the kitchen. I have leftover spaghetti. It won't take a minute to warm it in the microwave."

Eyes smiling, David said gravely, "Thank you."

As they turned, Grace saw the newspaper she'd left on the chair ripple and shift a few inches. It formed a good-sized tent.

"Lemieux," she said, when David raised a brow. "He thinks he's invisible."

"Ah."

In the kitchen, he picked an out-of-the-way corner and leaned one hip against the counter.

Self-conscious at being watched, Grace said, "If you want to sit down…"

David shook his head. "I've been sitting all day."

"And drinking coffee." She gave him a reproving look. "You'll get an ulcer."

He moved his shoulders indifferently, the tiredness showing again.

"Are things really going wrong at work?" She dumped the cold spaghetti into a bowl and popped it in the microwave, setting the timer.

"One of the unions is up for a renegotiation of their contract. There's no way in hell they're going to get what they want, although frankly I've been lobbying to make our offer better. Meantime, I'm getting undercut by some of the militants, who are agitating for a strike or worse.'' He grimaced. ''Today's disaster was a bunch of missing computer components. Having them not show up when they were needed may well cost DuraTech a million dollars or more in lost production. We're not talking a few packages, here.''

''Did you find them?'' she asked tentatively.

''Oh, yeah. Despite the fact that the tracing number located some horror writer's latest manuscript on its way to New York. Our planeful of computer components went to Bakersfield, California, to a small cosmetics company—no animal testing,'' he added wryly.

''You don't think two mistakes on the same shipment are coincidental, do you?''

''Hell, no!'' Jaw muscles knotted. After a moment he rotated his neck and visibly forced himself to relax. ''But how do you prove it? I spent the whole damned day on the phone, most of it with DuraTech executives who wanted to know how we could be so incompetent and what we were going to do to make up for our gross errors. And, oh, yeah, a union negotiator chose today to suggest we talk about some of the differences we'll be bringing to the table. He made a few veiled remarks about how angry his people were and how he wasn't sure he could 'control' them, which I took as threats.''

''Oh, dear.'' Grace was glad when the microwave beeped, giving her an excuse to turn away. In the middle of his wonderful day, *she* had hung up on him because he couldn't leave the office to pick up his daughter who had wanted to go to the library to flirt with her leading man—"man" being used loosely.

"'Oh dear' about sums it up."

She put sliced and buttered French bread on the plate with the spaghetti. "Come sit down and eat. What can I get you to drink?"

"Milk would be great."

At the table he started to sit and then stopped. "I should have asked. Any chance Claire is still up?"

"She'd gone to bed before you came."

With a sigh he sank into the chair and rested his elbows on the table, scrubbing his fingers through his hair. "Did I take two steps back with her?"

Grace sat, too. "In all honesty," she admitted, "she was more philosophical about you canceling than I was. She seemed..." Hesitating, Grace tried to choose the right word.

David finished for her. "Used to her father letting her down? Great."

"I think she was a little hurt, but only because your relationship is still fragile. Besides," Grace said with the first hint of amusement she'd felt tonight, "I *did* pick her up. Now, if she'd had to tell Josh, no, sorry, her mood might have suffered a little more."

David reached out suddenly and gripped her hands, laced together on top of the table. He gave one hard squeeze before letting her go and shaking out his napkin. "You don't like to hear it, but...thank you. It would appear that you bailed me out again."

That's what parents do. She opened her mouth, then, appalled, realized what she would be implying.

The words that had come automatically to her tongue died unspoken.

Claire wasn't hers. David wasn't hers, either. They shared a child only in an uneasy, temporary fashion.

"No problem," Grace managed to say lightly, before making an apologetic face. "Don't you wish I'd said that this afternoon, instead of chewing you out?"

"Yeah, I do wish." His eyes warmed. "Except that then I might not be sitting here, and I'm glad I am."

"My spaghetti is lots better than frozen." Perversely, she seemed determined to make light of his every attempt to tell her that he enjoyed her company even though she was hungry for such reassurance.

"Your company beats my own, too." A rare smile flickered. "And, yeah, your spaghetti is a helluva lot better than anything I have in the freezer."

As he ate, David asked about her day, which had been routine except for taking an hour of vacation to pick up Claire at the library. Grace chatted about personalities, a tangled murder case the firm was involved in, and about the one attorney she worked for who couldn't spell and had only a distant understanding of grammar, which meant that she had to severely edit his every letter and petition. "Then, of course," she said with exasperation, "he prowls by my desk wondering why I don't get his work done as fast as I do John Sawyer's."

David twirled spaghetti onto a fork. "What was your major in college?"

"English." Grace wrinkled her nose. "Useful, huh? Actually, I intended to become a teacher. But once I met Philip, I didn't finish the requirements for certification. Sometimes I think about going back to school.'' She shrugged.

''You'd be a great teacher.''

Conversation drifted, Grace contented to fill silences or let them linger—no, contented, really, just to watch him eat. David's every motion was neat and contained. Spaghetti didn't straggle from his fork. Crumbs didn't shower his shirtfront. No milk mustaches.

When he finished, David stretched luxuriantly. ''Thank you. That was great.''

Pleased, she said, ''You're welcome.''

''I'll call Claire tomorrow.''

''You're welcome to come to dinner.'' Grace hastened to add, ''If you can't make it, that's okay.''

''Are you sure?''

''I'm sure.''

''Tomorrow has to be easier. If something comes up, I'll let you know.'' His gaze rested on her face. ''Can we do something this weekend? You and me?''

''Claire…''

''I thought I'd see if she could have lunch with me one of the days. Sunday, maybe? Just the two of us.''

''Oh,'' Grace said inanely, the wind taken out of her sails.

''Can we have dinner Saturday night? We could go to a show, too, if you'd like. I can try to get tickets to *Phantom of the Opera*.''

She'd seen it once, and adored the glorious costumes, wrenching emotions and soaring voices of the Andrew Lloyd Webber musical.

"Could you really get tickets at such a late date?"

"I can try. If you want me to."

"That does sound fun," she admitted. In all honesty, anything sounded fun, if she were with him.

"Then we're on." He stretched again, giving her an opportunity to admire the play of powerful muscles in his neck and in his chest beneath the fine white fabric of his shirt. He suppressed a yawn and reached for his plate. "I suppose I should get home."

"Leave the dishes." She rose to her feet along with him. "I'll clean up after you're gone."

She walked him to the door, where he turned to her. He framed her face with his big hands, using his thumbs beneath her jaw to tilt her chin up so that he could kiss her briefly but very thoroughly. Grace couldn't help a whimper of protest when he lifted his head.

He smiled, laughter and something far warmer in his eyes. "Me, too." Without even a good-night, he turned and left.

Grace closed and locked the door, then leaned against it to give her knees a moment to regain strength. The smile, she didn't have to bother repressing.

HE COULDN'T GET *PHANTOM* TICKETS for that weekend, David told Grace apologetically the next evening as he took up his now familiar station in the kitchen and watched her putting together a salad to go with dinner.

"Do you want to go the next Saturday?"

The girls popped into the kitchen just in time to

overhear. ''What?'' Claire bounced on her toes, her face lighting. Poor Lemieux, slung over her shoulder, turned beseeching blue eyes on Grace. ''You're taking us to see *Phantom of the Opera?* Oh, that would be *so* cool!''

David's expression was even funnier than the cat's. For a remarkably inscrutable face, his showed a complicated tangle of emotions.

Grace laughed at him. ''You could, you know.''

Resignedly he said, ''I suppose I could.''

Suspicion furrowing her brow, Claire looked from one to the other. ''What are you talking about?''

''Nothing important.'' He gave a crooked smile. ''What do you say, girls? Do you want to go?''

They squealed and hugged each other, the Siamese cat escaping in the excitement of the moment. Claire even turned to David and, for a moment during which Grace held her breath, seemed about to hug her father, too. Then she settled for a more subdued ''Thanks, Dad,'' and followed Linnet to set the table.

''Is it possible for two parents to date?'' David asked in a low voice.

Still laughing at him, Grace shook her head. ''I have no idea. I've never seriously tried. Maybe a better question is, can you conduct a romance under the noses of your children?''

''Jeez.'' He sounded shaken at the idea.

Her laugh bubbled out of her. ''Better give it some thought,'' she advised, opening the oven to take out the casserole. ''Unless you intend for us to sneak around like two teenagers whose parents won't let them go out.''

JANICE KAY JOHNSON 193

His rusty chuckle followed her into the dining room.

"What are you laughing at?" his daughter demanded.

That set Grace off again, which earned her narrowed eyes from Linnet.

"Yeah. What's so funny?"

David set the salad bowl on the table. Only his eyes smiled. "You two. What else?"

"You weren't going to take us to *Phantom*, were you?" Claire asked suddenly.

Grace grabbed the basket of rolls. How was he going to handle this?

"Nope," he said easily. "To tell you the truth, I was trying to romance Linnet's mother." He put a subtle emphasis on "romance," his gaze touching hers briefly. "But, actually, I'm glad you came along. You and Linnet will love the show. Especially now that you're doing some acting yourself."

The phone rang. Both girls groaned in tandem.

"Ignore it," Linnet begged. "You know it'll just be somebody telling you they don't want to work on the stupid carnival."

Grace hesitated, her chair pulled out from the table. "Yes, but I *need* them to work on it."

"You can call them back."

At the hopeful look in her daughter's eyes, Grace sat down. "You're right. And whoever it is will probably say no anyway."

After the fourth ring, the telephone fell silent as voice mail picked up the call.

"What kind of work?" David asked.

"Um, Mom?" Linnet rolled her eyes toward him. "Maybe *he'd* like to...you know."

"I'm beginning to get a bad feeling about this," David said to nobody in particular.

Grace turned a toothy smile on him. "It's that wretched carnival and dance. The Friday before Thanksgiving. Linnet and Claire are really looking forward to it." Her glance quelled any chance of protest from them, if they chose to be traitors. "The thing is, we need lots of parents to put in a few hours that evening."

"Uh-huh." David dished up the chicken and cashew casserole. "Do I sense a pitch coming on?"

"Just two hours would be a big help."

"Uh-huh," he said again. "Doing what?"

"We need chaperons for the dance."

Claire moaned theatrically. "Not my own father!"

"Not a chance," he promptly told Grace. "What else?"

His daughter clasped her hands to her breast. "Thank you, thank you, thank you!"

"You could run a game." At his expression, she cleared her throat and hurried on. "Serve food? Announce raffle numbers? Oh, or run the cake walk. That takes muscle."

He mumbled something under his breath. Then he said resignedly, "Sure. Fine. Just nothing where I have to wear a stupid hat or act like an idiot, okay?"

"The cake walk." She smiled at him. "Bless you."

Out of the blue, Linnet spoke up. "You want to *romance* my *mom?*"

His gaze, unreadable, met Grace's. Then he turned to her daughter. "Yeah. Actually, I do. As in taking her out to dinner tomorrow night. Are you okay with that?"

She sat quietly, long enough to scare Grace. Then Linnet said gruffly, "I guess so. Sure. Mom dates sometimes. It's no big deal." Her tone challenged him to recognize that he was only one of a long string of brief, meaningless, casual dates passing through her mom's life.

Seemingly unperturbed, David nodded. "Good. Claire, would you pass the butter?"

Along with chicken casserole, he was served with a helping of talk about the glorious Josh. Relaxing in his presence, his daughter started by mentioning *Much Ado* and then artfully worked her way to the boy playing Benedick to her Beatrice. Once Linnet rolled her eyes, and David kept glancing incredulously at Claire and opening his mouth, presumably to change the subject, but never actually getting a chance to slip a word in edgewise.

Only near the end of the meal did he manage to interrupt. "Claire, I wondered if you'd like to have lunch with me Sunday. I thought maybe we could go down to the Seattle waterfront, maybe have fish and chips at Ivar's, then take a ferry ride over to Bainbridge and back."

She eyed him warily. "You mean, like, just us?"

"Just us," he agreed.

"Oh." She was silent for a moment—for the *first* moment in some time, Grace thought tartly. "Uh...sure." Her gaze sought Grace and her tone became hopeful. "If we weren't going to go shopping or something?"

"Nope. We can go tomorrow just as well."

She took a breath as if girding herself and said, "Then, I guess. Yeah. Okay." She stole a glance at him. "Um, I kind of wondered. Since we're going shopping."

"You need money."

"Well, yeah."

"No problem. Buy whatever you need."

Claire's deep breath rushed out, as if she'd been holding it all that time. "Thank you! I *really* need something new to wear to the dance."

A few minutes later, he made his departure. Grace left the girls to clean up the kitchen and walked him out.

"Lucky I just went to the bank," he said, and peeled off a couple of hundred dollar bills. "If she needs more than this, just let me know."

"Oh, I think she can manage on two hundred dollars. She's not exactly going around in rags," Grace said, dropping the bills into her purse, which sat on the hall table.

David opened the front door, then startled her by taking her hand and drawing her outside. Holding up one finger to hush her, he pulled the door closed so that they would be alone.

Since he hadn't turned on the porch light, they stood in darkness. A soft autumn rain fell, spattering under the tires of a passing car on the glistening wet street. Mist swirled around the street lamps and muffled sound.

Grace shivered, and David wrapped his arms around her. His warmth immediately enveloped her and she savored the solid, strong bulk of his body.

"Figured we could neck for a minute," he murmured. When she smiled and lifted her head, David's mouth closed on hers.

Grace could no more have denied her instant response than she could have resisted her daughter's first cry. This was instant, powerful, even frightening. Individual sensations—his big, restless hand on her hip, his tongue sliding along hers, the pressure of his thighs—melted into one. She wanted closer. To her frustration, there was no way to get close enough. She gripped him fiercely, kissed him back, would have given anything to have had the house without children just for tonight.

Oh, yes. However reckless, however potentially foolish, she would have invited him up the stairs to her bedroom. From the way he kissed her, from the way his hips crowded hers, he would have gone exultantly.

He tore his mouth from hers and groaned as he rested a cheek against her hair. His voice had roughened. "I feel like a teenager."

Her breath was tremulous. "Me, too."

"We've had this conversation before, haven't we?"

"Probably," she whispered.

"They're going to wonder where you are."

She burrowed her face into his chest. "Who cares?"

He gave a grunt she took for laughter. "I only do if they open the door."

On a sigh, Grace said, "Heaven forbid."

"It's getting harder to let you go." He still held her so tightly against him that she felt not only his arousal but the tension in every muscle.

Tomorrow night, you won't have to. She couldn't have said it aloud to save her life, modest child of her mother that she was. Ladies didn't throw themselves at gentlemen. Men did the asking. He hadn't exactly asked.

But she hoped, quite desperately, that he did. Come what may.

With the same aching reluctance that she felt, David gave her one last hard kiss, opened the door and all but dumped her inside. "Lock up," he ordered, and she didn't hear footsteps on the porch steps until the dead bolt clicked into place.

Once again she sagged against the door. Heaven help her, she was hopelessly, giddily, in love. She wanted him inside her, she wanted under his skin, she wanted in his head.

The last was the impossible part. David Whitcomb was not used to sharing very much of himself with anyone, including his daughter. Never mind a woman he had only just begun to date.

Grace drew a shuddering breath. What made her think he felt anything but lust for her?

The sad part was, she would take even that little from him. However wrenching it would be when he thanked her for the last time, took his daughter and walked away.

CHAPTER ELEVEN

FROM THE HEAVY WHITE tablecloths, lush roses in a crystal vase and delicately edged china to the rich Boeuf Bourguignonne and carefully presented wine, the restaurant was elegant. Tucked in a nook, a trio played soaring jazz pieces, the saxophone throaty, the piano riffs impossibly delicate. Waiters spoke in hushed voices, appearing even before they were wanted and then melting away. Tall white candles cast a gentle golden glow. David, in a dark suit and white shirt, was so handsome he stole Grace's breath. The evening should have been perfect.

It *was* perfect, except that she felt ridiculously awkward with David. Conversation seemed stilted, pauses too long, glances indirect.

Or was it all in her imagination? *He* talked with seeming ease about negotiations with the union, his plans for lunch tomorrow with Claire, a bill before the state legislature concerning the funding for more mass transit.

Grace, in contrast, couldn't quite remember what she'd done at work on Friday, and she was pretty sure David would have absolutely no interest in hearing about her day spent cutting orange, brown and gold crepe paper to deck the school halls for the wretched carnival. *Or* the increasingly whiny tone of her phone calls begging for assistance. Besides, all she could think about was him.

His large, competent hands, the fingers blunt tipped, calloused like a working man's. His strong neck, bulky shoulders, broad chest. His high forehead, the fine lines fanning from the corners of his eyes, the hint of a cleft in his chin. And, oh, that smile, piercingly sweet on those fleeting, rare occasions when it flickered across his face, softening the austerity.

Her trouble, she admitted, was that she was preoccupied with the all-important question: will he or won't he?

Not, of course, with *her* answer. She was crazy to think about sleeping with a man who might well want nothing but sex from her—well, she amended ruefully, sex *and* fostering for his daughter. But Grace had already made up her mind. Just once in an otherwise unexciting life, she was going to have one glorious affair, even if she did get her heart broken.

She emerged from this reverie to find that David was studying her with faint amusement, one eyebrow slightly lifted. Clearly, he had asked a question she hadn't even heard.

"Uh, I'm sorry." She cast about for an excuse. "The music caught my attention for a moment."

"Ah." He sipped his wine, his eyes never leaving hers. "Just wondered if you have the carnival in hand."

"You don't really want to hear about the carnival," she said frankly.

A smile twitched. He had a *very* sexy mouth. "Can't be any worse than union negotiations."

"Miles of harvest-gold crepe paper is worse than anything I can think of. Give me a few antagonistic labor organizers any day."

He flat out grinned, sending her pulse into overdrive. "You're right. Corralling reluctant parents may take the cake. If you'll excuse the pun."

"Since the cake walk is all yours—" she smiled cherubically "—pun away."

"I'm going to be sorry, aren't I?"

"Probably." Grace sighed. "*I'm* sorry. Never again. I swear off wasting time organizing trivial entertainment for unappreciative teenagers. I've heard about a no-kill cat shelter on Mercer Island. Maybe I'll volunteer there."

"Well, my daughter for one seems to be looking forward to the dance, at least."

"You noticed?"

"Oh, yeah." He shook his head. "Come to think of it, maybe I'll let you keep her until she gets over this Josh."

"Which will be very soon," Grace assured him, relaxing for the first time. She could talk in her sleep about children. "Middle school romances are fleeting. They 'go out' for a week or two, until one of them 'ditches' the other, which is momentarily a great tragedy. Until, of course, the next crush. Not, of course, that the pain isn't intense, maybe because their self-esteem is so fragile."

David fingered the stem of his wineglass, observing, "You're an expert."

Grace wrinkled her nose. "You know, it hasn't changed a whole lot since we were that age, except then we 'went steady.' Anyway, I hear all about it. Who is going out with whom, and why they broke up, and what everybody is whispering about. Although Linnet hasn't actually had a boyfriend yet, which depresses her unutterably. She's very jealous of Claire's romance, I must tell you."

David frowned. "Is that a problem?"

"She'd be jealous whether Claire lived with us or not. And her turn will come. Besides, she'll probably enjoy providing the shoulder for Claire to cry on." She hesitated. "Are you thinking Claire might be ready to go home?"

"Am I wrong?"

"No-o." She would miss the illusion of family they had had, Grace knew. Which wasn't excuse enough for discouraging him from reclaiming his daughter. "One thing worries me, though," she said honestly. "Nothing has changed. She's going through a good patch now because of Josh and the play and now her mother seems to be calling regularly. But remember what a short time ago it was that you had the blowup at the counseling session. Do you have any clue why she was so angry at you in the first place? And maybe more to the point, why she's not now?"

Silent for a moment, brooding, David leaned back in his chair. "No," he said at last, lines deepening between his brows. "I hoped we were just achieving some gradual understanding. And God knows, we've imposed on you long enough."

"Don't push it because you feel guilty. Do what's right for you and Claire. I'm fine with her staying." *And I will miss you so very much.*

David made a sound. "I haven't talked to her about this at all."

"I hope you two have fun tomorrow."

"Fun," he repeated, his gaze far away. "Do you know how many years it's been since Claire and I were close enough to have fun? She was maybe six, seven." He clamped his mouth shut for a moment. When he went on, his voice revealed the pain he usually hid so well. "We used to go to Golden Gate Park or the zoo or the ocean, just the two of us most of the time. We flew kites and went to Sunday outdoor concerts and art events for kids where she could learn origami or get her face painted. We were buddies."

"She'd be growing away from you now, no matter what you'd done," Grace said softly. "It happens to every parent."

He met her eyes with emotion stark in his. "But not every parent throws away the good years."

Her throat closed. "There can be more good years."

Regret still lingered in his eyes, but he also smiled. "There's my Pollyanna."

Grace made an apologetic face. "I can't help myself."

"I can tell." The look in his hooded eyes changed indefinably, warming her. "That's one of the things I like best about you."

"Oh," she said inanely.

"But only one of many." His gaze lowered to her

mouth, his eyes seeming to darken, before meeting hers again. "Are you ready?"

"Ready?" Grace squeaked. *Yes. No.* Did he have to throw it at her so bluntly? All of a sudden, she was less sure. She wanted him so badly, but she also wanted him to make the decision easier. Okay, in her heart what she wanted was for him to say *I love you.*

That eyebrow lifted. "Are you ready to go?"

Heat flooded her cheeks. All he'd been asking was whether she had finished her meal! And here she'd imagined... Totally humiliated, she closed her eyes for an instant. *Please, please, don't let him guess what I was thinking,* she prayed.

Striving to look poised—if also pink—she said, "Yes. It was delicious, wasn't it?"

He glanced at his plate as if he'd forgotten what he had eaten. "Yeah. It was good. No better than your spaghetti, though."

"Oh, *right.*" Hearing her own jeer, Grace laughed ruefully. "I sound just like Linnet or Claire. I'm sorry."

That smile lit his eyes. "It was cute." He signaled the waiter, who instantly materialized, taking the credit card. A few moments later, David collected their raincoats, helped her into hers before shrugging into his own, and steered her out with that hand on the small of her back. Even that minute touch made her weak. Grace was actually sorry, despite the downpour, when they reached the car and he let her go to unlock and open the door.

Behind the wheel himself, he put the key into the ignition but didn't immediately start the engine. Not looking at her, he said abruptly, "This is probably too soon to ask, but I'm going to anyway. Will you come home with me?"

Her heart lurched.

"To, um, see your etchings?" There she went again, trying to make light of something all too serious.

He turned his head, his expression making her pulse accelerate. "To make love with me."

A throbbing began, deep in her belly, shocking her with her instant readiness. Part of her felt curiously remote all of a sudden, as if this wasn't really happening, while her body was responding, most emphatically, as if it was.

There. He'd asked, as she had known somehow that he would tonight.

And she knew her answer, whatever a more sensible one would be. Even if he had only used the word *love* as a euphemism for crude, hot sex.

"Yes." Grace could hardly hear herself. "Yes," she said more strongly, more bravely. "I'd like to go home with you."

He didn't move for the longest time. When he spoke, his voice was hoarse. "I thought you'd say thanks, but no thanks."

"Why?"

Muscles in his jaw flexed. "Because on some level you must think I'm an SOB."

"No. Oh, no!" She turned to him impulsively, and he caught her hand in a strong grip. "I wouldn't say yes if I thought that."

David reached out his other hand and touched his

fingertips to her mouth, a tender touch that was shockingly erotic for her. "Thank you," he said huskily. The next moment, as if nothing had happened, he reached for the key and started the car.

The short trip passed in a state of bizarre unreality for Grace. David drove in his usual competent way, turning his head to check for traffic, gliding to a stop at lights, easing onto the freeway. Rain splattered the windshield and the wipers beat with a steady whump, whump. Grace looked out the side window at the water streaming along the glass, distorting the passing lights. As if hovering above, seeing herself from outside, she was very conscious of how primly she sat, belted in, hands folded in her lap.

Panic balled in her throat. Could she possibly be on her way to make passionate love with a man who, having withdrawn into himself, suddenly seemed like a stranger?

They passed through the tunnel, the lights eerily flashing, then emerged onto Mercer Island. One more bridge, and Seattle was behind them across Lake Washington, the high-rises of downtown Bellevue to their left.

Grace couldn't think of a single thing to say.

Absurdly, her mind tried. *My, look how it's raining!* Or, *Gosh, I hope it quits raining by tomorrow for your ferry ride.* Oh, better yet: *By the way, I've scheduled you for the seven-to-nine-o'clock shift at the school carnival.* She barely managed to swallow the bubble of hysterical laughter that rose in her throat.

What was *he* thinking? She stole a glance, to see

that he drove with both hands on the wheel, expression preoccupied and very distant. Was he even nervous? Did men get nervous about things like this, or did they—*he*—have sex with someone new way more often than she did?

She gave an inaudible sigh and resumed staring out the side window.

More often than she did? That wouldn't be hard. Her husband had been her one and only lover. She had not the faintest idea how different sex would be with someone else. The way she felt when David kissed her, she guessed it might be. But it could just as well be terribly disappointing.

When the car exited from I-90, Grace felt her mouth go dry. They'd be to his house in five minutes. Okay, she was having a full-blown panic attack now. *I didn't mean it!* she wanted to cry. *Take me home!*

She closed her eyes and tried to breathe deeply. Vaguely remembered lessons from childbirth classes seemed appropriate. In through the nose, out through the mouth. *Remember his kisses,* she reminded herself. *Remember the way you whimpered when he let you go. Scared doesn't mean you want to chicken out.*

She said suddenly, "I wonder if I should call the girls."

David glanced at her, his face unreadable in the dark. "They're thirteen years old."

"Yes, but..."

"And what are you going to tell them?"

Her fingernails bit into her palms. "I don't know. That we're not at the restaurant anymore. That we're going dancing."

He said nothing for a moment, then, "If you'd feel better."

No. Of course he was right. She didn't like to lie to Linnet. And she might sound funny. They might guess. This wouldn't take all that long, anyway, would it?

"Well, I had a little longer than ten minutes in mind," David said.

Grace gasped. She'd said it out loud! "I'm sorry," she said, pressing her hands to hot cheeks. "I guess I'm a little nervous."

They had turned into his exclusive neighborhood of fancy homes packed onto small, professionally landscaped lots. The road wound, cul-de-sacs opening to each side. She and Philip had lived in a neighborhood rather like this, in a house her husband had chosen and Grace had hated.

David turned into his cul-de-sac, then reached up to touch a garage door opener. For some reason, she studied the cream-colored house with the triple-car garage as if she had never seen it before.

Over the drumming in her ears, Grace asked, "Do you like your neighborhood?" The answer mattered an absurd amount.

David gave her an odd look. "Actually, not especially. When I was transferred up here, I bought this place sight unseen. I placed an order for one executive house, and this one was waiting for me. I rattle around in it. I don't collect cars to fill the garage— although I suppose I might get one for Claire when she's sixteen. So, no. I've thought about moving, but inertia has kept me from house hunting."

"Oh." Well, that was a relief, at least.

"Why did you ask? Have you detested my house from the moment you saw it?"

Her palms were sweating as the Mercedes glided into the huge, rather empty garage and the door closed behind them. "Philip and I lived in Eagle Crest. It suited him better than it did me." Through her light-headedness, she was briefly proud of her tact.

"Uh-huh." David turned off the engine. "And you're thinking your husband and I have yet one more thing in common."

"I'm sorry." How many times had she said that tonight? "I didn't mean..."

"That's okay." He got out of the car. Grace had barely freed herself from the seat belt and reached for the handle when David had the passenger door open.

He gestured her ahead. A short tiled hallway led past a bathroom and a laundry room darn near as big as her bedroom, to the kitchen. It was, of course, beautifully appointed, with bleached cabinets, granite countertops and the same gray tile floor. Grace found it very cold.

"Would you like a drink?" David asked. "Or wine?"

"I..." She was tempted, just to slow things down. "No. Thank you. I had enough with dinner. But go ahead if you'd like."

"No." He was silent for a moment, frowning. "Grace, if you don't want to do this, say so. I'm afraid I haven't been very romantic. I didn't deserve for you to agree to come over tonight."

"I...wanted to." The words almost stuck in her throat.

His gaze searched hers, the frown lingering. "You're sure."

No. She was very far from sure. But the curiosity and hunger he inspired in her were stronger than her cowardice.

Grace swallowed and gave a jerky nod.

The frown eased from his face; a smile crept into his eyes. "You look as if I'm about to wheel you to the guillotine."

"Oh, dear." Darn her blushes. "I really...um..." Mentally she threw up her hands. "Maybe I do need a glass of wine."

The smile grew, tender and amused at the same time. "Or maybe you need for us to quit standing ten feet apart here in this mausoleum of a kitchen."

Grace met him halfway. "That might help," she whispered, as she slid her hands around his neck.

He muttered something she couldn't make out, then kissed her. She felt the smile on his mouth; the tenderness was in the touch of his big hands as they caressed her face, smoothed her neck, squeezed her shoulders. Their lips clung, tasting and teasing until Grace felt a rumble begin in his chest.

Abruptly the hands that had been kneading her back moved down to grip her hips and pull her tightly against him. The kiss deepened, his tongue tangled with hers. She drowned in sensations that ran together like creeks joining in a rush for the larger river below. His sheer bulk, the strength of his thighs pressed to hers, his chest flattening her breasts, the bunched muscles in his shoulders and neck as he groaned again and lifted his head long enough to nip sharply at her ear before moving hotly down her throat.

"Grace Blanchet," he said thickly, "I have wanted you from the moment I saw you."

That couldn't be true, of course. She wasn't the kind of woman who inspired instant passion, but she thrilled at the words anyway. She needed him to want her.

"It was my voluptuous figure, of course," she murmured, her head falling back as he nudged aside the neckline of her dress to nibble and kiss his way along her collarbone.

"Mmm." He sounded considering. For the first time, he directly touched her breasts, both hands cupping them, weighing them, his thumbs stroking over her hardened nipples.

Grace's knees almost buckled. She gasped and then let out a shuddering little sound that would have embarrassed her in her right mind.

"I like a leggy woman." His cheek rasped against hers as he found her earlobe. "You could be a ballet dancer, like your daughter." He sucked gently at the same time as his thumbs made maddening circles on her breasts. "But, no," David murmured at last. "Actually, it was your hair."

Rubbing like a cat against him, she went momentarily still. "My hair?"

His hands left her breasts to begin plucking pins from her chignon. "It dances and shimmers." His voice, like his shaven jaw, was just scratchy enough to be intensely masculine and erotic. "It made me look at you again. And again."

"I love your eyes," she whispered, and kissed his closed lids. "The way they smile before you do. And, oh, when you do smile…"

His mouth covered hers, and she kissed him back with hunger as blatant as his.

He broke it off abruptly. "Upstairs," he growled, and planted a hand on her lower back, urging her ahead of him.

He hustled her past the characterless living room she'd already seen. At the foot of the staircase he kissed her; halfway up, he got the last pin from her hair, letting it cascade onto her shoulders. David threaded his fingers into her hair, lifted it and let it shower over his hands again. The deep, hot glow in his eyes made her feel like a sexy woman, an uncommon experience in her life.

She was one stair above him. David said, "Wrap your legs around me," and lifted her. With a squeak she did as he wanted, then became exquisitely conscious that she was riding his erection, each step he climbed upward sliding her against him.

A long, low moan emerged from her throat. He kissed her savagely, not stopping, bumping twice into walls as he carried her down a hallway. Once something crashed to the floor behind them and she heard a tinkle of shattering glass, but he didn't break stride.

The bedroom was dark. Not until he lowered her onto a bed did David reach for a lamp and switch it on. She had an impression of nubby cream carpeting and walls papered in a pinstripe, the bed king-size and covered with a duvet so thick she sank into it.

David planted one knee between her thighs and wrenched at his tie, tossing it aside. Grace swallowed and watched as he unbuttoned his shirt and shrugged it off. His shoulders were as glorious as she had imagined, broad and well muscled. Fine brown hairs formed an inverted vee on his chest, vanishing on his hard belly.

"Your turn," he said, sliding his hands under her skirt. Now she shivered as he hooked the waistband of her hose and peeled it and her panties off together. At one point he had to kneel on the floor to remove first one of her shoes and then the other. When he was done, he kissed the arch of her foot.

Grace's toes curled involuntarily. His attention shifted to her ankle; the next moment, he rubbed his cheek against her calf, then licked the underside of her knee. His hands shimmied up her skirt, his mouth following. Nobody had ever kissed the tender skin of her inner thigh like that; nobody had ever nipped just *there* with purely sexual intent.

If he lifted her skirt another few inches, she would be exposed to his gaze and his mouth. Part of her longed for just that; another part of her knew that to be unbearably wanton.

She didn't have to protest. He stopped, slid a hand up just long enough to tug gently at her curls, and then he rose to kneel between her sprawled legs.

"I want to see all of you at once." Heavy lids didn't hide the blaze in his eyes. "Come here."

Grace sat up, let him slide the zipper down her

spine. She closed her eyes and let her head fall back as the silk whispered over her body.

David made a sound of such rough satisfaction she had to open her eyes. He wasn't smiling, but his mouth had a twist that rocketed her heartbeat. The skin seemed to stretch taut over his cheekbones; his own pulse beat hard in his throat.

The next second, he reached for the hook at the front of her bra. Her breasts weren't full enough to spill out—she had always wished they were. But David brushed aside the lace and did smile now, as he stroked and rubbed her.

When he started to push her down again, Grace balked. "No." She didn't even recognize her own voice. "It's your turn."

His smile broadened, fiercely sexual even as humor crinkled his eyes. "Go for it."

Weren't these things supposed to happen the first time in the dark, a tempestuous coupling that required only mindless hunger, not conscious choices or the possibility of making a fool of herself?

Her hands shook as she unbuckled his belt, wrestled with a button, struggled with his zipper. She felt his shudders as her fingers grazed his length, as she slowly parted his trousers, impatiently tugged down his shorts, sucked in a breath at the sight of his erection. He stayed very still but for the muscle quakes as she touched, at first with tentative, feather-light forays, then more boldly as her courage and confidence increased.

Finally he broke, uttering a hoarse expletive as he pushed her back onto the bed and came after her, this kiss almost brutal in its stark need. She fought to yank down his trousers at the same time as he rolled to lift her so that he could rid her of the dress wadded at her waist.

They must be naked. Grace could feel hair-roughened skin against hers, his muscles bunching beneath her hands, his hard thigh separating hers. She heard the thump of a drawer and a growl from him, then the tear of a package. At last he was between her legs, bumping against her, tormenting her, until she lifted her hips in desperate need. He shoved inside her, so deep she cried out, and then cried out again when he pulled back. Of course he would come back, she knew he would, but she couldn't bear to lose him for even those fleeting seconds. She clutched frantically at his broad back, and he drove into her, again and again, until she convulsed helplessly and rivers of pleasure filled her veins. He jerked, made a guttural sound against her neck, and finally went still, weight heavy on her.

They lay unmoving for the longest time. Grace felt as if she were floating, the duvet a cloud beneath her, his big body warm and solid and protective.

Only slowly did she decide she needed to breathe. Even then she tried to hold out. She didn't want him to move. She wanted to stay just like this forever.

At her first tiny movement, David rolled to the side, taking her with him. She ended up with her legs tangled with his, her head resting on his shoulder, her arm draped across his chest. He nuzzled her hair and murmured, "Better?"

"I was already happy." Her eyelids felt extraordinarily heavy. Some of her hair was trapped beneath his arm, tugging at her scalp, but she didn't care.

His chest rumbled with a laugh. Fascinated, she flattened her hand right over his heart and said, ''Do that again.''

He did laugh, and she had to open her eyes to see.

''You should smile more often.''

''You haven't seen me at my best.''

She kissed his skin, tasting salt. ''Oh, I don't know.''

He lifted his head from the pillow, amusement again in his voice. ''Is that a compliment?''

''Maybe.'' Grace smiled and rubbed her cheek contentedly against his sleek shoulder.

How easy it was to slide into further exploration, into teasing and tenderness and a second long, slow lovemaking. She had a passing memory of her earlier thought that this wouldn't take long, and Grace almost laughed even though she was building toward another delicious climax.

She allowed herself only one regret: that she had to go home, that she couldn't for this one night be just a woman, not a mother. She wanted to sleep in David's arms, wake with her head pillowed on his shoulder, rub her palm over his morning whiskers and maybe shower with him.

The fears and longings that would crowd her tomorrow, she held at bay tonight.

CHAPTER TWELVE

CLAIRE STOLE A GLANCE at her father.

They stood together on the outside deck of the ferry, looking down at the last cars loading. A cold breeze blew off the Puget Sound. Dad had his hands shoved in the pockets of the jacket he wore over a thick sweater. She clutched the railing; he rocked on his heels and looked totally content, as though he had nothing else he wanted to do but ride a big, slow boat across the sound and back for no reason.

"Do you remember the time we went out to Alcatraz?" he asked unexpectedly.

Claire frowned. "Yeah. It was *creepy*." Guides had let them go inside the cells deep in The Rock, and little as she was, the clang of metal gates had made her want to run back out into the sunshine. She had panicked and cried. Dad had taken her out, and they'd sat on the rocky shore of the tiny island and explored tide pools until it was time for the boat to return to San Francisco.

"Yeah, but you loved the boat ride," Dad said.

Down below, workers fastened a chain across the stern. The ferry horn blasted, and Claire jumped. The engines rumbled and she felt the vibration in the railing. As water opened between the dock and the ferry, seagulls lifted off from the dark, creosote pilings and soared like hang gliders above.

She was embarrassed to feel a little excited, as if they were actually going somewhere. It was kind of cool, setting out onto the sound.

"Let's head up front now," Dad suggested.

They pushed through heavy doors and entered the warm interior of the passenger deck. Rows of booths let you sit by the windows and look out, if you didn't want to go outside. Maybe if you took the ferry all the time, you wouldn't care, Claire thought. One guy was already napping, lying on his back with his feet hanging into the aisle and his face covered with his arm. Others were reading. A bunch of teenagers played cards. A couple were guys, but not really cute ones. At the coffee shop in the middle, families were lined up to buy pop or snacks.

Up at the bow, the minute she and her father pushed through another big set of doors, the wind snatched at them. Claire almost had to lean forward to follow Dad out onto the observation deck.

Seagulls still floated above. The water was choppy and gray, with clouds thinner than yesterday but still looking like they might shed rain any minute. Out in the middle of the sound, a tugboat pulled a superlong series of barges, and toward land on the other side, Claire saw a whole bunch of sailboats, as if there was some kind of race. The sails were brightly colored, like some little kid who didn't know they should be white had drawn them.

Dad grinned at her. His hair whipped back from

his face, while hers stung her eyes. "I love it out here," he said.

"Me, too." Claire realized she meant it. "How do you learn to sail?"

"You take lessons. We could do it together."

"Really?"

"Why not?" He was still smiling, still looking happier than she was used to seeing him. "I could use a hobby."

"That might be okay," she said cautiously.

He nodded. "I'll find out more. We might have to wait until spring."

They didn't talk much on the way over to Bainbridge Island. It reared ahead, wooded, with a rocky shore and huge, fancy houses poking out of the trees. The town of Winslow was tucked behind an arm of land, shingled buildings above a marina. The bare masts poking up made Claire think of pick-up sticks shoved into their cylinder.

The ferry slowed, the water churning, then eased into the slip. Dad told Claire about a few accidents ferries had had, when captains misjudged and came in too fast. The two stayed outside, shoulder to shoulder, watching as first passengers and then cars unloaded, then new ones poured on.

Doing something like this, just the two of them, felt…weird. And…almost nice.

These past couple of years, when she thought about her father or saw him, Claire mostly remembered him leaving. The way he'd stripped her desperately clutching hands from his shirt and walked away without looking back even though she was screaming, "Daddy! Don't go! Daddy! Please!"

Lately she'd begun remembering before that, when he was the one to take her to the zoo or to the beach—they'd done that lots, she thought. They'd take picnics. Always peanut butter sandwiches, her favorite, and apples—back then, she wouldn't eat any other fruit. He would carry her on his shoulders, even up steep paths from the ocean, or sometimes at the park he'd grab her hands and swing her in circles until she was dizzy and the green lawn blurred and only he was steady in the kaleidoscope.

He had even gone on preschool trips. She knew that, because she had a couple of sharp memories, like snapshots or short videos. One was at an aquarium, that weird blue light in the background, and he was crouched helping this girl put on a sweatshirt while two others were clutching his shirt. She must have been standing a few feet away, she didn't remember why. Maybe she was jealous, and that was the reason the one meaningless scene had stuck.

The other time she remembered was a play. Some boy Dad had charge of had taken all of his clothes off while the play was going on and the auditorium was dark. When the lights came up, he jumped onto his seat and danced. Mostly Claire remembered everybody laughing and Dad mumbling under his breath as he tried to find clothes that had been kicked under seats and stuff this squirming kid back into them.

When she had been hurt or scared, she wanted Daddy, not Mommy. She still didn't really know why he'd gone away and only come back once in a while. He told her the divorce didn't have anything to do with her, but she never had believed him, or else why hadn't he taken her then?

It confused Claire, remembering the time when she would squeal and race to the door just because Daddy was home from work, when only Daddy could tuck her into bed. It had been easier to hate him when all she thought about was the sight of his back as he left her. Now she was all muddled. She used to dream about him coming back, and now here he was, but what if he didn't stay?

Even hoping a little that he did made Claire feel guilty, as if she'd betrayed her mother. Mom really had needed her, Claire knew she had. Who else would get Mom up, when she forgot to set her alarm or turned it off and put the pillow over her head? A familiar worry nudged at Claire. What if Mom couldn't get another job without a letter of reference? Would Pete give her money? Was she remembering to pay bills? What if she never ate real meals? Would she get sick?

Guilt roiled in Claire's stomach when she admitted to herself a secret relief that she didn't have to do all that stuff anymore. Living with Mom, she could never have been in the play or hung out at the library with Josh. She didn't even *have* any friends, because she couldn't ask anyone over and her mom could never drive her anywhere.

But then she'd think about what might happen to Mom without her, and she'd get mad because Dad wouldn't care if something awful *did* happen. And the confusion would start all over, because she didn't really want to go back to California anymore but she felt like a horrible person for being so selfish.

The ferry horn blasted again. Claire and her father watched as Bainbridge Island fell away and the ferry headed out into choppier waters. The wind felt colder and she suddenly shivered.

"Let's go inside," Dad said. He held open the door for her and they found a window-side booth that was empty. When they'd sat down facing each other, he asked, "Can we talk?"

"I guess." She looked down at her lap.

"Despite what I said at the counseling session that day, you can't stay with the Blanchets forever. I'd like you to come home."

All her confusion sharpened into fear. "They don't want me anymore?"

"Want you?" He leaned forward as if he was going to touch her, but then didn't. "No, Grace hasn't said anything like that. It just seemed to me that…well, we're getting along better. That maybe you feel ready to come home."

Just a month ago she would have snapped that *home* was with Mom in California. Now she sat with her head bent. Picking at a frayed spot on her jeans, Claire tried to figure out what to say.

She *liked* things the way they were. Sometimes she wished…oh, that Linnet really was her sister and Mrs. Blanchet was her mother and that Dad might marry her, so then he'd still be Claire's father, even in this dream.

If she was Claire Blanchet, then she wouldn't have

to feel left out the way she sometimes did. Her bedroom wouldn't be the "guest" room. She wouldn't feel embarrassed every time she had to ask for a note for school or money—money was the worst! And she wouldn't be so jealous when Mrs. Blanchet gave Linnet a private smile or hug as if Claire was invisible. No, not invisible—in the way. Mrs. Blanchet was super nice, but she didn't love Claire the way she did Linnet. And that sometimes gave Claire a hollow feeling inside.

At least her father was really hers. Back when she was little, he had given *her* those kinds of hugs and smiles. Lately, instead of looking baffled and angry with her all the time, he had begun to seem as if maybe he was sorry and he did love her.

Not that she trusted him! She would never totally trust him again, but maybe she could...well, give him a chance.

"Maybe," she said finally. "How would I get home from rehearsals?"

"Grace and I have been taking turns anyway. There's no reason we couldn't keep on, is there?"

"But what if I wanted to be in something and Linnet wasn't. You wouldn't have time to do all the driving."

"Claire." Dad waited until she looked up. He looked at her steadily. "I promise I'll figure out a way for you to do everything that's important to you. Heck, if nothing else, we've got a great bus system. We can figure out routes."

"Would you trust me?"

He smiled, and her heart did something funny. "Yeah," he said. "I trust you."

Pleased despite herself, she went back to picking at the hole in her jeans. "If I come home, can we get a cat?"

"You want a *cat?*" Dad sounded startled, and not totally happy.

"I'd miss Stanzi and Lemieux." Which was true. She'd never had anybody to sleep with before. "You know. Linnet's cats. They're really good company."

"A cat."

She frowned at her father. "What? Do you think it would ruin your furniture or something?"

"I don't give a…" He cleared his throat. "I don't care about the furniture."

"Then why don't you want a cat?" Claire asked stubbornly.

"Because you're thirteen years old and *I'm* the one who'd end up with a cat when you go off to college."

"Wouldn't you like the company?" Her tone became wheedling. "Lemieux likes to snuggle under the covers. I lift them up and he whisks in, turns around, and then tucks his head under my chin. It's…it's nice." The word was inadequate for the comfort and trust the big snowshoe Siamese gave her, but she couldn't think of another.

Dad let out a sigh. "I'd rather not get a kitten."

"That's okay. Mrs. Blanchet says the grown-up cats have a harder time getting homes. Everybody wants kittens 'cause they're cute and fluffy. I want a cat that maybe wouldn't get a home if I didn't choose him."

Dad had a strange expression on his face. After a moment, he said, "Okay. It's a deal. When you come home, we'll pick out a cat."

"Cool." She had him over a barrel. What else could she ask for, while he was in the mood to give her anything she wanted? "Can I have Linnet spend the night sometimes?"

He lifted his eyebrows. "Of course you can."

"Like maybe the first night?" Seeing his surprise, she bent her head again. "The house is so big. And empty." She looked up hopefully. "Maybe we should get two cats?"

Dad just laughed. "Or maybe we should move."

Alarm flared. "You mean, away?"

"No, I mean, buy a different house. We could stay in Lakemont. I wouldn't want you to have to change schools. I've just realized that I don't much like our house. I'd like something...warmer."

"More like the Blanchets'?"

"Yeah." Another odd expression passed briefly over his face. "Friendlier."

"That would be okay," she decided. "I don't like your house, either."

"There's just one thing, Claire." He sounded serious, now. "I want you to promise me something."

"What?" she asked warily.

"You won't take off without talking to me first. Give me a chance if I foul up or something happens. Yell at me if you want. Just don't sneak out and disappear."

Her eyes suddenly burned. She was even madder

at herself when her voice came out super tiny. ''Mom's coming for a visit anyway.''

''That's true.''

''Okay,'' she said, still in that small voice.

''You'll talk to me, you won't take off.''

Claire nodded. ''Can we pick out a cat right away?''

''Why not?''

''Like, tomorrow after school?''

''Shouldn't we wait until you've moved home?'' She considered. ''Maybe.''

''If you're not ready…''

''No. That's okay.'' She liked the idea of having her own cat, although she would miss Lemieux.

''Next Saturday? We can move you, then get dressed up to go to The Fifth Avenue to see *Phantom of the Opera*.''

Tension eased inside. That gave her a few days to…well, *adjust*.

''Okay,'' she said again.

''Then—'' Dad rose to his feet and held out a hand to her ''—unless we're going back to Bainbridge, it's time for us to get off this ferry.''

Startled, Claire looked out the window and saw that the ferry had docked back in Seattle and that the other booths were empty.

Hesitantly she laid her hand in her father's and let him pull her to her feet. It felt weird, having her hand in his. For a minute, she was a little girl again, with Daddy keeping her safe. When he held her hand, nothing bad could ever happen.

The tears stung again and Claire tugged free, hurrying ahead of him so he wouldn't see how much she wished it was true.

IT WAS A GREAT WEEK, as far as David was concerned. First, he felt good about the time he'd spent with Claire; amazingly, the time-out Grace had given him and his daughter seemed to have worked. Claire was ready to come home, and he thought he had a better idea how to be a father she could rely on.

Then, he and Grace managed to get away twice in a week that hadn't looked good at the beginning: Wednesday at lunchtime and then Friday night when Linnet and Claire went to a movie with a gaggle of other girls.

He had intended to take Grace out to lunch on Wednesday, but when they got out to the car and he asked, "What are you in the mood for?" she had looked at him and said simply, "You."

His house was five minutes from her law firm. They made it that far, but the minute the garage door started rolling down, he kissed her with all the patience of a randy teenager, and she kissed him back the same way. He swore when he tried to pull her into his arms the way he wanted to and the console and stick shift got in the way.

Pink cheeked, Grace laughed and said, "I don't think this is going to work."

He leaped out of the car and met her in front. They necked all the way into the living room, where he unbuttoned her very proper white blouse, unhooked her bra and exposed her breasts at the same time as she was shoving off his suit jacket and tugging at his shirt buttons.

There was something damned erotic about not bothering to get entirely undressed. He shoved her skirt up and pulled her hose and panties off. She unbuckled his trousers and freed him just as he rode her down onto the leather couch. She made soft, desperate sounds that turned him on in a way he couldn't remember ever happening before. He barely had the presence of mind to put on a condom. They grappled and tangled and then he was inside her.

There was nothing tender or romantic about this sex, but it felt unbelievably good. She arched to meet every thrust, her fingernails biting into his back. Grace had been as hot and ready as he was, because her inner ripples began almost immediately, shivers that escalated into a full, rolling climax, drawing him with her.

Hell, they even had time for a sandwich before he had to take her back to work, her prim suit only slightly wrinkled.

Friday night was as good. Having resigned himself to seeing her only with both their daughters present this weekend, David was still in the office when his secretary put Grace's call through.

"Are you stuck there?" she asked, muted excitement in her voice. "A girl from school asked a whole bunch of her friends, including Claire and Linnet, to go out for pizza and a movie."

He mentally junked the pile on his desk without compunction. "We can go out to dinner." David knew better than to express what he thought was a better idea: repeat Wednesday. Forget the meal and go straight for the sex.

"Or I could make something simple. Potato salad wouldn't take long, and we could grill steaks."

Nice compromise. He was hard just thinking about the two of them alone again. He did manage to corral his animal instincts long enough to make civilized conversation over dinner before he finally couldn't keep his hands off her.

She shot the bolt on the front door, just to be sure they wouldn't be surprised by two thirteen-year-olds, then led him up the stairs to her bedroom.

David almost felt nervous, perhaps because of the way she took his hand and drew him with her so solemnly. That, and the fact that she was inviting him into her own bedroom. It seemed a step beyond having hot sex on his living room couch.

Just inside the door, he wrapped an arm around her waist, pulled her close to his side, and looked around.

Funny, he hadn't noticed until he started hanging out here how sterile his own house was. After the designer was done, he'd bought one or two pieces of furniture he liked and picked out some artwork when he happened to wander into a gallery. The trouble was, compared to Grace's home, his looked unlived-in. He was a tidy man who didn't leave books or papers lying around, didn't have messy hobbies, didn't even entertain if he could help it.

Downstairs here, her hobbies overflowed onto chairs or the tops of tables. She'd mentioned that she was helping sew costumes for the play, and fabric heaped the buffet. He liked the way she'd unselfconsciously left out her sewing machine. Tonight, dried flowers and herbs and some kind of woody stems wound into circular shapes cluttered one end of her kitchen counter. She was making wreaths, she'd mentioned casually.

But her bedroom, he had figured, was her inner sanctum, so to speak. An intimate place stamped with her personality.

He'd been right.

The whole room was done in blue and white, the window shaded with white wooden slat blinds, the valance made up of blue-and-white quilted squares. The iron bed was painted white, the coverlet was a rich blue, while a faded blue-and-white quilt that must be old was folded at the foot. The cherry bedside tables had lushly curving legs with intricate cutouts; rag rugs covered wood floors. Her dresser was white-painted and simple, the beveled mirror above it an unframed oval suspended from a ribbon. The room had a clarity and simplicity he found restful—no feminine fripperies, only books heaped beside the bed and a few photographs of family.

He could live in this bedroom, or one like it, if this thing with her went where he thought it might.

"It looks like you," he said with a nod.

"And here I hoped I looked like a silk-and-lace kind of woman." Grace sounded rueful.

"I prefer clean lines—" his hand demonstrated on her long slender waist "—and directness." He turned her to face him, bumping her hips up against his. "You always look me right in the eye and tell me what you think."

Grace wrinkled her nose. "Not the sexiest of qualities."

"I don't know." He gave a slow smile and pulled her a little tighter so that she couldn't miss noticing that he did, indeed, find her sexy as hell. "Works for me."

She wriggled and then slid her hands up around his neck. "Apparently," she admitted, satisfied with his demonstration.

Tonight's lovemaking was more leisurely than either of the last two times. Which wasn't difficult, since he'd started both the previous times with little finesse and no patience.

This time, he found plenty of spots on her slender body that brought sighs from her, and she was a little bolder, seeming to enjoy her exploration of him just as much. In the end, his control snapped and he had to take her hard and fast, but she was eager, too.

David lay beside her afterward, for the first time aware of a silence when maybe something should be said.

What was she thinking? Expecting from him? He had to assume she was expecting more than a few sexual interludes. Grace Blanchet was too classy a lady to indulge in casual affairs.

Her head was tucked on his shoulder. Knowing she couldn't see his face, David frowned at the ceiling. He didn't much like the idea that she might think of him as a convenience and not as the man she wanted to have and to hold.

Probably they should talk soon about the future. He knew he wasn't much good at courtship—the only other experience he'd had was pushing twenty years ago. But without him fully being aware of any incremental step, this *was* a courtship. Just the other day, when he'd thought about house hunting, for example, he had automatically taken into account what she would like, as well as the fact that they'd need a bigger place than this, with two girls and three cats.

Still, it seemed a little soon to say *Marry me.* Part of him thought he and Claire needed a little time to themselves first, anyway.

What amazed him was how incredibly he and Grace connected not just in bed, but in conversation. Damn it, he liked her! This week, he'd taken to calling her the evenings when he wasn't coming here after work, just so he could hear about her day and tell her about his. In the bleak months after his divorce, he had hated going home from the office to nothing but solitude. In the years since, David guessed he'd gotten antisocial, because until this past month or two, he had liked living alone, not having to deal with people in the evening, storing up energy for the next day's problems.

Grace renewed his energy in a different way, with sharp perceptions and her basic kindness and generosity. After making love with her, he felt a bone-deep relaxation. In fact, tonight he was too relaxed to get into a talk about a mythic future he wasn't sure would arrive.

So he said nothing important, eventually giving her a back massage that evolved with startling speed into more sex, as good as the last.

Oh, yeah, they did connect incredibly well here, at least.

They both got dressed and David left before the girls were due back. He didn't want them wondering what their parents had been doing together all evening at home. He was pretty sure Grace wouldn't be much of a liar.

"See you in the morning," he said, with one last kiss that made him regret he had to go home to his empty house. He would have liked to spend the night. See what Grace looked like in the morning, when her hair still floated loose on the pillow and her eyes were sleepy.

"Damn it," he muttered, and left.

She stared after him.

It occurred to David in the middle of the night that having Claire living here and Linnet with Grace was going to make getting together without a kid around even tougher. He frowned at faint bars of streetlight coming in where the blinds weren't tight enough. He couldn't keep picking Grace up ostensibly for lunch but really for a quickie.

Marrying the woman was the obvious solution.

What made him edgy was knowing she'd want the words every woman demanded. He'd made himself say *I love you*, to his daughter because his all but absence from her life gave her good reason to doubt his feelings.

For Grace…swearing under his breath, David rolled over and pounded the pillow into shape. What he felt for her might be love; he didn't know. He guessed it was. He wanted her as he'd never wanted another woman. She fulfilled him even as he was left needing more. He liked her, he hungered for her company, he couldn't imagine now doing without her.

Was that love? He hadn't seen enough of the real thing to be sure. The very word made him uncomfortable. A man showed how he felt about a woman or his children by what he did, how he cared for them. Flowery words were easy to say. Staying through the hard times—he winced at the self-condemnation—that was how a man said *I love you.*

And, since he hadn't stayed the course last time, how did he know he could?

He could start, he thought the next day, by proving to Claire that he was the father he should have been all these years. As he carried her suitcase back down the stairs at Grace's house and out to the trunk of his car, he felt the symbolism. They loaded his car and the trunk of Grace's, making him wonder how his daughter's possessions had swelled in only six weeks or so.

At his house, everybody trooped upstairs lugging Claire's stuff. In her bedroom, she unrolled one of the posters she'd just dumped on the bed.

"I never even liked *him,*" she said with curled lip about some pop singer, just before she wadded him up and trashed him.

Grace and David eventually left the two girls to rearranging Claire's room. He shook his head as Linnet's voice drifted after them.

"If you put the dresser here, then the desk could go…"

Where, he didn't hear.

"Are girls born with some kind of decorating gene? Who cares where the dresser is?"

Halfway down the stairs, Grace poked him with her elbow. "Well, now. I'll bet you're particular about where your desk is at work, or here in your home office. You just don't care about dressers."

Or sofas or end tables, he added silently. She was right. He did care how his desk was situated and where the lamp stood to cast light when he read. The printer had to be to the right of the computer; he liked a keyboard that slid out of the way when he wasn't using it. Fax machine to the left. Two pens, two pencils, no more, no less, in a clay pot Claire had made in kindergarten.

"Point taken," he conceded.

He showed Grace his home office, and even christened it, in a way, by lifting her onto the desktop and kissing her until he was between her thighs and his hand was up her T-shirt and they were both breathing raggedly.

"You know—" she nibbled on his neck "—we can't..."

He weighed her breasts and groaned. "There must be somewhere in this house they wouldn't find us."

She gave an airy giggle that tickled his throat. "But just think how it would cramp your style, knowing they were looking."

Girlish shrieks and the thunder of footsteps coming down the stairs made her point all too effectively. He damn near leaped back at the same time as Grace sprang from the desk, tugged down her shirt and ran her fingers through her hair. Both assumed casual poses.

Then they met each other's eyes and laughed.

"Okay," he said. "Time to get ready for our big night on the town."

"They *will* enjoy it." But she sounded the tiniest bit wistful.

David was sardonically aware of how the longing in her voice stroked his ego. That awareness didn't keep him from feeling richly satisfied. If he couldn't take her right here and now on his gleaming cherry desk, he did like knowing she was as regretful as he was.

As the girls ricocheted into his office, he smiled at Grace and murmured, "What would you say to lunch on Monday?"

She gave him one flash of those sexy, deep blue eyes. "That sounds very nice," she said primly, before turning to their daughters. "Well, girls, what do you say we go get ready for *The Phantom of the Opera?*"

The excited face Claire lifted to David erased any lingering regret he felt.

"This will be *so* cool," she declared.

He had a brief, self-important image of himself as man of the house, making all his womenfolk happy. His basic insecurity wouldn't let him cling to such idiocy.

But, damn, it did feel good to have not just Grace and her daughter, but Claire, too, gazing at him with glowing eyes.

Maybe he could have a family again, and do it right this time.

CHAPTER THIRTEEN

ON SUNDAY, LEMIEUX WANDERED around the town house poking his head into rooms and wailing.

When he padded into the kitchen, his slightly crossed blue eyes agitated, Grace set down the bundle of dried lavender she had been separating and scooped him up. Slinging the big cat over her shoulder, she ran her fingernails down his spine. "Poor baby. You miss Claire, don't you?"

He agreed mournfully.

"She'll visit."

Not reassured, poor Lemieux struggled and, when Grace released him, leaped with a thud to the floor. A moment later, wincing, she heard him caterwaul in the living room. Thank goodness the wall between her town house and the neighboring one was well insulated!

Linnet wandered into the kitchen. "Gol! He's really noisy." She hooked a stool with one foot and sat. "What're you doing?"

"Making wreaths." Grace poked a lavender stem into the moss she was using for a base. The lovely, pungent scent of the herbs filled her nostrils. "I was going to donate a couple of them to the raffle at the carnival."

Her daughter looked, as if automatically, toward the telephone. "How come nobody's calling?"

"A momentary lull," Grace said, making a face. "Right this second, I have enough volunteers lined up to run every single game and chaperon the dance. I'm jinxed. They're going to start canceling any minute."

Linnet flashed a grin. "Nah. You've made 'em all feel too guilty to ditch on you."

"Pray God," Grace muttered.

Linnet watched her work for a moment. "It seems weird not having Claire here," she said suddenly.

"Lemieux evidently thinks so." Grace studied her surreptitiously. "Do you miss her?"

"Kind of," the teenager admitted. "I'm sort of bored. I thought, I'll go bug Claire, and then I remembered she's gone."

"You could call her." Grace reached for a freeze-dried rosebud.

Linnet's face brightened. "Yeah. Maybe I will." She hopped off the stool, grabbed the cordless phone and disappeared after the cat.

Wondering how things were going with David and Claire, Grace continued working. She tried to always have the house clean by Saturday night so that Sunday was hers to spend as she chose. Sunday was for sewing or quilting, or for doing something special with Linnet.

Or, more recently, with Linnet, Claire and David.

They'd had a wonderful time last night. The girls had both adored the costumes and the glorious music and the dark romanticism of *Phantom,* plus the excitement of dressing up and eating out at a nice restaurant. But Grace didn't think it had sunk in for either that they were going home to separate houses, that they would no longer be the next best thing to sisters.

To her, the evening had felt distressingly like a goodbye party. She was convinced David had bought the expensive tickets as a thank-you gesture for her and Linnet, a last fling with all of them together.

Her hand stilled and she stared blindly at the wreath. How much would she hear from him, now that he had his life back the way he wanted it?

She couldn't seem to help the weight of depression that had settled over her the moment she opened her eyes that morning and remembered that Claire was gone, that David was no longer obligated to visit. She'd tried to argue herself out of the black mood. If nothing else, it shamed her to discover how selfish her willingness to keep Claire had been. Truly, truly, she liked his daughter. She could even love her.

She and David had made plans for tomorrow, of course, but the reminder didn't lift her gloom. From his point of view, why not grab the chance to make love to a willing woman on his lunch hour? What man wouldn't?

Oh, she was being unfair to him, Grace knew she was. The trouble was, he hadn't said a word to make her think he felt anything more than mild liking and considerably more than mild lust.

Grace let out an unintentionally heartfelt sigh. She had known perfectly well what she was letting herself in for. The man had never promised her anything—

except that he would be there for his daughter. It would appear, after a few glitches, that he was keeping that promise.

And it was the one that really counted, wasn't it?

She was having the wild fling she had told herself she would enjoy. *So enjoy it,* Grace thought fiercely, *and quit bellyaching!*

SHE DID MANAGE TO ENJOY their Monday rendezvous.

Gentleman that David was, he courteously asked where she would like to go for lunch.

She smiled. "We wouldn't be alone in a restaurant."

He leaned over to give her a quick, hard kiss. "No," he agreed roughly, "we wouldn't. But I thought I'd offer."

"You made a mean sandwich."

Already looking over his shoulder and backing the car out of the slot, he laughed. "It was probably peanut butter and jelly."

Grace hadn't known it was possible to want a man so very much. She had actually considered that her sex life with Philip had been perfectly okay in the early years, before his indifference and her anger grew. Now she knew better.

This was...all consuming. That sounded so trite, and was so true. When he touched her, she went weak at the knees and completely single-minded. She *ached* to have him inside her. She'd glance at his hand and imagine it on her breast. Her gaze might lower to his neck above the crisp white collar of his dress shirt, and she remembered the shameless way she had nipped and kissed her way down to his chest. His powerful thighs, she craved to have between hers.

All she wanted was to arrive at his place so that they could make love. Her pride had gone the way of the typewriter, which had been relegated to garage sales.

No sooner had the car rolled into the garage and David signaled the door to shut than they started kissing. Once again they met at the front bumper. This time they progressed to him tugging up her skirt and lifting her to the hood of the car. Only her shriek when the cold metal came in contact with her bare legs kept them from doing it right there, in the garage, on his Mercedes.

Laughing, he lifted her and wrapped her legs around his waist, carrying her into the house. She used the opportunity to pull loose his tie and open the buttons of his shirt so that she could press her open mouth to the hollow at the base of his throat. His laugh became a groan.

Once again, the black leather couch was as far as they got.

Grace hadn't known women like her actually had affairs like this. Actresses in movies did, but they shrugged and moved on with blithe ease, the sequel calling.

Grace was terribly afraid she would never be able to move on. At the exact moment when David thrust slowly, exquisitely into her, she thought, *What if this is the last time?* Her heart seemed to break even as her body convulsed in slow-motion ecstasy.

On the way back to her office, David frowned

ahead at traffic, his expression already preoccupied. "The rest of the week doesn't look so good for me. The strike vote is Wednesday. I'm flying to Atlanta tomorrow. In fact," he cleared his throat, "I was going to ask you…"

"If Claire could spend the night?" Grace finished smoothly. "Of course she can! Linnet will be thrilled."

And you, she told herself in disgust, *are pathetic. You* want *him to be obligated to you!*

"You'll be gone for just the one night?" she asked, as he pulled into the parking lot of her building. Perhaps her pride wasn't totally gone, she marveled. She had somehow managed a tone of pleasant inquiry, much as she might have used if one of the attorneys for whom she worked had mentioned an out-of-town trip.

"One night." David set the emergency brake, grinned and leaned over to kiss her, a brief brush of the lips. "Can't miss the cake walk."

Perhaps it was relief that allowed her to laugh at him. "However much you'd like an excuse to."

"Did I say that?"

"You didn't have to." Grace got out of the car and bent to look in. "Have a good trip. Call if you get held up, and Claire can stay another night."

He gave her one of those smiles that opened another crack in her heart. "Thank you, Grace. I'll call tomorrow night anyway."

"Then goodbye." She slammed his car door, waved and walked into the lobby.

How would she survive until she saw him again?

There, waiting for the elevator among a crowd of dark-suited attorneys, Grace knew how deeply and irrevocably she had fallen in love. She felt like sobbing with fear. How could she bear life without him?

How could she love a man who had already broken his daughter's heart?

In the way of the world, she didn't have a chance to crumble. Instead, she smiled at the junior partner blocking the elevator controls and said, "Fifth floor, please."

DAD TOLD HER he had to go to Atlanta tomorrow, but Claire didn't mind so much because he also said, "Shall we go choose a cat today, or would it be better to wait until I'm home?"

She frowned thoughtfully. "Well, we could look. I might not find the right one the first time we go to the shelter anyway."

He gave her a funny, lopsided grin. "Oh, I think you'll find one. What worries me is that you'll find ten or twelve."

"You did say maybe two." She eyed him slyly. "If they came together."

"Whoa." He pretended to reel back. "I don't remember saying that."

"You did!" She hesitated, then opted for honesty, "I think you did."

Dad laughed again. "Let's just see, okay?"

"*Can* we go look? Now?" She waited hopefully.

"Why not?"

So they went to the Humane Society in Bellevue, which made Claire really sad until the nice lady there told them that ninety percent of the cats got homes. The only ones euthanized were the terribly sick or injured cats, or the ones with really bad behavioral problems.

Dad was right. There were so many friendly cats coming up to the bars of their cages to rub and purr, she couldn't make up her mind without adopting all of them.

Finally she said, "We can't take a cat home until the day after tomorrow anyway, because Dad has to go out of town and I'm staying with a friend. So I'd like to think about it."

The woman smiled. "That's a good decision. You want to be home to give lots of attention to your new cat."

She and Dad went out to dinner—she'd noticed he used any excuse to go out instead of cooking. Afterward, they were passing right by the Bellevue Square shopping mall when Claire spotted a small pet supply store on a corner.

"Oh!" She sat up straight. "I forgot. Mrs. Blanchet said they have a couple of cats there at a time from another shelter. Can we go look?"

"You haven't seen enough for one day?" Dad grumbled mildly, but he was already turning into the parking lot.

Claire knew the minute she set eyes on Kitkat. A pretty, dark short-haired cat with a snow white chest and shoulders, she was trying to hide in her cuddle bed, her big scared eyes peeking over the edge. But when the lady who worked in the store opened the cage so Claire could pet her, she bumped her face hopefully against Claire's hand and then started to quietly purr.

"Be careful on her left side," the lady said. "Kitkat was found hiding in some bushes, absolutely skin and bones, with her flea collar under her arm. It had cut into her flesh, and it's healed very slowly. She almost died. If someone hadn't heard her cry..."

Dad, seeing the expression on Claire's face, said, "Why don't I buy a litter box and bed and what have you." He lifted his eyebrows at the clerk. "If you can make suggestions?"

"Are you going to adopt her?" she said with delight.

He glanced at Claire.

She nodded vigorously.

"Is there any chance you can hold her until Wednesday evening?" He explained. "We could take her home now, but then she'd be alone for twenty-four hours, which doesn't seem like a good introduction to her new home."

"Oh, no! We love Kitkat. Of course we can hold her." She smiled at them both. "I do have a few questions I need to ask you."

She wanted to know if Kitkat would be indoor-only and to be sure they wouldn't declaw her. Purrfect Pals asked people not to declaw cats from them, because it was like amputating a person's fingers from the last knuckle. Once she was satisfied that they weren't the kind of people who would lose interest in Kitkat and move and leave her or something, she went off with Dad to pick out "goodies," as she put it.

Dad ended up back near the cat cages to study the

scratching posts. Cuddling Kitkat, who had buried her face under Claire's arm, Claire went to help him. He ended up spending *tons* of money on this really cool climber with sisal-wrapped posts and ramps and a hidey-hole at the top.

Then they filled out the paperwork for Kitkat, paid for her and all the stuff, and loaded it in the car—which meant tying down the trunk. Claire said goodbye to Kitkat and whispered against her soft fur, "I *promise* I'll be back for you. Okay?" She and Kitkat looked deep into each other's eyes, and then she kissed her goodbye and hurried out before she could start crying.

At home she helped Dad unload everything and decide where it would go.

Then he said, "Any homework, kiddo?" and she remembered the math she had to finish.

She nodded. "Dad?"

He had started to turn away, but he paused, that eyebrow up.

"Thank you." Before she could change her mind, she launched herself at him, wrapped her arms around his waist and hugged him, hard. "I promise to take care of her!"

His arms came around her and he hugged her back. "I know you will." His voice sounded funny, a little muffled.

Embarrassed, Claire backed away quickly. "You'll love her, too, won't you?"

"Probably." He sounded wry now.

"Mom would never let me have a pet," she blurted.

After a moment he said, "I think she was allergic to cats, and you really didn't have a place for a dog."

She nodded, glad he hadn't dissed Mom. Usually she was careful not to say anything critical about her mother. Mom had said she was allergic, but Claire had never been quite sure she believed her. But if Dad said it, too, maybe it was true.

Tuesday was rehearsal—Claire could hardly believe that the performances were only eleven days away. Mrs. Hinchen had to spend all her time working with Brendon Korstad, who was playing Don John like he was this totally *nice* guy instead of really evil, and Arnie Gould, who was Claudio—or would be if he could remember his lines. Linnet and Mrs. Hinchen were *completely* patient with him, but once Linnet rolled her eyes toward Claire, like she was saying *Help!*

It would have been so-o boring, except Josh sat next to Claire and whispered jokes into her ear. Once the teacher had to shush them before she turned with a sigh and prompted Claudio again.

"'As chaste as is the bud ere it be blown.'"

He frowned. "Right. 'As chaste as is the bud ere it be blown; But you are more...'" His mouth worked, but nothing came out.

"'Intemperate in your...'"

"'Intemperate in your blood, Than Venus or...'" His brow crinkled again.

"*I* know his lines better than he does," Josh whispered.

"*Everybody* knows his lines better than he does." Claire shook her head. "Mrs. H should have given him some tiny part, and Brendon could have been Claudio, so it wouldn't matter if he can't be mean."

"Yeah, but who is really wicked to play Don John?"

They couldn't decide, but Claire loved just being with him, both of them slumped low in the auditorium seats, their faces close to each other, their shoulders bumping. He hadn't actually asked her out yet, but everybody said he would. Maybe Friday, after a slow dance…

She shivered in anticipation.

Wednesday Dad got home in time for them to go out for dinner—again!—and pick up Kitkat. She was scared at first in Claire's bedroom, but after lots and lots of cuddling, she got down on the floor and crept around investigating. Claire made sure she knew where the litter box was in the bathroom. She was hiding under the bed when Claire went to sleep, but in morning the cat was stretched along Claire's hip.

"You're not a Kitkat, you're a hipcat," she murmured. When Claire drew her up for a snuggle under the covers, the cat purred and purred and kissed her. She had the cutest lips, as if she wore cream-colored lipstick.

Thursday Linnet came home with her from school to meet Kitkat. They talked about the play, "Which is *so* hopeless!" Linnet declared. "And Josh—he flirts with you *all* the time." Linnet was flopped on her stomach on the bed, petting Kitkat, who was rolling and growling every time Linnet's hand slowed. "I can't believe he hasn't asked you out yet."

"Do you really think he will?"

"Are you kidding?" Linnet said incredulously. "Everybody knows he's going to. People talk about you two all the time."

"Really?" Claire pretended she didn't know it was true. "Like, *why?*"

"Because you're *so* cute together. Besides," she grinned, "all the girls are jealous. Tamara Rogers would *kill* to have Josh stopping by her locker." Her expression changed. "Did you see that baby tee she wore yesterday? I swear, it was *glued* on. If I wore something like that, I'd get sent home."

"Yeah, but she looked really good in it."

The two girls reflected gloomily for a moment, but then Linnet's face brightened. "So what? Josh likes *you.*"

Claire was surprised when Mrs. Blanchet picked up Linnet that Dad didn't suggest they all go out to dinner or something. She guessed he was just tired. He had barely gotten home, his eyes bloodshot and his manner abrupt.

The moment the Blanchets were gone, he said, "Would you mind making yourself something for dinner in the microwave? I really need to work."

"No, that's okay, but don't you want something?" she asked.

"Not hungry," he said, and disappeared into his office.

Claire heated a frozen lasagna and took it upstairs, where she discovered that Kitkat liked lasagna, too. They watched TV and, when she got bored with that, Claire took out a feather dangling from a wand and played with Kitkat, who went totally berserk and acted like a kitten, making Claire laugh.

Friday was absolutely going to be the best day of her life. She wore her favorite flare jeans and a cute top and did this thing with her hair where it was pulled up in a couple of butterfly clips and then tumbled down. Of course, she'd be changing before the carnival and dance, but she wanted to look great the whole day.

She had the second lunch, which she hated since Josh had first. Lunch tray in hand, Claire was looking around for Linnet when this cluster of girls blocked her way.

"Did you hear the big news?" one of them asked. Angie French was wide-eyed like she was being super friendly, but her friends were watching Claire with avid expressions.

Stomach knotting, Claire braced herself for news she already knew she would hate.

"Josh McKendrick asked Tamara Rogers out. They are absolutely hanging *all* over each other."

Pain and humiliation crashed over Claire, who struggled not to show either. "Really?" she said, trying to sound bored.

"They are so perfect for each other," one of the other girls chimed in. "Don't you think?"

"I guess." Claire shrugged, and the milk she'd already opened tipped over on her tray. "Excuse me."

She went straight to the busing station, dumped her whole lunch, and hurried out of the cafeteria. In the bathroom she locked herself in a stall and sat silently crying. Once she heard a bunch of girls come in, and she pressed her hand over her mouth so she wouldn't make a sound until they left.

She washed her face with cold water over and over. She still looked puffy and blotchy in the harsh light as she examined herself in the mirror, but the bell would ring any minute, so she just hurried to her locker and kept her face averted from anyone looking at her.

The afternoon crawled, with her staring down at her open notebook, the teachers' voices buzzing around her head. *Do* not *think about Josh,* she told herself fiercely, over and over. *You cannot let anybody see you cry.*

Somehow she made it; the final bell rang. Linnet called out to her on the way to the buses, but Claire waved and kept walking. Right now, she didn't want to talk to anybody at all.

How could she go to the carnival tonight? Or to the *dance?* Every slow dance, Tamara and he would be out there on the floor, leaning on each other.

But if she *didn't* go, everyone would know she was heartbroken, which was just as unendurable.

At home, she went straight to the telephone to check messages. Maybe he'd called to tell her people were saying dumb stuff that wasn't true, and he wanted to make sure she was going to the dance.

"First new message," chirped the voice mail. Her mom came on, which was weird on a weekday. She *sounded* weird. "Claire, I just wanted to say how much I miss you. I thought maybe your father was right and this was better for you, but it's really hard."

That one was from 10:05 a.m. The second message

was from Mom, too. Her voice was getting slurred, and she talked about what fun they'd had last year on vacation at Lake Tahoe—12:37 p.m.

In the last message, Claire's mother was crying. "Your dad ish—*is* right." She was trying to enunciate clearly, and not doing very well. "I do drink too much, and I want to quit for your sake, but I can't help myself." She sobbed noisily. "I'm so sick when I don't get my drink or two in the evening!" For a moment, there was nothing but hiccuping, whimpering sounds. Then, in this small, wobbly voice, she said, "Clairabelle, please call. I'm so sad today. I don't know what to do. You're the only person who cares whether I'm alive or dead."

Claire's hand was shaking when she dialed. Mom wasn't sick or…or thinking about killing herself, was she? Her face crumpled. *Please, please, please,* she prayed.

On the fourth ring, she screamed, "Mom, answer! Please answer!"

"Hello?" Mom sounded…scared. Like she didn't know who'd be on the other end.

"Mommy!" Hot tears poured down Claire's cheeks. "I just got your messages. I'm sorry I couldn't call sooner!"

"Oh, honey!" She began to cry again, too. "I shouldn't have called you. I'll figure something out."

"What's wrong? Haven't you found a new job?"

"Nada." A sloshing sound made Claire wince— Mom was pouring a drink. "I've been applying everywhere, but without a reference I can't even get an interview."

"Are you out of money?"

"I'm two months behind on the rent." Mom took a drink; it seemed to steady her. She tried to laugh. "Hasn't been my month. Pete's getting back together with his ex, can you believe it?"

Claire ignored that. "You scared me earlier. When you said that about not knowing what to do. I *love* you," she said intensely.

Mom started to cry again. This time she sobbed and sobbed, and admitted that nothing had been right since Claire left. "You take such good care of me! We took good care of each other. Didn't we?"

Claire wiped her wet face on her sleeve. "Of course we did!"

"But you're probably happier now with your father. You probably don't want to come home anymore. I'm being selfish."

"You're supposed to visit next week. You're still coming for that, aren't you?" Claire begged.

"Oh, sweetie! I don't know where I'll be next week. I have to be out of here." She took another drink and kept crying, too. "I don't know where to go. Your father sent me money to visit you, but I needed it."

For alcohol, Claire thought with a zap of bitterness that shocked her. She buried it right away. Mom couldn't help herself. It was like being sick.

Mom was talking about how she'd kept Claire's room exactly the way she'd left it. "If you were here, we could just pack everything we own into the car and drive away." She seemed to be pleading. "Maybe we *should* find some little town in Idaho, and I could get a job at the local diner, and you could baby-sit or have a paper route. Or maybe we could just keep going. All the way across the country if we had to. We wouldn't stop until we found a town we really liked. Maybe someplace with snow in winter, like Minnesota or Maine. Or would you like sunshine and beaches?'' She was suddenly eager. ''How about Florida? Or the Chesapeake Bay. I read a book once…well, it doesn't matter. What does is—we could start all over.''

It was like being ripped in half. Huge tears ran down her cheeks and dripped unheeded from Claire's nose and chin. Her mother needed her. How could she not go? This was what she'd wanted so desperately not very long ago.

She could never, never say *I am happier with Dad. I don't want to start over.* She couldn't say *I'm scared to go off where nobody can find us and you might not be able to get a job and I'll be alone at night when you're at the bar and I won't have any friends.*

What if they couldn't afford any place to live? Would they end up parked in their car on dead end roads and not having enough to eat?

And what about Kitkat? Would Dad really love her and take care of her, or would he ask the shelter to take her back because Claire had been the one who wanted her?

Dad…she squeezed her swollen eyes shut. She'd *promised* Dad she wouldn't take off without talking to him. She grasped at a faint beam of hope. Could he help Mom somehow? Give her money, or find her a job, or...? Claire didn't know what he could do, but *something*.

So she didn't have to do it.

Sniffing, wiping at her cheeks, she said, "Maybe Dad would send you some more money. And you could come up here."

"We don't need him." Mom was still excited sounding. "It was always just you and me. We can do it, Claire-a-belle. Just you and me," she repeated with suddenly slurry satisfaction. "My little practical one. What did I ever do without you?"

Claire finally got off the phone with her mother after promising to call back as soon as she figured out what to do.

"Your dad gives you money, doesn't he? Maybe you could take the bus," her mother said boozily. "You'll find out the schedules and all that, won't you?" She took a drink. "My little practical one."

Claire went into the bathroom and stared at herself in the mirror. Her eyes were so puffy, her vision was all squinty. In the brilliant white illumination, the face staring back at her could have belonged to this horribly dead person in a slasher movie. A person who had been terrified before she died.

She blew her nose and peered more closely at herself in the mirror. No. What she looked like was a little girl who had hurt herself and needed her mommy or daddy to take care of her.

On a billowing wave of fear, she knew Dad was right. It wasn't fair of her mom to ask. She *wasn't* old enough to be the mommy or daddy instead of the kid. But in her head she heard her mother's wobbly voice saying *I don't know what to do. You're the only person who cares whether I'm alive or dead.*

Claire swallowed. It was true. There wasn't anybody else. Which meant Claire had to be the one to take care of Mom.

But first, she would keep her promise to her father.

Turning off the bathroom light, she went to find his work number.

CHAPTER FOURTEEN

HIS BOSS'S CALL HAD COME just before David was ready to leave the office for the day.

The union reps are refusing to talk if you're not here. I told them you'd be in Atlanta and ready to sit down at eight o'clock tomorrow morning. You have a rep as tough but fair. They'll believe you when you say the company can't go for their demands. Hell, toss 'em one percent more on the bonus. They'll snatch it, coming from you.

Disbelieving—why tonight? why did he have to be the bad guy?—David was nonetheless scrambling to rearrange his plans. As he punched the numbers to reach Grace at work, he hoped like hell she'd understand.

His secretary appeared in the doorway to his office and he gave a distracted glance up.

"I've booked you on a flight leaving at six." She glanced pointedly at the wall clock. "That doesn't give you very long."

"Thanks, Barb."

Damn, Grace wasn't picking up. She should still be in the office.

"Grace, this is David." He explained the crisis: the striking union refused to come back to the bargaining table unless he sat down with them. The CEO wanted him in Atlanta by morning; he had to get there early enough to catch a few hours' sleep. "I hate to let you down," he concluded. "And to ask a favor at the same time. But here goes. Will you take Claire home with you tonight?" Frowning, he hung up.

"Is your suitcase here at the office packed?" His secretary hadn't budged.

"Yes." He paced to the windows and back to his desk. What else did he have to take? But his mind kept jumping. "Hell. Let me call Claire."

"Yes, sir." Finally, discreetly, Barb withdrew.

His daughter had left two increasingly frantic messages, just as things blew up here. In the last, she'd said, with an edge of hysteria in her voice, "Mom doesn't have any money and she's getting evicted and...I'm scared. Please, please, will you call?"

Damn Miranda, he thought viciously. She'd been on a downward spiral since she'd taken her first drink. Any sympathy he might have had for her had been obliterated by her willingness to take Claire with her. He'd offered countless times to foot the bill for treatment, but no cigar. She liked her booze too much.

Well, this was the end of the road. License revoked. In his book, you didn't call an unstable thirteen-year-old and dump your adult problems on her. He'd take care of Miranda—when he got back.

Claire snatched up the phone on the first ring. She had to have been hovering over it.

"Hello?"

He mentally girded himself. "Claire, listen. I've got problems with tonight."

"I don't care about tonight!" She breathed raggedly. "You got my messages, right? It's Mom."

"Until your mother quits drinking, she's going to have troubles. They're going to get bigger and bigger, but *they're not yours.*" David paused to let the punch sink in. "They're hers. You're a kid, not an adult."

"You never listened when I said I took care of her!" That semihysterical note was back. "She says nobody else loves her, and it's true!"

"Yeah, probably, but think, Claire. What can you do? You can't earn a living, you can't pay the rent."

His secretary poked her head around the door frame. "Call from Mr. Sealey. Line two."

He glanced down at the blinking red light. Great. All he needed were more instructions from on high.

"Claire," he said, "you can't help your mother."

"You said we should talk!"

"When I get back from Atlanta, we will."

"Atlanta?" Her voice sounded thick, teary.

"I'm sorry. The strike has gone sour, they need me there. You go home with Linnet after the carnival tonight. If you can't reach Mrs. Blanchet now, if she's gone over to the school early, call a cab. There's plenty of money in the top drawer of my desk. Got that? I should be back Sunday. We can talk then."

The blinking light indicating the waiting call went out. He swore.

"Dad?"

"I have got to go." He pinched the bridge of his nose and tried to speak calmly. "I know you're looking forward to tonight. Just have fun, don't worry about your mother, and tell Mrs. Blanchet how sorry I am. I'll see you Sunday.'' Without waiting for a protest, he hung up the phone and reached for his Rolodex.

"David, you really should leave for the airport." The woman he paid to nag was doing her job. "I'll explain to Mr. Sealy if he calls again."

"Yeah. Okay." Stomach eaten by acid, he grabbed his briefcase and stuffed in every file that seemed relevant. "My laptop?"

She had it waiting with his carry-on bag. Of course.

On the way to the airport, he realized he hadn't called Grace at home. Predictably, the batteries on his cell phone were dead.

At the airport, he checked in, then found a pay phone and dialed her home number. No answer. *Damn it!* Had she already left for the school?

"We're now ready to commence boarding Flight 2386 for Chicago and Atlanta," intoned the PA announcement. "Seats one through twenty-six, please go to the gate now."

David left a hurried message on Grace's home voice mail, then tried to think what to do. Would anybody be answering the phone in the school office? He knew better.

"Seats twenty-seven through fifty-two, please prepare to board."

How could he get on the airplane without knowing Claire was taken care of for the night?

The cell phone, which had been dead as a doornail, chose right then to ring.

"Hello?"

He heard a crackle, and then it died again.

His stress level was so high by then, he almost threw the damn thing to the floor in frustration. What if Grace had been calling?

"Seats fifty-three through…"

David joined the line. What else could he do? The strike was crippling the company. As it was, this flight didn't get in until three in the morning. If he took a later one, assuming he could still change his ticket, he wouldn't get even a few hours of sleep before sitting down at the bargaining table tomorrow. He never had acquired the ability to sleep on an airplane, however much he traveled on business.

David rotated his shoulders and tried to erase some tension.

Claire was a big girl. He'd left maybe a hundred bucks in his desk. She could take a cab to the school. She'd be all right.

In his second row seat, David stowed his carry-on and took out his laptop. He'd better spend these few hours going over numbers.

Focus.

In Atlanta he took a cab straight to his usual hotel. The night clerk handed him a sheaf of messages. The top one was from Grace.

The clerk watched him. "We assured Ms. Blanchet that you were booked here. She seemed…quite anxious."

Fumbling, heart slamming, David paged through the rest. *Sealy. His secretary about something he'd forgotten. Carmichael, a labor arbiter.* The message slips were falling to the floor in a flutter of pink.

Another from Grace. *Claire never came to the carnival tonight. She's not answering the phone at home. Please call.*

He looked up blindly. "Telephone?"

"There's a courtesy phone at the desk right over there, Mr. Whitcomb. I'll bill any calls to your room."

David almost fell into the chair, then couldn't remember Grace's number. Head buried in his hands, he yanked his hair. Damn it, *think.*

It came slowly, from the sludge his brain seemed to have become.

Four in the morning. That made it one o'clock at home. She wouldn't have gone to bed if she was worried about Claire, would she?

He dialed, listened to the rings. On the fourth, Grace answered, her voice quivering with tension.

"Hello?"

"It's David," he said tersely.

"Thank God. Where's Claire?"

"She's supposed to be with you. Didn't you get my messages?"

"Messages? You only left one, and no, I didn't hear it until I got home at eleven."

He shot to his feet. "She was supposed to take a cab to the school if she couldn't reach you. You're sure she didn't show up?"

"If she did, neither Linnet nor I saw her, and we were looking. Especially after you didn't show, either."

David swore. "I'm sorry, Grace. This couldn't be helped."

"Canceling on me is one thing. Canceling on Claire is another."

"I work. I have to travel."

"You still don't get it, do you?" She made a soft, exasperated sound in which he read a frightening finality, as though in that one moment she was giving up on him. "Forget it, David. Let's concentrate on figuring out where Claire is."

"I'm afraid I know." The sense of urgency still rocketed through him, but he might as well have been behind bars for all the good he could do his daughter from here. "Her mother called today. Several times, if I understood Claire right. She's apparently lost her job and is broke. She was no doubt drunk. What she thought Claire could do..." His jaw clenched.

"I have no idea what she thought, but it's obvious what Claire believes she can do. Take care of her mother," Grace said simply.

You never listened when I said I took care of her!

Claire was right: he hadn't really listened.

"She swore she wouldn't run away again." He dropped like a stone into the chair when the truth slammed home.

No, that wasn't what Claire had said.

What she had actually promised was that she wouldn't take off without talking to him first. Without giving him a chance.

She'd tried to keep her promise. He hadn't listened carefully enough to realize that was what she was doing.

Grace interrupted his self-flagellation. "I'll call the police."

"I don't think I can get a flight in the middle of the night," he said stupidly.

"Probably not." She didn't sound like she gave a damn. "You can't do anything anyway."

"She might call."

Very coldly, Grace said, "Why would she? She knows you aren't there, doesn't she?"

They left it at that. Grace would use the key he hid outside to go into his house and be sure Claire wasn't there and just not answering the phone. He would call Miranda in the morning and get home when he could.

If he didn't sit down at that bargaining table to-morrow—no, today—he would undoubtedly be un-employed when he caught that flight home.

David found that he didn't give a good goddamn.

He left orders for a wake-up call. In his room, he showered and climbed between the covers. Exhaustion weighed on him as if the blanket were knit from a lifetime of regrets, but at the same time he was too full of adrenaline and dread to sleep.

David could admit to himself now that, the other times Claire had bolted, he has been as much angry as afraid for her: she had inconvenienced him. He'd been frustrated by his inability to get through to her. In many ways, she had been a stranger to him, as he was to her.

But no longer. She was not only the little girl who had ridden on his shoulders and laughed with pure delight. She was a teenage girl who had been hurt by too many adults who should have protected her. She was a magnificent actor, someone animals trusted, a gutsy child-woman who felt such responsibility toward her mother, she couldn't *not* help when she was asked. She was someone David liked as well as loved.

And she was out there somewhere with her thumb out, frightened and despairing because her father hadn't listened when she'd begged for help.

David groaned and laid his forearm across his face, as though he could blank out the pictures that flicked before his inner eye like hideous slides.

His daughter wasn't the only one he might have lost tonight. He hadn't had to ask to know that Grace had written him off. She wasn't a woman who could love a man who failed his child. Generous to a fault, she had given him second and even third chances.

Three strikes, you're out.

Why had it taken him so long to see what counted? Or to recognize that, uneasy though the word *love* made him, he damn well wanted to hear it from Grace.

When he was deep inside her and she cried his name, he wanted more. He wanted her to look into his eyes and say, "I love you, David." He needed words he hadn't given her, about an emotion he hadn't known he felt.

Until tonight.

He had once thrived on the high stress of his job. It made him feel alive, in control. He was damned good at putting together the thousands of tiny puzzle pieces that made up the big picture, moving them all around until they fit, manipulating, ordering and persuading, insuring that packages were on the right plane, the right truck, delivered when they'd been promised.

The past month or two, David had become sick to death of it all. The angry strike had hit him hard, as though he'd failed in some way. Was the company offer that unreasonable? *Was* management—including him—trying to screw the employees? Did he want to be a part of that? Did the shareholders matter more than the rank-and-file employees, the men and women who wore the company uniform and busted their butts to get the job done?

He felt enormous distaste for his role in the morning negotiations. He had gone over the figures again during the flight. Why let the strike go on when the company could—and ultimately would—meet demands? Why not have created positive union-management relations and morale in the first place by saying, "Yeah. Six percent raise across the board? Sounds fair."

Time was, he hadn't minded traveling. Why should he? Home could just as well have been another hotel room. In under two months, he'd done a one-eighty. He wanted to be able to count on seeing his daughter's school play. He wanted to go home from work to Grace, wake up with her in the morning, not alone in a featureless bedroom paid for by the night.

David gave a grunt of bittersweet amusement. He had actually looked forward to refereeing the cake walk. That's how domestic he'd become.

He wanted it all: family, hearth and home.

He just hadn't realized it until too late.

Business, he was good at. Love, he sucked at.

He turned his head and sought the red numerals on the clock—5:12 a.m.

Let Claire be safe, he prayed. *Get us all through till morning.*

THE EARLIEST FLIGHT he could book a seat on left Atlanta at 10:12 a.m.

At eight on the nose, David sat down at the bargaining table and laid it out. "Here's the numbers. Here's what we can afford. I'm not authorized to offer it, but I'm going to cut through the crap here and now and tell you the truth."

Then he stood up, said, "Ladies and gentlemen, I have a family emergency and I have to catch a flight home. Please excuse me," and walked out, leaving a murmur of shock in his wake.

Sealy roared, "Whitcomb!" but he didn't stop. Outside, he grabbed the first cab.

From the airport he called Grace. "Any word?"

"Nothing." Her voice was strained. "Have you talked to her mother?"

"Her telephone service has been cut off. I called an old friend and asked him to go over there. Pray she's not out of the apartment already."

She sucked in a breath. "But she asked Claire to come!"

"Yeah," David said with quiet ferocity. "Well, while you're at it, pray that she remembers she did."

Grace made a sound.

"I'm coming there rather than going to San Francisco. Claire's got to be able to reach me. My flight gets in just after noon. I'll call when I'm home."

"Okay."

Conspicuous by its absence was a reassuring, *Don't worry, David*. Hell, Grace probably *wanted* him to feel the agony of this wait.

He got home to a house empty but for the cat, who meowed piteously at the sight of him, and a note from Claire, which Grace had missed. It lay in the top drawer of his desk, in place of the money she had taken.

In a teenager's loopy script, she'd written, *Dad, I'm sorry. I don't know what I can do to help Mom, but she does need me. At least I get her up in the morning so she makes it to work. I'll call you in a few days, so you know I'm okay and don't have to worry*. At the bottom, the handwriting suddenly cramped, she concluded, *Love, Claire*. And then, *P.S. Please, please, don't take Kitkat back to the shelter*.

An anguished bellow ripped its way from deep inside him, and he slammed both fists onto the desk, glad for the pain.

Where was she? Why hadn't the cops found her? What good were they, anyway, if they couldn't find one teenager?

He listened to phone messages, none from Claire, all pretty much summed up by Jeff Sealy's snarled, "What in hell was that crap you pulled this morning, Whitcomb? Why not just write a letter of resignation? We might have given you severance." Slam.

David deleted every message, then sat there at his desk with no idea what he should do. He had never in his life felt more useless.

$100. Would she have used the money to take a

Greyhound bus? He grabbed the phone and called the police officer in charge of locating his daughter.

"Yes, sir, we did check. No one of her description has boarded a bus. They're still watching up and down the I-5 corridor, in case she has trouble hitching a ride and decides to take a bus the rest of the way. I'm sure she knows she'd be spotted as a runaway and hauled back. She's experienced at this."

David hadn't needed the reminder.

Nick Sanchez called an hour later. Miranda was still in the apartment, drunk as a skunk. Professed to be shocked that Claire was hitching to California. Of course she hadn't asked her to come! David had custody now; why would she do that? Would she call if she heard from Claire? Of course she would!

David thanked his friend, and at last heard somebody say, "Don't worry. She'll be fine. You're imagining the worst, which doesn't happen very often. Kids are smarter and tougher than we think."

David knew he spoke from experience and the heart. Nick's son was currently in remission.

"Thanks, Nick. I'll keep you posted."

In the early evening, Grace did come by. She surrendered her coat reluctantly, making David think she didn't intend to stay long. He offered her a drink; she shook her head, her shining hair swinging.

Going ahead of him into the living room, Grace asked, "Are you sure your ex-wife will call when Claire shows up?"

"I don't know." Tiredly he rubbed a hand over his face. "No, that's not true. Yeah, at this point I think so. She actually phoned an hour or two ago. Sounded like she'd sobered up some. I think now she's scared, too. It's been—what?—twenty-four hours. Claire should be getting there unless she's holing up at night—and, at her age, she can't be renting motel rooms. Bad enough to think of her with her thumb out during the day, but at night?'' He let out a strangled oath. ''Why haven't the cops spotted her?''

Face troubled, Grace suggested, ''If Claire's getting rides easily…''

''Oh, yeah. Cute young teenage girl…'' He was surrounded now, by those nightmarish visions. Darkness had fallen outside; it was cold as hell, and would be most of the way to the Bay Area. She had a good coat, and at least it was gone from the closet.

A coat didn't protect a pretty girl from human predators.

Grace bit her lip. ''There are decent people out there on the road, too.''

He turned on her in his fury. ''Then why haven't any of them driven her straight to a police station? Tell me that!''

''I don't know!'' she snapped, her stare just as fierce. After only an instant, she dropped into a chair as if her knees had collapsed. ''I'm sorry, David. Maybe…'' He could feel her groping for an explanation. ''Oh, probably she's got a great story. She's imaginative, you know that. Can't you picture her conning a nice older couple into believing they're helping her out by taking her as far as possible on her way? And people just don't *think*.''

David sank down, too, on the couch facing her. As little sleep as he'd gotten last night, he was now swinging wildly from a state of nervous energy to complete enervation. His emotions swerved as unpredictably. Hope, rage, giving way to a morass of guilt. Fear, love that was painful, wrenching despair.

Voice guttural, he said, "You blame me, don't you?"

Her eyes showed white like a spooked horse's. "I...don't know. I...at first..." She swallowed, said honestly, "Yes. I admit that was my first reaction. But I can see that you almost had to go to Atlanta. Your job just isn't one that lends itself to being a single parent."

"I didn't want to recognize that." Elbows braced on his knees, David looked at the floor. "I had a deal with her," he said softly. "Did you know that? She'd talk to me before she took off. Give me a chance." His face contorted. "She tried."

"David..."

He shook his head violently. "What if some sicko murders her? Because *I wouldn't listen?*"

"That won't happen."

He lifted bloodshot eyes to glare. "How do you know that?"

Their gazes locked. Suddenly her eyes flooded with tears and she shot to her feet.

"I have to go."

David stumbled to his feet. "Don't go. I'm...oh, hell. You're trying to help, and I'm taking my guilt out on you."

"I could have noticed she was missing sooner, too." She swiped at her cheeks. "I did notice! But I was so busy obsessing about...about some missing

raffle item or the volunteer who left his game unat-
tended, I didn't take the time to worry about her. If
only I'd gone home and checked messages, we might
have found her right away."

He took a step toward her, but stopped dead when
she backed away.

"No!" she said. "No. Don't...don't touch me
right now. I'll just cry."

"Because of Claire?" he asked raggedly. "Or because you're intending to say 'nice knowing you but
goodbye' to me?"

New tears brimming, she said, "You aren't Philip.
I know that. But you're like him, in ways I don't
know if I can bear. I..." She pressed tremulous lips
together. "This isn't the time to talk about it, or...or
to make decisions. Can't we...can't we just concentrate on finding Claire?"

His shoulders slumped. "Yeah," he said leadenly.
"Go home, Grace."

She hesitated. "You'll call?"

"Of course I will."

She gave a tiny nod, opened her mouth as if to say
something else, then closed it and left. For the first
time ever, David didn't even walk her to the door.

At the sound of it closing, his whole body jerked.

SITTING AT HIS DESK, David dozed despite himself as
the evening crawled into night. Somehow, he
couldn't bring himself to go to bed, to put his head
on a pillow and stretch out luxuriously under a down
duvet when Claire was out there somewhere, cold and
afraid. What if he slept too heavily, missed her call?

At some point the cat found him and settled on his knee, her comforting purr fading into soft breathing even as he dropped off.

The shrill ring of the telephone shocked him awake. The cat shot away. David banged his knee against the desk and knocked his desk organizer to the floor with a crash.

Swearing, he grabbed for the phone, stabbed the wrong button, finally found Talk.

"Hello? Claire?"

She sounded far away and terribly young. "Daddy?"

"Claire." His throat closed. "Honey, where are you?"

"I don't know." She began to cry. For a moment nothing but whimpers and the muffled sound of traffic came through the line. "I'm scared."

He jumped to his feet. "Is somebody with you? After you? Claire, *what's happening?*"

"This…this trucker wants to give me a ride. I told him no, but he's still waiting, and…and I can see him right now. The way he looks at me is…is so creepy." A sob escaped her. "I wish I was home!"

"I love you," he said, knowing it was useless but somehow feeling she needed to hear the words anyway. He clenched his jaw. "Okay. Tell me where you are."

"It's some truck stop." She sniffed, tears still threatening. "I don't know. Near Redding, I think."

Northern California. Did Redding have an airport? he wondered on one level, even as he said, "And are you inside, with other people?"

"No!" Her breathing was shaky. "I'm in a phone booth, and it's across the parking lot from the café. It's...it's really dark out here, with all these trucks parked, and nobody's around except *him*."

Feeling cold, he said, "Okay, honey. Here's what I want you to do. You're going to drop the phone and run like hell for the café. When you get inside, you're going to grab the first waitress you see and tell her you're a runaway, you're scared of a man outside, and you want to call first your father and then the police. If that son of a bitch tries to cut you off on the way, you scream, and you keep screaming until everyone inside that truck stop comes pouring out. Got that?"

She repeated his instructions.

"Now, don't hang up. Just drop the phone and *go*."

"Daddy?"

"Yes?"

"I love you, too."

The phone thudded, and he knew she'd dropped it. Traffic noises intensified when she opened the booth door. A small gasp came to him, then the whack, whack of her first running steps.

David stood utterly rigid, straining every fiber to hear.

Distantly he made out a muffled male shout, but no scream. Nothing. Faraway traffic. Finally the roar of a big diesel engine starting up.

His muscles spasmed in protest, his eyes burned from not blinking. Had she made it?

Call, Claire. Damn it, call.

He paced a few steps, then froze again in fear he'd miss a sound. Any sound.

Call.

An eternity seemed to pass. His anguish and fear grew. She hadn't made it. He shouldn't have told her to run. She might have had to pass right by the bastard. He should have told her...what? he asked himself savagely.

Call.

A beep came. His hand was shaking as he pushed the button to switch calls.

"Claire?"

"Daddy?" Exhilaration and tears mixed in her voice. "I'm okay. I'm okay."

He made a sound that felt...raw. "Thank God."

"I...the truck stop manager is going to phone the police. Will they put me in jail or something?"

"No. I think they'll find you someplace safe to wait for me."

Sounding woefully uncertain, she said, "You'll come for me?"

"I'll charter a small plane and be in Redding by morning. Sweetheart, will you put the manager on the phone for me?"

David thanked the man, who said kindly, "If you want to leave the police out of this, the wife and I live in a little house out back. We have a pullout couch. It wouldn't be any bother if you want us to take care of her until you get here. She looks hungry and tired."

David ended up accepting his offer. After writing down the address and phone number, he talked again to Claire, who told David, ''He already called his wife. She's making him get me some dinner. I, um, I tried to tell them I have money to pay for it, but he said he wouldn't take it.''

A moment later, David hung up. A few phone calls found him a pilot who was willing to fly him to Redding, for a price. His next call was to Grace.

Her hello was taut with anxiety that he vanquished with a few words.

''Do you want me to come with you?'' she asked. ''I can get someone to stay with Linnet.''

''No. Go back to bed.'' Frowning, realizing he had sounded curt, he said, ''Claire and I need to finish this ourselves.''

She was silent for a long moment; he heard her breathing.

Then she said quietly, ''I understand. You're a family. It's just that…'' She stopped.

He finished for her. ''We felt like one all together.''

Her yes was very soft.

''That,'' he said, ''is something we need to talk about.''

Dawn had painted the sky lavender with luminous rose highlights when David left the taxi waiting behind the truck stop. He walked down a cinder lane to the small white house with a sagging porch and a clothesline strung out front over an improbably green lawn surrounded by brown weedy fields.

His knock on the door sounded unnaturally loud. It was followed by a thump and a flurry of running footsteps. His daughter undid the dead bolt lock and flung open the door.

The next moments, when she cried with relief and joy and threw herself into his arms, were the richest of his life to this point, outdoing the night she was born.

His Claire was safe and she was coming home of her own free will.

Holding her tight and laying his own wet cheek against the top of her head, David snatched at one whisper of hope.

If his daughter of all people could truly forgive him and come to trust him, wasn't there some chance that Grace could do the same?

CHAPTER FIFTEEN

GRACE STOOD TO ONE SIDE in her living room, drinking in the sight of Claire, alive and well if also tired and puffy eyed. At the moment, Grace was trying *not* to be caught staring at David.

"You mean, your dad hired an airplane, just to go get you?" Linnet was asking, wide-eyed.

Claire plopped, cross-legged, on the floor in front of the couch. "Yeah, he came to get me right away." She cast him a shy glance, her voice subdued. "He paid somebody to fly him to California in the middle of the night. I was so glad. It was scary." After a moment she brightened. "Actually, flying in a little plane was lots better than being in a big jet where you don't even know you're off the ground. I might like to get my pilot's license someday."

Now Grace had an excuse to turn her gaze to David. He stood in front of the fireplace, his arms crossed, his hair damp from a shower. In faded jeans and a black T-shirt, he was breathtakingly sexy.

At his daughter's hopeful look, he laughed and shook his head. "Don't hold your breath."

Only Grace seemed to notice the lines carved by tiredness in his forehead, or the guarded way he had greeted her.

He and his daughter had stopped by at Grace's invitation. She'd told herself it was for Linnet's sake, and Claire's. Linnet had asked to sleep with her last night.

The thirteen-year-old had stood in the bedroom door hugging her pillow, one spaghetti strap hanging down her thin arm. "I'm just...kind of scared," she said, hanging her head. "I mean, I know nobody is going to break in or anything like that. I just keep thinking about Claire."

She had slept like a log once David called, but this morning she kept saying, "Are they home yet? Do you think she's okay? I mean, nothing bad happened to her, did it?"

Grace's reassurances didn't cut it: Linnet needed to see her friend.

And Grace needed to see David.

Except that, at the same time, she *didn't* want to see him. Not yet. She was still too unsettled.

What had he been implying last night, when he said, *That's something we need to talk about?* Did he have in mind resuming their twice-weekly trysts? Was he ready to end their relationship, such as it was? Or could he possibly have been thinking about melding their families? About *marriage?*

Not that he'd ever said a word to make her think he was considering a proposal. When she got right down to it, their relationship had been pretty much a "slam, bam, thank you, ma'am" kind of thing. She had apparently checked her pride at the door.

So here was the question she had to ask herself: was she willing to keep doing so?

She tried to make herself think about what a poor example she would be setting for Linnet and Claire if the girls ever found out their parents were having casual sex. But the truth was, the sex had never been casual for her. She had fallen in love with David Whitcomb a long time ago. She had even begun dreaming—hoping—that the tenderness in his eyes when he looked at her meant something. He hadn't agreed to run the cake walk at the school carnival for Claire's sake; he'd done it for her—Grace, although the very idea must have been horrific for this very reserved man.

Which led her to the real point. He *had* agreed, and then something more important came along and he ditched her and Claire with a few hurried phone calls.

Yes, he'd been under a huge amount of pressure. He was a vice president of a large company; men like him didn't have the luxury of saying *Gosh, this isn't convenient right now, I'm volunteering tonight at my daughter's school.*

Her first reaction had been negative. He'd let Claire down yet again. But the truth was, everyone let down the people they loved sometimes. It was hard to balance job and family. His was harder to balance than most.

But did she want to let herself fall ever more deeply in love with a man who, on a regular basis, had to put his job first? At that, with a man who either didn't reciprocate her feelings, or who didn't see any need for emotional nonsense?

Or, worse yet, a man who had just plain never learned how to be a husband and father, who had grown up without love, without role models?

What if he did ask her to marry him? Of all possibilities, it was this one that scared her the most. They had great sex, he seemed to like her, and, gosh, what a convenience it would be for him, now that he had to think of Claire, to have a wife to help raise his daughter.

How could she turn him down, when she missed him an hour after he walked out her door, when only his look or touch or voice on the telephone made her feel alive, when she ached to smooth those harsh lines in his forehead or to solve his every problem?

How could she marry him when she loved him so desperately and he *didn't* love her? Wouldn't her heart over time erode like a cliff crumbling into the ocean? All she had to do was remember the years with Philip to know how easily bitterness grew until it consumed you. Wonderful sex wasn't enough; grave courtesy might protect her pride but not her heart.

"Mom?"

Grace blinked and looked around, to see that they were all staring at her. Flushing, she said, "I'm sorry! Did I miss something?"

"Weren't you listening *at all?*" her daughter asked with amazement.

"I'm afraid my mind was wandering." She smiled at Claire. "We worried about you."

The girl ducked her head, her cheeks turning pink. "I'm sorry. I wish I'd called you before I did something that stupid."

"You wouldn't have been able to reach me, either," Grace admitted. "Friday was a confluence of wretched days for each of us."

Apparently feeling left out, Linnet sprang to her feet. "Hey! You want to come upstairs? I'll show you what I won at the carnival."

"Sure!" Claire rose so lithely Grace felt old just watching.

In a second, the two girls were racing up the stairs.

David didn't move from his position in front of the fireplace. His unreadable gaze rested on her face.

To cover her self-consciousness and her aching fear of the future, Grace hastened into speech. "Tell me quick, while they're upstairs. What are you going to do about Miranda?"

Although something flickered in his eyes, David accepted her gambit, shaking his head. "Not much. Claire and I talked for a long time about her mother. If I bail her out and find her a new job, she'll keep drinking. You and I both know she's got to hit bottom."

"Did Claire understand?"

The lines on his face deepened further. "I hope so. I am buying a plane ticket for Miranda to come up next week and see the play, spend a day or two with Claire. I've told her before and I'll tell her again that

I'll pay for alcohol treatment. But just offering a crutch…'' He moved his shoulders uncomfortably. ''I don't think I'd be really helping. The next crisis will come anyway, and the sooner she meets it, the sooner she'll decide to get sober.''

Grace nodded.

''Do I sound cruel?''

''No. Oh, no! I think…you're wise,'' she said awkwardly. She ached to touch him, to smooth the harsh lines on his forehead.

His voice roughened. ''Grace…''

Upstairs one of the girls squealed.

He shot a hunted look toward the stairs. ''We need to talk.''

She twisted her fingers together. ''Is what you have to say quick?''

''That depends.'' His chest rose and fell. ''I hope not.''

Her heart swelled, filling her chest to the point of pain. *Say it!* she wanted to cry.

Both started when Linnet's bedroom door burst open, and suddenly the two girls were coming down the hall above.

''How can we get rid of them for a while?'' David said hurriedly. ''Buy 'em a pizza and slip out the door?''

''You look exhausted.'' Grace tried to tell herself she too was being wise, but knew cowardice when she committed it. ''What about tomorrow night? You bring Claire over, and I'll have a dinner ready for them while we go out.''

Claire and Linnet tumbled down the stairs like a pair of puppies, their high, light voices interspersed with giggles.

David gave Grace another look in which she read sheer desperation, but all he said, rather expressionlessly, was, "Six o'clock tomorrow. You have a date."

SHE DRESSED UP, although she didn't know if they were really going out to dinner, or just to David's house to talk.

What if all he had wanted was to find a graceful way to end their relationship? That worry had haunted her ever since he had left with Claire yesterday. Now, because of the girls, they almost had to spend at least a couple of hours in each other's company. But he was right. The time had come for them to talk, whatever the outcome. She just wished she had the slightest idea what he intended to say.

How could she not have *some* idea? It amazed and horrified her to be in love with a man whom she apparently understood so little.

His daughter at his side, he came to the door in his usual well-cut dark business suit. This one looked completely unwrinkled, the shirt crisp and the knot of his tie straight, as though he had gone home and changed for Grace's benefit.

"Hello, Mrs. Blanchet." Claire started in the door and then turned to give her father a tentative but somehow fierce hug before whirling and darting past Grace.

She raised her eyebrows.

"We're…working things out," he murmured.

Grace called out a few last instructions on heating dinner and not opening the door to anyone, which earned her rolled eyes and a sarcastic "We're not little children, Mother. I *know* not to go to the door."

"All right, all right! Just be good."

In the car, David put the key in the ignition, then didn't start the engine. Instead, he looked at her. "Can we skip dinner and go straight to the talking?"

Her heart took a dizzying leap. "Yes. Of course." Her voice came out high, little-girl uncertain.

He nodded, started the car, and without a word chose a route that would take them to his house. Grace sat stiffly, clutching her small purse, gaze fixed straight ahead although she was preternaturally aware of him. His hands, wrapped around the steering wheel, his shoulders, filling the car, his face in profile.

His silence.

They were briefly on I-90 when he said suddenly, "I quit my job this weekend." He grunted. "More accurately, I chose to set myself up to be fired."

Her mouth literally dropped open. "You what?"

"I'm unemployed."

Still staggered, she said, "But why?"

"Partly because of Claire. Partly out of general disillusionment. And partly for you."

Now her heart was drumming so hard, she felt dizzy. He had quit his job for her? What came out of her mouth was another example of cowardice. "I…what do you mean, general disillusionment?"

He cast her an enigmatic glance before returning his attention to the freeway and the upcoming exit. "I was fed up with the company position on the contract negotiations. The stockholders always come first. To hell with the workers. The sabotage ticked me off royally, but the anger I understood. I was slated to go in there Saturday morning and be the bad guy, tell them why we couldn't squeeze out more than a two-percent raise even though earnings have skyrocketed." He smiled grimly and told her what he had done. "I made it impossible for the company to do anything but give in to the demands. Union members are back to work today, and I'm out on my ass."

"Oh, David! I'm sorry!"

"Are you?"

Grace examined her tangle of emotions and finally said yes and meant it. "You loved what you did."

"Once upon a time. Not lately."

"Really?" She scrutinized his profile, for what little it told her.

"I want to know I'll be able to see *Much Ado* this week. I want Claire to be sure I'll be there." He reached above her to press the button to open his garage door.

"But what will you do?"

David shrugged. "I can find something with a local or regional company that doesn't involve so much traveling."

He drove into the garage. The door rolled down behind them just as he set the emergency brake and turned off the engine.

Into the silence, Grace blurted, ''I didn't ask you to quit your job for me.''

''Didn't you?''

''No!'' Her fingers bit into her purse. She struggled to moderate her voice. ''I've reacted sometimes because of Philip. His job always came first. That doesn't mean I'm incapable of understanding that sometimes it does have to.''

He watched her. ''Friday night, you blamed me. I blame myself,'' he added quietly. ''The thing is, given the demands of my job, I couldn't have done anything but catch that damn flight.''

''Yes.'' She looked down at her hands and said with difficulty, ''I do see that.''

''There was a time I didn't mind giving twelve-hour days, going out of town at the drop of a hat. Now I do.''

Grace braved herself to meet his eyes. ''Why?'' she asked simply. ''Because Claire needs you?''

''Because I need her.'' His mouth twisted; his voice roughened. ''And you.''

How? How do you need me? her heart cried.

''Grace…'' David cleared his throat. ''Maybe it's too soon. Maybe you have too many doubts. But I'm going to ask anyway. Will you marry me?''

This felt unreal. They sat in the car, both still belted in, the huge, almost empty garage around them. He hadn't touched her. He didn't have flowers or a ring; the lighting was stark white overhead bulbs, not the flickering, warm glow of candles.

"You've never said anything..." she began awkwardly.

"I know." He drew an audible breath. "Grace, I'm not good at this kind of thing. The place and time probably stinks."

"I don't care about that." Being completely honest was more difficult than she'd expected. "I care about why you want to marry me. Did you just decide this? Was it what I said, about how we'd felt like a family? Do you think I expect a proposal, because we made love?"

"No, I don't think it's because you expect one. In fact—" his big shoulders moved, as if he sought to ease tension "—I've been afraid you wouldn't welcome a proposal at all."

"You're kidding," she said blankly.

A reluctant smile tugged at his mouth and disappeared as quickly. "You're not leaping to accept."

"I've told you my reservations." But never that what she needed most was his heart.

"And I'm hoping I can reassure you."

"How are you going to do that?" she asked straight out.

"I'll do whatever I have to." He gripped the steering wheel, his fingers flexing so that his knuckles showed white. "Tell me whether I have a chance, Grace. Have you even considered me as husband material?"

"I don't sleep with men casually." She looked away. His tools hung with military precision on a rack; not even a clump of grass from the parked lawn mower marred the spotless pale gray concrete floor of the garage. "In fact," she admitted in a low voice, "you're only the second man I've ever slept with."

"Then I'm very lucky," he said quietly. A faint frown creasing his forehead, he faced her. "Grace, marry me. I can't do without you."

"Why?" she asked again. "You know I'll always be available to help with Claire, if that's in your mind."

Anger sparked in his eyes, edged his voice. "Is that all you think of me? That I'd try to buy you with a wedding ring?"

Her chin shot up. "Be honest. Isn't that what you're thinking? We do make a comfortable family. Life is easier when you have a partner to depend on. I'm not accusing you of child molestation."

"No, you're just accusing me of being pretty damned self-serving," David snapped. He hunched his shoulders, scowled at her. "What I'm trying to tell you is that I love you."

She quit breathing, only stared.

He released the steering wheel to rub his palms on his thighs. "Is that so unlikely?"

"You...you've never said," Grace whispered.

"I told you once before that it's not a word I'm in the habit of saying."

"You love me." She couldn't help sounding incredulous.

He took her incredulity as disbelief, because he swore. "I tried to tell myself that we were good together, that I like talking to you, that you'd be the wonderful mother Claire needs. In Atlanta, when I heard in your voice that you'd lost patience with me, I knew I felt a whole hell of a lot more.'' His habitually quiet, almost impassive voice became ragged. ''I don't want to go to bed without you, or wake up without you. You've made me realize how empty my life was. It'll be empty again if you won't have me.''

Tears sprang into her eyes. ''You're...sure?''

He made a raw sound that might have been a laugh. ''Surer than I've ever been of anything in my life.'' Finally he reached out and gripped her hand hard. ''Grace, put me out of my misery. Will you marry me? Yes or no?''

She struggled to turn her hand in his so that she could squeeze back. ''Yes,'' she said.

He sat motionless for the longest moment, only his eyes vividly alive. ''Then,'' he said hoarsely, ''let's get out of this car.''

She dropped her purse, fumbled for the door handle, then climbed out on legs that felt shaky. She'd taken only a few steps when David met her. His arms closed around her in a bruising embrace she returned with equal fervor. She laid her cheek against his chest, dampening it with tears. He rubbed his cheek on the top of her head.

After a moment she looked up. His mouth captured hers in a kiss that combined raw passion, barely banked, with exquisite tenderness. Tears kept running down Grace's cheeks, making the kiss salty and damp, at the same time as joy quietly fizzed to life inside her.

He loved her. He really loved her.

Insincere men didn't propose in the garage. They used flowery words, not simple, starkly emotional ones. If he'd used candlelight and roses as weapons, she would not have felt so moved.

David lifted his head at last. She had never seen such vulnerability on his face. "Are *you* sure?"

She smiled tremulously. "I love you."

He closed his eyes for an instant, but too late to shield the hot light of relief from her. "You love me."

Grace laughed. "Now you don't believe me."

Troubled lines formed on his forehead as he searched her face. "I don't deserve your love."

Grace laid a hand on his hard jaw. "Why not?"

"For the same reason I don't deserve Claire's. I deal so poorly with emotion, I've hurt everyone else along the way."

"You've never hurt me." At his arched brow, she admitted, "Disappointed me a few times, maybe. But nobody's perfect, David. I think that's your trouble. Look at this garage, and your house, and…and even your suit." She smoothed her free hand over the fine-textured wool. "Do you ever allow anything to be messy, or flawed?"

He gave a grunt of reluctant amusement. "I seem to be learning. The cat threw up on the living room carpet yesterday."

"The point is," she said earnestly, "a person doesn't *deserve* love, or not deserve it. It's a gift. So you see, you can't turn mine down."

"Turn it down?" His eyes held that stunning look of vulnerability again. "I'd hold your heart hostage—" he laid a hand beneath her breast "—if I thought I could get away with it."

"You can," she whispered.

Suddenly he was kissing her again, the passion torn free. "I love you," he growled against her throat, before he swung her into his arms.

She held on tight and pressed her cheek against the rougher texture of his. "I think," she murmured, "I fell in love with you the day you showed up on my doorstep, so horribly bad tempered."

"I wanted you like hell from that day on."

Which, for a woman who thought of herself as plain, was an erotic and satisfying statement.

Without pause, he carried her past both the living room and a startled Kitkat, taking the stairs as if Grace weighed nothing.

"I can walk," she protested.

"If I put you down, I'll kiss you, and then we'll make love on the stairs." His mouth found hers briefly anyway. Shouldering open his bedroom door, he said roughly, "Sex on the couch—or the stairs— is great fun but not very romantic."

"Oh, I don't know," she said reminiscently.

He flashed a grin at her that speeded her already galloping pulse. "Shall we go back down?"

She pretended to consider. "The bed *is* conveniently close."

The smile was gone as he looked at her with naked hunger. "That's becoming rather important." He let her down beside the bed so that she slid the length of his aroused body. Yet when she reached for his tie, he stilled her hand.

Voice husky, he said, "If you love me, why did you hesitate when I asked you to marry me?"

Tears prickled in her eyes again. "Because I didn't think you loved me."

"Not because of my job, or because I was a rotten father." He spoke carefully.

"I think I made excuses," Grace admitted, a lump in her throat. "If you didn't give Claire what she needed, that meant you *couldn't* love. And if your job always came first, then I was just...handy sex and a convenient baby-sitter. So you see, it's okay if your job does come first sometimes, or if you forget our anniversary or...oh, anything like that. Because what really matters is whether I believe, deep down, that you love me."

"Despite my ineptness." He still seemed to be waiting for the other shoe to drop.

Grace found his uncertainty to be sad. Had nobody ever loved him unconditionally?

"Actually—" she lifted his hand and slid it inside the low-cut neckline of her dress "—you seem, um, skilled enough to me."

As if he couldn't help himself, David caressed her breast. His breath came more harshly.

"Most men propose on bended knee. After an elegant dinner." He nuzzled her throat. "They have a diamond ring and a bouquet of red roses on hand."

With a soft moan, she arched her back. "I liked it

just the way you did it. Although I wouldn't say no to a diamond.''

''My pleasure.'' He nipped the tender flesh where her neck met her collarbone.

Breathlessly she said, ''And it's never too late to go down on bended knee.''

To her shock, he did just that. Clasping her hand between his, he gave her that sweet, tender smile. ''Will you be mine?''

''Yes.'' She smiled back even as her eyes, infuriatingly, filled with tears again. ''Oh, yes.''

David groaned, lifted her in his arms, and together they fell onto the bed, where she became his, heart, mind and body.

CLAIRE TOOK A SIP of her soda and watched covertly as Linnet flicked the remote control from a boring sit-com to MTV.

Sounding super casual, she said, ''Yesterday Dad left me at a music store for half an hour. He doesn't know I saw him, but he went into a jewelry store.''

Linnet bopped in time to 'N Sync's hit single. ''Yeah? So?''

''I bet he's going to ask your mom to marry him.''

The remote control dropped with a soft thump to the floor. Gaping, her friend didn't notice. ''You think?''

''Uh-huh.'' Claire tried to sound as if it was no big deal. ''Will your mom say yes? Do you know?''

Coming out of her shock, Linnet frowned thoughtfully. ''Maybe. She really likes him. But...*married?*''

"We'd be kind of like sisters."

To Claire's intense relief, Linnet's face brightened. "We would, wouldn't we? That would be cool! I've always wished I had a sister or brother."

"Me, too." Maybe she wouldn't have felt so scared and alone after Dad left.

"Did he *say* he was going to ask her tonight?"

"No, but you saw how dressed up he was. He worked on his tie, like, *forever*."

Linnet wrinkled her nose. "Mom tried on at least *eight* dresses before she decided."

They looked at each other, soberly for an instant, and then Linnet squealed and hugged Claire, who hugged back.

"We're going to be sisters!" they chanted.

Suddenly Linnet drew back. "You don't suppose they're…well, you know. Doing it? Right *now?*"

Claire was starting to get interested in the whole idea of…well, not sex, exactly, but boys. And things a boy might do with a girl. Like kissing. And maybe more. Ignoring the pang of hurt thinking about him gave her, she remembered how once, when Josh had reached for something and his hand brushed her breast, she'd had this funny feeling down there and even thought that if he actually laid his hand on her breast, she might like it.

Her own vague longings were one thing. She did *not* want to picture her father doing it.

"Eww," she proclaimed.

They both shuddered.

"They were going out to dinner," she said, not even convincing herself. "To a restaurant."

Wide-eyed, Linnet said, "Unless they lied. You notice they didn't leave a phone number like usual."

Claire gave another shiver. "Let's make a pact. If they get married, we will never, *ever,* think about what our parents do once they go in the bedroom."

"Deal!" her friend agreed without hesitation.

They shook hands solemnly. Then, at the same moment, they shrieked and flung themselves at each other again.

"We're going to be sisters!"

HARLEQUIN *Super*ROMANCE®

They look alike. They sound alike.
They act alike—at least
some of the time.

Twins

THE REAL FATHER by Kathleen O'Brien

(Superromance #927)

A woman raises her child alone after her boyfriend,
the father, dies. Only his twin knows that his brother
isn't the real father....
Available July 2000

CHRISTMAS BABIES by Ellen James

(Superromance #953)

One twin masquerades as the other. Now they're both
pregnant. Did the same man father both?
Available November 2000

Available wherever Harlequin books are sold.

HARLEQUIN®
Makes any time special ™

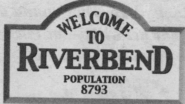

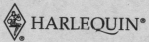

Presenting...

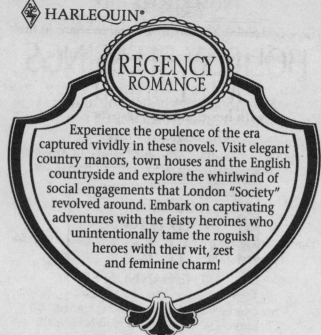

HARLEQUIN®

REGENCY ROMANCE

Experience the opulence of the era captured vividly in these novels. Visit elegant country manors, town houses and the English countryside and explore the whirlwind of social engagements that London "Society" revolved around. Embark on captivating adventures with the feisty heroines who unintentionally tame the roguish heroes with their wit, zest and feminine charm!

Available in October at your favorite retail outlet:

**A MOST EXCEPTIONAL QUEST by Sarah Westleigh
DEAR LADY DISDAIN by Paula Marshall
SERENA by Sylvia Andrew
SCANDAL AND MISS SMITH by Julia Byrne**

Look for more marriage & mayhem coming in March 2001.

HARLEQUIN®
Makes any time special ™

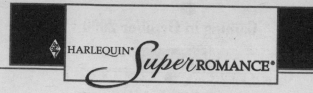

COMING NEXT MONTH

#948 A CHRISTMAS LEGACY • Kathryn Shay
Riverbend

When his father betrayed him, Jacob Steele left Riverbend, vowing never to return. Now he's back—because of his father's strange will—making sure he and his aunts are protected from Kate McMann, the gold digger who stands to inherit if he doesn't fulfill the terms of the will.

Riverbend, Indiana: Home of the River Rats—a group of men and women who've been friends since high school. These are their stories.

#949 MY SISTER, MYSELF • Tara Taylor Quinn
Shelter Valley Stories

Christine Evans is due to arrive in Shelter Valley to begin her new teaching position. A woman who *calls* herself Christine shows up—but it's her sister, Tory. Christine is dead and Tory can protect herself only by assuming her sister's identity. Tory needs to keep her secret safe, but that becomes harder as she falls in love with the town of Shelter Valley—and with a man named Ben Sanders.

Come home to Shelter Valley—a place where love lasts and families matter.

#950 A HOME OF HIS OWN • Judith Bowen
Men of Glory

Lewis Hardin—ex-cowboy, ex-con and now a successful man in the oil business—is ready to come back to Glory. Phoebe Longquist, Glory girl and rancher's daughter, has finally managed to escape. Phoebe fell in love with Lewis long ago and now, when they meet again…they do something impetuous. They elope. But they keep their marriage a secret from family and friends—until Christmas. A Christmas in Glory.

#951 THE FIRST FAMILY OF TEXAS • K.N. Casper
Home on the Ranch

Adam First's family has run the Number One Ranch in West Texas for generations. His daughter's spiteful act is about to bring an end to that. If Adam is lucky, the bank that will take control of the Number One will let him stay on and oversee it. But Adam has to agree to management consultant Sheila Malone's recommendations. That's asking a lot. Adam is as inflexible as Sheila is strong willed. And the sparks that fly between them aren't *just* about the ranch.

#952 'TIS THE SEASON • Judith Arnold
The Daddy School

Evan Myers, divorced father of two, needs a baby-sitter fast to get him through a work crunch at Christmas. He also needs a few Daddy School lessons to help him cope with some larger issues regarding his children. Filomena Albright can certainly help Evan with the kids—and a whole lot more, if Evan would only stop fighting her spell and she would only stop fighting her heart's desire.

#953 CHRISTMAS BABIES • Ellen James
Twins

When Danni Ferris walks into the home of a complete stranger, the last thing she expects him to do is take her in his arms and kiss her passionately. But that's exactly what happens. There can only be one explanation—handsome, sexy Bryan McKay has mistaken Danni for her twin sister, Kristine. A mistake that could change their lives forever.